Murder On Spruce Island

Murder On Spruce Island

a Louis B. Davenport mystery

Gene Brewer
author of *The K-PAX Trilogy*

Copyright © 2006 by Gene Brewer.

Library of Congress Number: 2005910034
ISBN: Hardcover 1-4257-0290-2
Softcover 1-4257-0289-9

All rights reserved. No part of this book may be reproduced or transmitted in any form or by any means, electronic or mechanical, including photocopying, recording, or by any information storage and retrieval system, without permission in writing from the copyright owner.

This is a work of fiction. Names, characters, places and incidents either are the product of the author's imagination or are used fictitiously, and any resemblance to any actual persons, living or dead, events, or locales is entirely coincidental.

This book was printed in the United States of America.

To order additional copies of this book, contact:
Xlibris Corporation
1-888-795-4274
www.Xlibris.com
Orders@Xlibris.com
30139

Contents

Cast Of Characters	15
A Call Comes	17
The Island Haven	19
Spruce Island	22
A Dead Body	25
The Big House	30
The Guests at Porpoise Bay	37
Nobody Knows Nuttin'	40
A New Assistant	45
Porpoise Bay Cottages	49
The Scene of the Crime	52
A Bird's-eye View	56
Happy Hour	60
The Old Lighthouse	63
A Display of Pyrotechnics	65
At Death's Door	69
The Lady Butterfield	72
Davenport Finds a Clue	75
The Coroner's Report	78
A Late Visitor	81
Birdwatching	85
The Big Banana	88
A New Theory	92
The Shower Bower	95
Hard Evidence	97
The Mayor of Spruce Island	102
Dulse Cove	106
A Debt Repaid	109

Another Victim	111
An Invitation	116
A History of Spruce Island	119
A Face at the Window	126
APTGAFIA	131
Blueberry Hill	135
A Hike in the Woods	138
Some Muddy Footprints	141
The Doctor Makes a House Call	146
A Stroll in the Dump	150
A Cup of Tea	153
The Catalog of Poisons	158
The Missing Key	162
Kill the Umpire	165
A Stranger from Away	168
The Dulse Festival	172
Another Threat	176
A Hot Night	182
Dangerous Ground	185
A Secret Passageway	187
The Lights Go Out	190
An Assessment of Damages	194
Indian Cave	198
A Confession	201
The Missing Dory	205
A Denouement	208
The End	212
Acknowledgments	215

In memory of

Rea Wilmshurst
1941-1996
Jean Presley Bowles
1923-1996
Kathleen Buckley
1916-2005

On a wrinkled rock in a distant sea
Three gannets sat in the sun.
They shook the brine from their feathers fine,
    And lazily, one by one,
They sunningly slept while the tempest crept.

In a painted boat on the distant sea
Three fowlers sailed merrily on;
They each took aim as they came near the game,
And the gannets fell one by one,
And fluttered and died, while the tempest sighed.

There came a cloud on the distant sea,
And a darkness came over the sun,
And a storm wind smote on the painted boat,
And the fowlers sank one by one;
Down, down with their craft while the
    tempest laughed.

—Walter B. McLaughlin

COASTAL MAINE ISLANDS

SPRUCE ISLAND
1- airport
2- Cranes
3- Byron
4- gro. store
5- Caitlin's Park
lighthouse
Ferguson's Cove
Nor'east Head
pier
Bald Head
cliffs
Red Trail
dump
Porpoise Bay
lighthouse
cottages
cliff road
bog
smokehouses
cliffs
Deer Hill
Deer Pond
SPRUCE
Blueberry Hill
road
Owl Creek
Deer Creek
main
Dulse Cove
Blue Trail
Dulse Cove Road
high school
FOREST
Eagle Point
Trail
1- Drs. office
2- ball park
3- drug store
4- license bur.
5- garage
6- cemetery
Bass Lake
Centerville
pier
Scallop Bay
Yellow Trail
Lake
Rainbow Creek
dump
The Flukes
cove
Fog Cove
Indian Beach
Sand Harbor
Dog's Tail
Seal Beach
Seaview B&B
lighthouse
1- lumber yard
2- church
3- gift shop
N

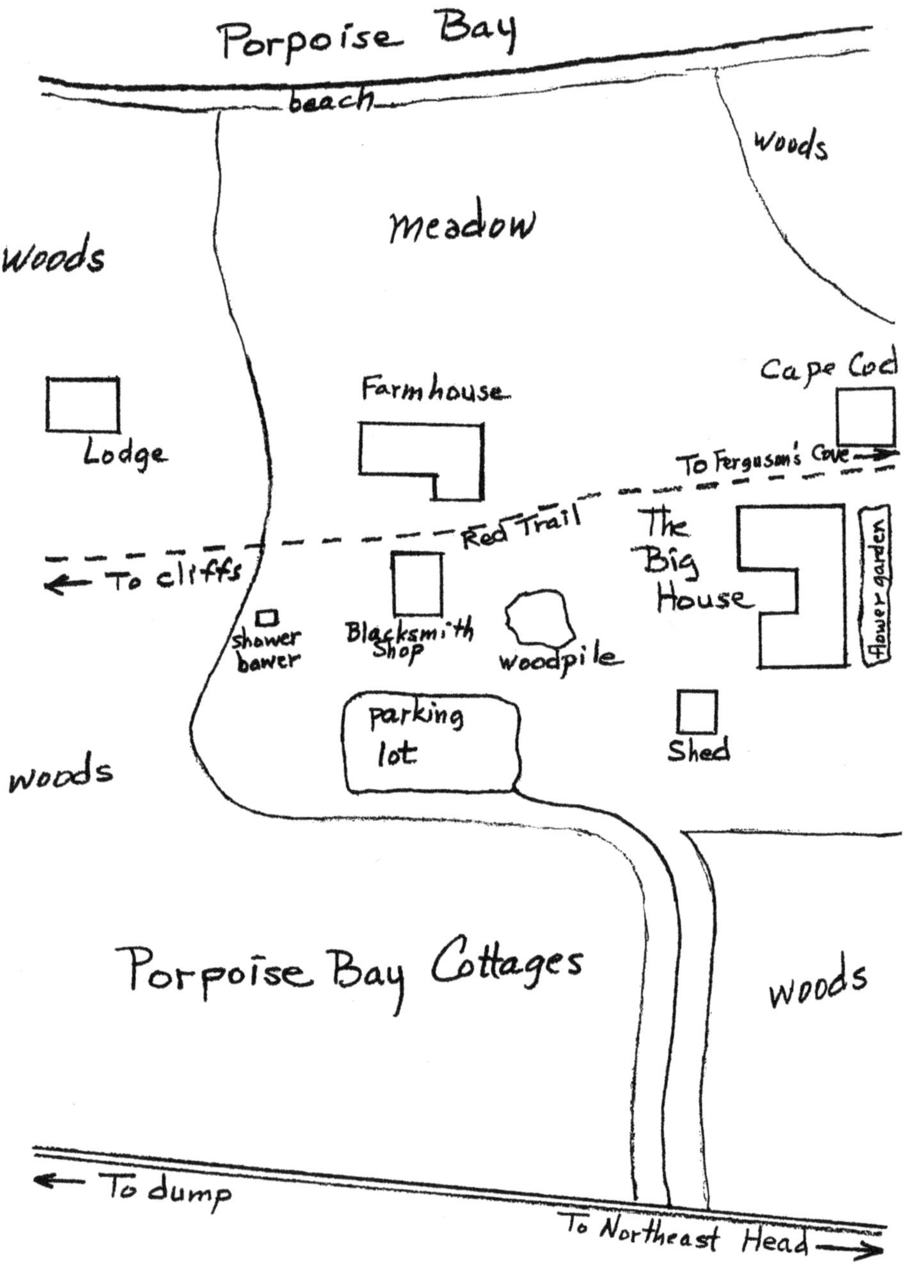
Porpoise Bay
beach
woods
meadow
woods
Cape Cod
Farmhouse
Lodge
To Ferguson's Cove
Red Trail
The Big House
Flower garden
To cliffs
shower bower
Blacksmith Shop
woodpile
parking lot
Shed
woods
Porpoise Bay Cottages
woods
To dump
To Northeast Head

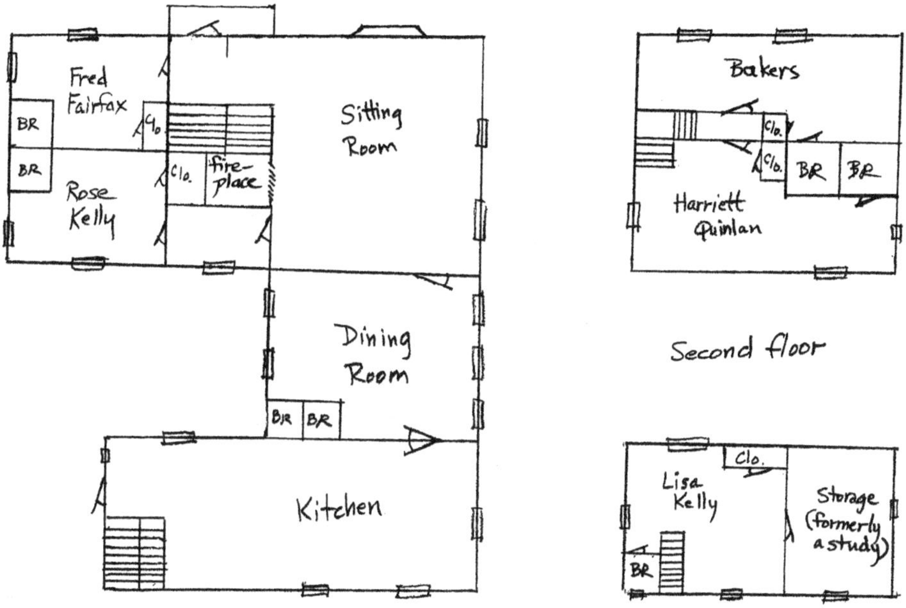
Fred Fairfax
BR
Clo.
BR
Rose Kelly
Clo.
fire-place
Sitting Room
Dining Room
BR
BR
Kitchen
Bakers
Clo.
Clo.
BR
BR
Harriett Quinlan
Second floor
Clo.
Lisa Kelly
Storage (formerly a study)
BR

THE BIG HOUSE

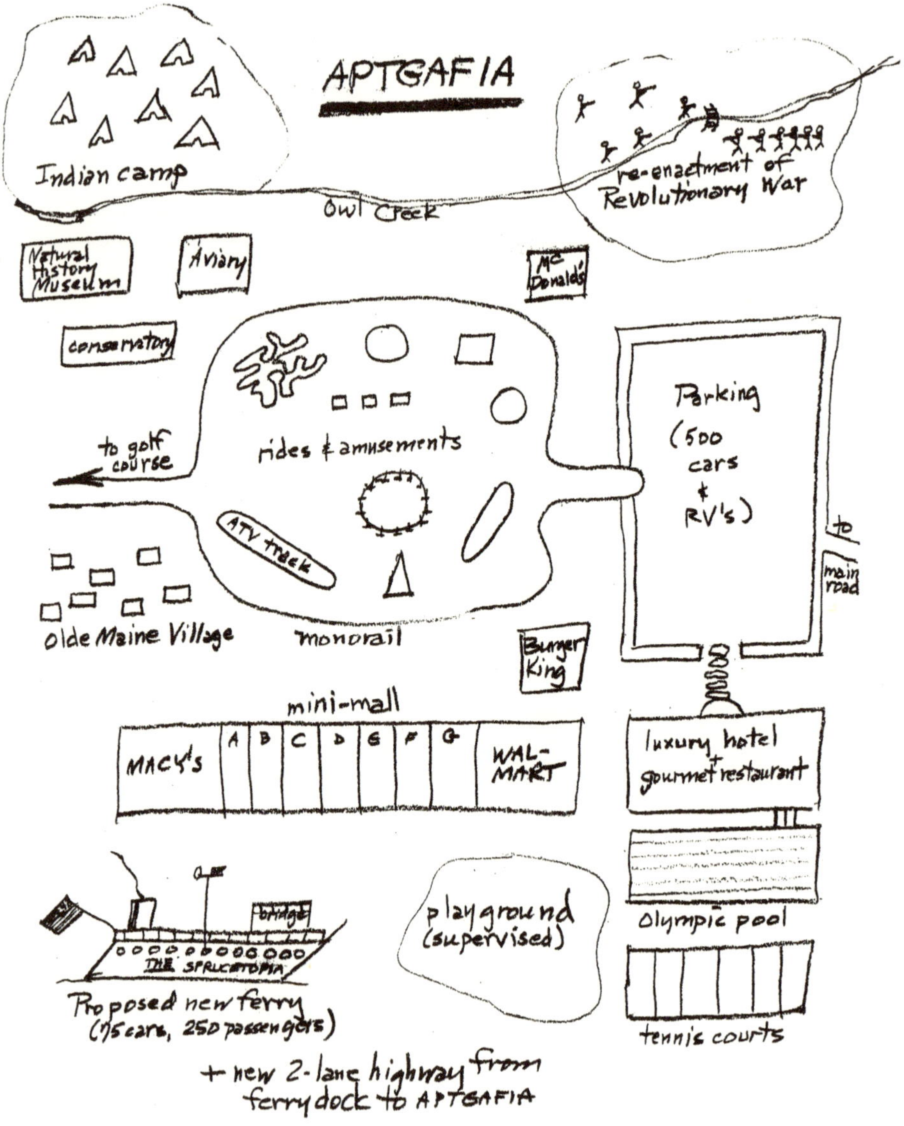
APTGAFIA
Indian camp
Owl Creek
re-enactment of Revolutionary War
Natural History Museum
Aviary
McDonald's
conservatory
rides & amusements
to golf course
ATV track
Parking (500 cars & RV's)
to main road
olde Maine Village
monorail
Burger King
mini-mall
MACY's
A
B
C
D
E
F
G
WAL-MART
luxury hotel + gourmet restaurant
bridge
THE SPRUCETOPIA
Proposed new ferry (175 cars, 250 passengers)
playground (supervised)
olympic pool
tennis courts
+ new 2-lane highway from ferry dock to APTGAFIA

Cast Of Characters

Louis B. Davenport   special deputy sheriff, Washington County, Maine
Lochinvar Tate   sheriff, Washington County
Rose Kelly   proprietor, Porpoise Bay Cottages
Lisa Kelly   her daughter
Kelly   their dog
Joey Small   handyman
Marjorie Jordan   waitress

Guests, Porpoise Bay Cottages

Fred Fairfax	banker	the Big House
Dr. Walter D'Arcy	retired diplomat	the Cape Cod
Patricia D'Arcy	his wife	"
Alice Barnstable	Pat D'Arcy's sister	the Lodge
Harriett Quinlan	New York Public librarian	the Big House
Frank Parkening	insurance executive	the Farmhouse
Paul Thornhill	stockbroker	"
Maryellen Thornhill	his wife	"
Edith Manhart	retired actress	the Blacksmith Shop
Callie Black	her companion	"
Jim Baker	molecular biologist	the Big House
Cathy Baker	nurse	"
Debby Baker	their daughter	"
The Topats	former guests	"

Spruce Islanders

Worm Mallory   captain, the ferry Island Haven
Shep Farmer   crew, the Island Haven

Dr. Peter Houseman	Spruce Island physician
Harold T. Henderson	flight instructor
Richard Blue	fisherman
Rog Banner	mayor, Spruce Island
Byron Henderson	no known occupation
Hermit Blue	dulser
Don Crane	lobsterman
Mary Crane	his wife
Grandma Nan	his paternal grandmother
Crane kids	their children
Perry Crane	Don's brother
Art Dazzledorf	pharmacist
Henry Sanders	grocer and insurance agent
Sherri Blue	director, license bureau
Gannet Banner	mechanic
George Banner	manager, liquor store

A Call Comes

Special Deputy Sheriff Louis B. Davenport was on his way out the door for a long-overdue visit with his grandchildren when the telephone rang. Once. Twice. Three times. He hesitated. Four. Five. He dropped a frayed cardboard suitcase to the cement porch. Slowly, as though trapped in a bad dream, he grunted the door ajar and mumbled his way to the phone. In falsetto: "He's not here."

"Lou, boy! Glad you're still there!"

Davenport didn't like "Lou, boy," nor the sheriff's deep, commanding voice. Nor, for that matter, did he like the sheriff. He visualized the strong, deeply cleft chin, the confident smile, the involuntary jerks of the oversized head. "What's up, Loch?"

The sheriff slurped a mouthful of coffee that his special deputy knew was white with milk and thick with sugar. "I've got a deal here you can't refuse."

Davenport's rust-brown eyes scanned the dirty carpet, flicked up to the beige sofa with the hair stain on the arm. He fished for a Maalox tablet.

"Something's happened out on Spruce Island, my friend. Ever been there?"

"No, I haven't."

"I was there once. Rained the whole damn weekend. Weird people over there. Stare at you like you're some kind of Frankenstein."

Davenport gazed at the wet spot on the ceiling. "What happened on Spruce Island?"

"Got a call from some woman runs a lodge called—uh—Porpoise Bay Cottages. Somebody found one of her guests at the bottom of a cliff. It would seem like an accident except for the note."

"Suicide note?"

"Just the opposite. Note said, 'YOU'RE GOING TO DIE.'"

"Why me, Loch?"

"C'mon, Lou. Most of the guys are off someplace for the holiday weekend. The rest have families they want to be with. You understand."

Davenport did understand. It was Tate's subtle way of reminding him that, despite his age and experience, he was low man on the pole.

"Here's the thing, Lou: why not pack up a bag and make it a working vacation?"

"Isn't there a deputy already stationed on that island?"

"There used to be, but we brought him back."

"How come?"

"Nothing ever happens out there."

Davenport refrained from stating the obvious. "What's the rest of the deal?"

"All right, all right. Full pay and expenses. I can't get away or I'd go myself. Got to give that damn speech at the Fourth of July shindig. You understand."

Davenport did understand. Sheriff Lochinvar Tate was running for the United States House of Representatives. "How do you get out there?"

"Only one way. Take the ferry from Milbridge. Leaves every couple of hours, if I remember right."

"Any other details?"

"Not many. They took the body to the island's only doctor for a prelim. Find him and away you go."

The torn curtain, the lamp with the ink stain on the shade. "Victim have a name?"

"Oh. Yeah. Let's see . . . slurp . . . SLURP! . . . name was Fairfax. Frederick. Older guy. Left a wife and a pack of dogs. The woman who called was a Rose Kelly. Got that?"

"Kelly. Rose."

"I won't forget this, Lou. You know, somebody's got to take over for me when I move down to Washington."

"Nobody could fill your shoes, Loch."

"Say a good word for me on the island, will you? I need every vote I can get. Got to run, Lou. Give me a buzz when you've got everything sorted out."

Davenport hung up, sighed miserably, stared at the smudges on the filamentous yellow curtain, the shiny spot on the broken TV antenna, the cobweb on the ceiling—imprinting them all in his memory, wondering, as he always did when starting a new case, whether he would ever see them again.

The Island Haven

Davenport's thoughts circled around and around the black hole of his life. For the millionth time he found himself pointing his weapon at the heart of the suspected killer of a prominent Boston attorney, hesitating to pull the trigger until it was too late, watching as a fellow detective, one of his few friends, fell dead at his feet. Absolved of guilt, he was nonetheless ostracized by the rest of the department and forced to resign after twenty-five years on the job, taking with him to Machias, Maine, a gaudy plaque and a cheap watch. He felt a wave of nausea and cursed himself for eating something he had found in the back of the refrigerator in a fat-free margarine container.

There was only one sign for the ferry, miles from Milbridge on Highway 1. He took a wrong turn and finally got to the dock just as the rusty red scow, which looked almost homemade, was pulling away with a milk truck, half-a-dozen cars, and a few staring passengers on board. It dissolved in the fog like a ghost ship, trailing a raggedy flag behind.

Davenport leaned over the pier and studied the oily water. Below him a jellyfish pulsed and undulated grotesquely under the iridescent oil, whose pungent aroma reminded him of the clanking garage he had worked in as a youth. The jellyfish reminded him of his ex-wife. A wave of vertigo nudged him away from the edge. He popped another Maalox tablet.

The thick boards under his feet were cracked by salt and weather. Some were warped, a few were actually missing. He could see the water below, which made him feel queasy again, and he lifted his gaze to the now invisible ferry, its horn growing softer with each receding blare. He looked around for a boat schedule.

A few evil-looking gulls stood on the posts glaring at him, waiting. Smears of greenish-white guano decorated the pier, splattered paint on a ruined canvas. He could hear the water plashing against the pilings, but the town and the entire ocean had disappeared in the fog. Except for the birds and the jellyfish, he was utterly alone.

Truth is, Louis B. Davenport didn't mind being alone. Despite his fear of water he had always wanted a boat, the loneliest of ventures. Perhaps, he thought, a person can learn to overcome seasickness, even in late middle age. He took in a great draft of redolent sea air and wandered around listening to the wail of a nearby foghorn, the slap of waves, the occasional warning cry of a distant ship. Somewhere out there is a murderer, he thought grimly.

The old Plymouth didn't like the humidity, but, with a pathetic whine, came grudgingly back to life. He tapped the horn to warn the gulls loafing on the pier. It barely uttered a squeak. Slowly he circled back to the little red diner he had passed on his way to the dock.

The frisky waitress explained that the ferry left at 9:30, 1:30 and 5:30 every day except Sundays and holidays, when there was only the 9:30 and 1:30. She was dressed in classic pink with a decorative microapron and matching cap, and stood on one foot, the other resting on its tip behind her. Today was a holiday, she reminded him before sashaying into the kitchen, leaving him with a copper-colored thermos, a coffee stain running down its side. He could hear pots and pans banging in back, but the freckled teenager made no further appearance. Sipping black coffee, he gazed out the big plate-glass window into the pock-marked street and waited until it was time for lunch to be served, his ruminations caught in the blinding glare of photographic memory.

After forty years he still knew every square inch of the orphanage, from the grimy skylight windows in the attic to the moldy walls of the basement storeroom, the damp abode of spiders and cockroaches. He remembered the grounds from front to back, side to side, the quirks and blemishes of the teachers and staff. Miss Constantine, for example, who limped slightly and smelled of moth balls, and ancient Mrs. Edwards, who made Noel Gerringer stand on his toes with his nose against the blackboard until he passed out. And, especially, the headmaster, Mr. Bissell, who couldn't look anyone in the eye, not even a six-year-old, but who had some information on little Louie B's background that he could not, or would not, divulge. Davenport had disliked bald men with rimless glasses ever since, even though his own forehead was growing and his eyesight fading almost by the minute.

From the window his own shadowy face stared back at him. What a conglomeration of serendipitous occurrences a life is, he mused. All the events of his past, major or minor, had led to this precise moment, drinking too much coffee in the Milbridge Diner, waiting for a ferry to nowhere.

He had become a cop for the flimsiest of reasons, gone to Boston on a whim. Even his wife had been a chance encounter, two ships colliding on a starry night, drawn to each other like moths to the other's flame. Out of their passion arose two strong-willed daughters, one obstinate, like him, the other demanding, like her mother. The marriage had ended abruptly: one night she simply wasn't there. She had taken the girls with her, leaving him with a stack of bills and a huge pot of chili bubbling on the stove. He had eaten it every night until he could no longer stand the smell of it and threw the rest out.

A few customers ambled in, stared at Davenport for a moment, then ignored him as if he were invisible. He would never feel at home in a place like this despite all the time he spent in diners and coffee shops. The waitress finally reappeared. Certain he was going to be seasick later on, he ordered only juice, toast, and poached eggs. Afterward, still hungry, he asked the girl about their homemade pies, as the menu instructed.

"The homemade pies haven't come in yet," she chirped. "But there's one slab of blueberry left from yesterday."

His mouth filled with bitter saliva. "Blueberry? It's too early for blueberries, isn't it?"

"Not for the frozen ones." She popped her gum. "You want it?"

"Sure. Why not?"

He ate it with dispatch while studying a pattern of irregular black chips in the gray-white Formica tabletop, stones in a cloud. Feeling suddenly self-conscious, he wiped his mouth on the paper napkin and glanced around at the other tables, which were filled with people who kidded one another and laughed together, an experience virtually unknown to him. He finished off the thermos. Already he could sense a massive case of heartburn coming on. He fished for a Maalox tablet and reminded himself of his New Year's resolution to go on a diet soon.

Spruce Island

By one o'clock he was back at the pier, ninth in line for the ferry. "How many cars does the boat take?" he shouted at the old man leaning against the car ahead of him. The geezer slowly lifted his eyes from a book called *Femmes Fatal*. Though there was no sun he squinted at Davenport and opined, "You'll never get on, and the next boat ain't till tomorruh." His face was the color and texture of a worn belt.

Davenport could hear the ferry honking in the fog. "Why not today?"

"You'll never get on," the man said with finality. He strolled over and spat down the bank into the water.

An even older couple approached him, grinning. "That's what we like about this place," said the woman, poking her head into his car. "It's so unpredictable." Davenport soon learned, without asking, that they were retired school teachers from Indiana. They had been coming to Spruce Island every summer for four decades.

"The island must have changed a lot since you started coming here," supposed Davenport, fighting another wave of nausea.

"Hasn't changed a bit," said the old man, butting the woman out of the way. His hair was white with splotches of color, like a morgue sheet. "That's why we keep coming back."

The ghostly Island Haven drifted silently into view, pirouetted neatly around and snuggled up next to the dock. He could see the captain pointing in his direction. The one-man crew shrugged.

"Maybe they can squeeze you in," said the teacher hopefully. One of his front teeth had passed away long ago and his breath was bad, like a three-day-old corpse. Davenport wondered if he were carrying some vile disease. Just when he thought he could hold his breath no longer, the old fart pulled his head out of the car. "Come and see us if you ever get over to the island!"

"Good luck!" echoed the wrinkly woman. Davenport took a deep breath of the fresh salt air and watched them climb into their shiny new Jaguar, three cars up. He had once read a white-jacketed book with the blood-red title, *The Murdering Type*, whose author had studied several hundred case histories and reached the conclusion that anyone was capable of murder if the motive was strong enough. Even feeble old couples like this one. Find someone who disliked Fred Fairfax, he reckoned, and you'll find his killer, no matter how unlikely a candidate he might seem.

After the incoming traffic had disembarked and the cars ahead of him had been crammed on, Davenport was waved forward. He pulled into the remaining space. A foot of the Plymouth hung out past the stern. The captain and crew scratched their chins. He was waved off. After some discussion between crew and passengers all the cars in front of him inched up a little. He was wedged in again; this time he almost fit. The gate rose up; his rear bumper cried out like a woman screaming. In another second the engine roared and they were under way. It was only then that he realized he had been so preoccupied with getting on the ferry that he had neglected to take a good look at the passengers getting off.

He made an effort to twist out of his car, at which point he was jolted by a blast from the foghorn. When he jerked his head, a sharp pain seared the back of his neck, which he was sure was broken. For a moment he had the horrible feeling that he was going to be sick and then trapped for hours wallowing in his own vomit. But there was no swell and he made the trip in relative comfort. In fact, despite the regular snorts of the horn and clanking of the engine, the invisibility of land and sea put him promptly to sleep. He was surprised when he awakened to find the boat drifting toward a run-down pier.

With much waving and grimacing of the crew, each of the vehicles disgorged itself from the ferry and rattled up the plank ramp onto the paved road. He was about to follow the last car off when someone rapped on his half-open window. "Hold 'er, fella."

"Huh? What's the problem?" He swiveled the broken neck and found a pair of steel-blue eyes staring in at him. "You forgot to pay," said the crew.

"Oh. How much?"

"Car and driver—twelve bucks. Didn't want to disturb your beauty sleep." A guffaw filtered down from the wheelhouse.

Davenport fiddled for his wallet, pulled out a twenty, handed it to the crew. "Where can I find the doctor?"

"Pete Houseman? You sick?"

"No. Business." He waited for the change.

The crew nodded. "Ah. You must be the deppity." He painstakingly counted out eight dollars, then leaned down and peered into the open window. "Just follow that last car—the Fiat. Up the main road till you come to a big blue house. Can't miss it, even with the fog."

But the Fiat, and everything else, was long gone. Judging that "up the main road" meant north, Davenport rattled onto Spruce Island and turned right at the T. He frowned into the fog for blue houses, eventually found one on the left, and pulled into the rutted driveway. The wet weeds slapped at the bottom of his car as he chugged slowly toward the old house.

A Dead Body

There wasn't a sign anywhere of a doctor's office. The only hint that he might be in the right place were the few vehicles parked haphazardly at the head of the lane. He pulled in beside them and squished his way toward the front door. A man with coal-black hair came out the side entrance, his arm in a sling. The guy stared dourly at Davenport before proceeding along the narrow walkway to his pickup.

Like the house itself, the side door needed painting. He entered through a short passageway lined with yellow rain gear and stepped into a room furnished with unmatched chairs in various states of repair. The walls were papered in faded pink roses on a dusty green background. A few picture postcards were tacked to the wall alongside a diploma. The chattering ceased as soon as Davenport appeared, and a dozen squinting eyes glared at him suspiciously, like those of so many gulls. Some of the patients, like the man he had just encountered, were dark and stocky, others blondish or sandy-haired and pale, like the crew of the Island Haven. He mumbled an unrequited greeting and looked around for magazines. There were none. A fat yellow cat sidled into the room and settled down between two middle-aged women on the high-back sofa. It yawned at Davenport, who wanted a cigarette.

Gingerly he lowered himself into an old wooden chair that might once have been part of a dining room set, feeling, as he did so, a number of aches and pains that he hadn't noticed before. To the plumpish woman on his right he observed that it was a "pea souper."

"Yes," she murmured, glancing at him as if he were an idiot. "Yes, it is." Later she added an afterthought, more to the others than to him: "They're giving sun for tomorrow." Each of them nodded gravely. Everything of importance having been settled, they cleared their throats and whispered amongst themselves.

Davenport considered each of the patients briefly. All the eyes, whether green, blue, or brown, had the same look of suspicion and determination. He studied the photo of a fishing boat on the wall, read the diploma next to it: "This is to certify that Peter L. Houseman has fulfilled all the requirements for the degree of Doctor of Medicine, Tufts University Medical School, June 10, 1945...."

A boy of about twelve banged through an inner door and danced into the room. Obviously whatever had brought him there had not been a serious matter. The grin faded when he spotted the stranger in their midst. His mother crooned, "See, I told you it was nothing," before offering her good-byes to the others, who seemed relieved that the kid was all right. As soon as they had gone a man appeared in the inner doorway. He wore no white coat and dangled no stethoscope, but he was obviously in charge. His snow-white hair was uncombed and his face deeply lined, as though he hadn't slept for days.

Davenport rose quickly. "Doctor Houseman?"

The man squinted. "Yes?"

"I'm—uh—Davenport. Did someone let you know I was coming?"

"Maybe so. But you'll have to wait your turn. All right—who was next?"

Davenport could feel his face getting hot. He asked where the bathroom was. "Thermos of coffee," he murmured. Houseman stared blankly at him and motioned to the other door.

A plumpish woman got up and was escorted into the office. Davenport was amazed to find that she had left her purse on the coffee table, a former tree stump. He started to say something, but one of the others cut him off. "Don't worry," she snapped. "Nobody's going to take it." There was an enormous space between her two front teeth. Davenport nodded sheepishly and stepped into the bathroom.

Embarrassed by the sound of tinkling, he flushed the toilet, but it finished before he did. All eyes watched as he returned to his seat, where he fidgeted for the next hour, counting the roses in the wallpaper, counting them again. Unpleasant memories of injections and tongue depressors darted around in his mind, all wielded by the unsmiling young doctor who visited the orphanage once a year.

At last everyone had been seen and the waiting room was empty. The cat slept soundly on the sofa. Houseman came out drying his hands on a towel. "You a detective?"

"The official title is 'Special Deputy Sheriff.' But yes, they send me when they want some detective work done."

"He's back here."

Davenport followed the wrinkled pants through an ominous-looking office and dimly-lit corridor. Two of the side rooms contained robe-clad patients. At the back of the house a stairway led down to an unfinished basement, familiarly cold and damp. He looked around for spiders and cockroaches. Lying under a bare bulb on what appeared to be an old kitchen table was a body in torn clothing. He studied the grotesque facial expression and wondered, as always, what it was like to die. The victim was in his late fifties, pale, wiry. The blind eyes stared pleadingly at Davenport as he examined the gashes and contusions about the face, the ripped and bloody clothes. The small feet were encased in dusty Italian-made dress shoes. How fragile we all are, he thought. Little points of light in a shell of dust. At least it was mercifully quick. "Looks like he died from a fall."

"That's what it looks like."

The corpse was not yet discolored. "How long ago?"

"Ten or twelve hours, maybe a little longer. Rigor is already fairly well along."

"Are you fairly certain about the time?"

"Nope. I'm no expert on dead people. I try to keep 'em alive if at all possible."

Davenport managed a weak smile. "You know the man?"

"Name was Fairfax. Been coming to Spruce Island every summer for years. Sometimes stopped in to see me about some minor ailment. Then squawked like an irate gull if I charged him anything."

"Any evidence that something else might have happened to him? Before he fell down the cliff?"

"Nope. But I haven't looked very hard, either. The body goes back on the first boat for autopsy."

"You mean tomorrow."

"That's what I said." He peered over the wire-rimmed eyeglasses. "Required in cases like this. No point in my messin' with it beforehand."

"Then you know about the threatening note that was found in his room."

"Yep."

"Isn't there a helicopter service, in case of emergencies?"

"There's no emergency with Mr. Fairfax here, wouldn't you say?"

Davenport, recoiling slightly from the cold flesh, checked the victim's fingernails. They were clean, suggesting that he hadn't lost his balance and slid down the cliff, clawing all the way. "Anything like this ever happen before on Spruce Island?"

"Nope."

"What's the population here?"

"'Bout nine hundred."

"What do people here do for a living?"

"Fishing, mostly. Everybody else provides some sort of service or other."

"Do you mind if I just take a look at the torso?"

"Help yourself."

Davenport unbuttoned the ragged shirt, peeled it back from the body. No sign of a bullet hole. A knife wound was harder to rule out, given the nature of the gashes. The upper body was thin, but there was a donut of fat around the gut. "Can you help me turn him over?" The doctor complied without a word. Despite the rigor, the victim's head flopped nonsensically on the broken neck. The back of the skull was severely damaged. Could have been a boulder. Or a blunt instrument. He rubbed his own sore neck and shuddered. "All right. Thanks."

Something flew past his ear. He jumped back involuntarily, and the yellow cat landed in Houseman's arms. After the chills subsided, Davenport gingerly examined the victim's pockets, finding only lint. He turned to the doctor. "Anybody seen anything suspicious going on around here lately?"

"Rog Banner—he's the mayor—said he saw a stranger yesterday. Left the island this morning, according to Worm Mallory. Maybe you saw him get off the boat in Milbridge."

"What did he look like?"

"Like he didn't belong here."

"Who's Worm Mallory?"

"Captain of the Island Haven."

"All right. I'm finished here. Can you tell me how to get to Porpoise Bay Cottages?"

Houseman led him out of the makeshift morgue. "Follow the main road to the cliff road. It'll be the left fork—the main road curves to the right. Follow the cliff road to the cottages. If you come to the dump, you've gone too far." The physician led the way back to the screen door.

"And where's the nearest motel?"

With a hint of a smile on his unshaven face, the old doctor turned to face Davenport. A splotch of egg clung to his flannel shirt. "There are a couple of bed and breakfasts. In fact, there's three. One for each town. Can't miss 'em."

"Thanks. You always work on the Fourth?"

"If people get sick on the Fourth, then I work on the Fourth."

Nodding sympathetically, Davenport stuck out a hand. Houseman stared at it for a moment, as if unsure what to do with it. Finally he grasped it and led him out the door. "By the way, we can do something about those tics if you like."

Davenport made his way along the narrow path to his car, now marked by a crooked rear bumper. After several wet failures, he got it going, turned around in the empty parking area, and rattled back to the main road. In the rearview mirror the doctor and his cat gradually faded into the dense gray fog.

The Big House

Davenport puttered to an unmarked fork in the road, veered left, and started up a seemingly endless hill. The ancient Plymouth protested, but rattled on. The cliff road was thinly populated by well-kept houses. An occasional ghostly lane led off somewhere, but there was no sign of any lodge or cottages. Suddenly someone careened out of the woods and into his path. Davenport veered hard to avoid running over him. The swarthy, middle-aged man turned onto the road without looking back, and waddled ducklike into the mist.

A mile later he pulled up behind a horseman, whom he followed into a wide driveway, dislodging dozens of resident gulls and one feral cat. When the horse stopped alongside a pile of smoldering refuse, Davenport rolled to a stop behind it. A few gulls squawked and squabbled among themselves; others looked as though they wanted to kill him.

"Afternoon!" he shouted to the man unloading trash bags from the saddle. The cowboy was wearing overalls embossed with silver studs, and was topped by a ten-gallon hat from which tufts of blond hair protruded here and there. The strains of a plaintive country tune seeped out of the pocket of the fancy shirt. "Know where I can find Porpoise Bay Cottages?"

The bow-legged horseman lifted his hat and wiped his forehead with a sleeve. He squinted at Davenport. "'Bout three-quarters of a mile back."

"Didn't see any cottages."

He heaved a final bag well into the dump, dislodging several angry gulls and a disgruntled raven. "Can't see 'em from the road."

"All right. Thanks."

The man nodded. "'Bout three-quarters of a mile," he said again, in case the stranger didn't understand English.

Davenport drove back exactly 0.75 miles and turned into an almost invisible lane, which led down and around to an open space surrounded by several cabins, a gravel parking lot, and an enormous pile of firewood, black in the mist. He clunked to a halt and stepped out of the Plymouth, reassured somehow by the sound of a distant foghorn.

One of the cottages was bigger than the others, with an extension protruding from the back. At the crown of the roof creaked a large wrought-iron weathervane in the shape of a porpoise. A wisp of blue smoke rose from the main chimney. Davenport made his way around the cedar-shingled structure, dark gray with age. A mane of ivy covered the front and part of the sides. He knocked on the door. No answer. He rapped louder. Still no answer. He tried it. It was unlocked.

Calling out a "Hellooo!" he passed hesitatingly through a small entryway and entered a warm living room furnished with a large sofa and several overstuffed chairs, and embraced by shelves of old books. An open roll-top desk cluttered with envelopes and papers stood along the wall to the left, in the light of the bay window, whose wide sill was covered with porpoise bric-a-brac, an oil lamp, and a vase of yellow flowers. An unfinished game of Scrabble waited patiently on a card table stationed at the end of the sofa. Seascape photographs were hung here and there around the room, along with a pencil drawing of a handsome young man wearing a captain's hat. A sweet-smelling blaze crackled in the fireplace. "Anyone home?"

He stepped into a dining room filled with small wooden tables, already set for dinner. A number of delicate china cups and plates lined the shelves along two of the walls. Outside he could make out a large flower garden, the colors barely dampened by the fog. "Hello?"

He pushed through another door into the kitchen, where he found a woman about his age standing at a stove. She was wearing a blue and white checked shirt and orange slacks with matching apron. Without turning around she muttered, "Shoulda come to the back door. Saved yourself a lot of walking." She was not a large woman, but firmly packed.

"How did you know—"

"Saw you go by." She wiped her hands on a damp towel and turned to face him. "You must be the deputy sheriff."

He looked around. The spacious kitchen was well-equipped. "Special Deputy Sheriff Davenport."

"That's quite a mouthful." She looked him over with interest. "Got a first name?"

"Louis. Louis B. Davenport."

"All right, Louie. You can call me Rose."

"Fine. I see you're busy, Mrs.—uh—Rose. I'll try to be as brief as possible."

"No need. I'm just waiting for Lisa to get back with some stuff we need for dinner. Glass of sherry?"

"No, thanks. I'm on duty. You go ahead."

"Thanks. Think I will."

She led him back to the room with the fireplace. "Sit down, Louie." As if anticipating the question, she added, "Lisa's my daughter." She filled a smoky glass from a bottle standing on the ornately-carved side table, dropped into the chair next to it, threw her legs onto the matching footstool, and sighed loudly. "Toss a log on the fire, will you?" She took a sip of the sherry. "Fog makes everything damp."

He did so clumsily, nearly knocking over the screen. The fire went out immediately.

She motioned him to a seat on the sofa. When he was firmly rooted she got up, dragged the screen away, and gave the log a brisk kick. The fire blazed up. "Well? What can I do for you?" She replaced the screen and dropped back into the chair.

"I guess you know why I'm here. I just came from Doctor Houseman's office. Did you know the—uh—victim?"

"Of course I knew Fred Fairfax. He's been coming here for thirty years."

"Was he a friend of yours?"

"Like I said, I've known him for thirty years."

"I see. Who found the body?"

"Richard Blue found him at the bottom of the cliff up the bay here. You talk to Richard yet? Married to Pete's sister—"

"Richard Blue is Dr. Houseman's brother-in-law?"

"That's what I said." She took another sip of sherry. "Second marriage for both of them. First wife was no good. Drinkin' and carryin' on. She was a Henderson. Father was old Matt Henderson. Used to be on the boat. Ran into the dock once and never took it out again. They say he had Alzheimer's. I think he was just plain dumb. Olivia might have had a touch of it, though. Never could remember where her own house was. Left the island, finally, and never came back."

"What time did Mr. Blue find the body?"

"'Bout six this morning."

"What was he doing out in the bay at six in the morning?"

"He's a fisherman."

"And he took the body to the doc?"

"If he hadn't it'd still be lyin' there, wouldn't it?"

Davenport gazed into the smiling eyes a moment before looking away. "I'd like to talk to Mr. Blue. Where can I find him?"

"I think he said he would be out fishing today and tomorrow. Will you still be here Monday?"

"If need be. Now—I understand you found a note."

"In his room. I went to look for him when he didn't come in for breakfast."

"Where is it?"

She pulled a piece of paper from the kangaroo pocket of her apron and handed it to him. He took it with a frown, but said nothing about the possible destruction of fingerprints. The 4 x 6 lined paper had been torn from a small tablet. On it a handprinted message warned: YOU'RE GOING TO DIE.

"Had he slept in his bed that night?"

"Somebody did."

"According to my information he left a wife and—uh—a pack of dogs. Is that right?"

She swallowed noisily. "Yes, he had a wife. And dogs."

"Didn't the wife sleep in his bed?"

"Not very likely."

"Why is that?"

"She's in Boston."

"She didn't come with him?"

"Never does."

"Why not?"

"Fred told me she gets bored quite easily. Not much to do on Spruce Island. No bars, no tennis courts, no golf courses, that kind of thing."

"What do people do for fun around here?"

"Why, we *live*, Louie. We *live*."

He smiled uncomfortably. "How well did they get along?"

"How should I know?"

"You never met her?"

"Nope. She's his fifth wife. First one left him a long time ago. I liked Emma. She was a fashion designer. For a big department store, I believe. Used to sit right out there on the lawn with her sketch pads and draw the prettiest things you ever saw—dresses and hats and whatnot. Didn't mind letting people look over her shoulder. She was as common as an old shoe. Never did know what she saw in Fred. The rest of his wives you can have. A rum bunch, the lot of 'em."

"You have his current wife's address?"

"Maybe. I'll see if I can find it for you later on."

Davenport nodded patiently. "Anything else you can tell me?"

She drained her glass. "What else do you want to know?"

"Mind if I take a look at his room?"

"Nothing much to see."

"I'd like to take a look anyway, if you have no objection."

She sighed again, stood up, stretched, and led the way to the little entryway where he had come into the house. Across from the stairs was a door, which was unlocked. The room was furnished with a bed, a reading chair, and a dresser, on top of which stood a vase bursting with a variety of fresh flowers. A pitcher and bowl waited on the little washstand. The wallpaper was decorated with breaching porpoises. A light breeze lifted the chintz curtains and brought in the smell of the sea to mix with the pleasant aroma of soap and flowers.

"I thought you said he slept in his bed."

"I said somebody did."

"This bed's been made."

"It's Saturday. We change everything on Saturdays."

"I see." Davenport scratched his stubbly chin. "Where did you find the note?"

"On the dresser."

"Folded, not wadded up?"

"Yep."

"Find anything else?"

"Nope."

"His clothes in that closet over there?"

"Yep."

"Mind if I take a look?"

"Why should I?"

Nothing of interest inside: a few pairs of new-looking jeans, the same kind the victim was wearing when he died, two pairs of dress slacks, a matching seersucker jacket, a few hand-painted ties. Underneath all this stood a couple of expensive-looking suitcases and a pair of LL Bean hunting boots, size seven.

"He wasn't wearing these boots when he was found," Davenport pointed out.

"Evidently not."

"Why do you suppose he wasn't?"

"I haven't got a clue."

He rummaged through the dresser drawers. Shirts, socks, colorful silk boxer shorts. "He have any enemies that you know of?"

"Just about everyone who ever knew him, I imagine."

"That include yourself?"

"Can't say that I liked the man, though he wasn't so bad at first, when he was poor and married to Emma."

"What was he like later on?"

"Arrogant. Tight-fisted. Selfish. Mean. Especially when he was drunk. Nobody liked Fred, but they all tolerated him for his financial advice. He could have made money on Edsel stocks."

"Did Fairfax carry a lot of cash around with him?"

"I doubt it. Anyway, he didn't spend much on the island."

Davenport nodded. "Okay, Rose, I'm through here. For now." He checked his watch. "I understand there's a bed and breakfast in town. Any restaurants?"

"No need for that. You can eat in the dining room with everyone else." She looked at him as though she wanted to fix his tie, if he were wearing one. "Dinner's at six."

"That really won't be—"

"You can sleep here."

"In *this* room?"

"Why not? You afraid of ghosts?"

"Well, no, but—"

"All right, then."

"I'll have to send all his personal things back to the lab for analysis."

"Analysis for what?"

"You know: hair, fibers—things like that."

The front door squeaked open and closed with a bang. Rose called out: "Lisa?"

"Yeah, Mom, it's me." Davenport thought he detected a hint of resignation.

"C'mon in here a minute!"

A thirtyish woman loaded down with paper bags appeared in the doorway. "What do you want? These things are heavy.... Oh. Who are you?" A Skye terrier followed her in, sniffed around Davenport's legs.

"This is Louie Davenport. From the sheriff's department over in Machias."

"Name's Lisa," she frowned. "The dog's name is Kelly. But we'll have to do this later. It's almost five-thirty. You remembered to set your watch ahead, didn't you, Louie? It's Atlantic time here." Without waiting for a reply she turned and disappeared. The dog followed her out.

"I have to tell you right now: she's stubborn, just like her father."

"Will I be meeting him at dinner?"

"I don't think so. He's been dead nearly ten years."

"Oh—I'm sorry."

"So am I," she murmured, gazing out the window into the impenetrable fog. "So am I."

A distant shriek: "Mom!" Davenport sensed they were on the cusp of transition. Some day soon the daughter would become the mother.

"Well, I'd better get out to the kitchen. You need anything, let us know."

"Is there a key?"

"I suppose there is—someplace. Nobody ever asked for one before."

"Maybe you'd better find them all. The other guests might want one after what's happened."

"Why should they?"

"Until we find out what killed him, we had better take proper precautions, don't you think?"

"Not really. But I'll see if I can find them."

"MOM!"

"I've got to go. Whatever happened to Fred, people have to eat." She hurried out of the room. He gazed again at the porpoised wallpaper, the colorful flowers, the bowl with its matching pitcher. It was homey, simple, complete. Not like the orphanage, with its empty gray walls and creaking floors, or the house near Boston, with its stiff modern furniture. He inhaled the fragrant air and thought, with a mixture of happiness and doubt: this is what a home must feel like.

The Guests at Porpoise Bay

After dusting the dresser and doorknobs for fingerprints, Davenport packed the victim's luggage and sealed it with tightly-knotted twine, a spool of which he had spotted lying near the woodpile. Then he brought in his own tattered suitcase. As he stripped off his damp trench coat he heard yelling: "Somebody stole my string! Somebody stole my string!"

He hurried outside and found a small giant with wildly disheveled hair, waving a hatchet. His eyes had the dull look of the mentally impaired. Davenport backed away. "Sorry. I borrowed it."

"I want it! I want it!"

Davenport led him into the house, retrieved the twine, and handed it over. Clutching it to his chest, the burly young man ran out the front door, still wielding the hatchet. Davenport stepped outside and watched him disappear into a shed behind the house.

In the mist ahead of him stood two of the cottages, smoke curling from their chimneys. He ambled along a well-worn path toward them. Like the main house, the cedar-shingled cottages were choked by long tentacles of ivy, and both appeared to be very old. Beyond them the trail led into a dense forest. Tapping his hip to be sure his .38 was there, he followed the path and promptly found himself immersed in a dark world of earthy silence. The wildflowers, their petals wrapped around themselves for warmth, dripped with moisture. A bird warbled overhead. As he searched for it among the spruce branches he skidded on an exposed root. Under these conditions, he suspected, it would be a simple matter to push someone off a slippery path and over a cliff.

Engulfed in the quiet, he paused for a moment. There wasn't a hint of wind, no voices, no vehicles, no splashing waves. It was a kind of sublimity he had rarely experienced, and could only describe in terms his grandchildren might use: awesome. Transfixed, he wandered slowly from the trail into the unspoiled forest itself, where the spongy earth was littered with needles and half-eaten mushrooms. The pungent, inseparable aromas of growth and decay filled his nostrils. The only disruption to the perfect peace was the occasional warning cry of the foghorn and the desultory nip of a mosquito. The feeling, if not the scene, seemed vaguely familiar. He tried to remember....

It was almost time for dinner when he finally made his way back to his room. He poured some water into the porcelain bowl, which somehow reminded him that it had been more than forty-eight hours since he had had a bowel movement. After washing up with a bar of porpoise soap and shaving off a two-day growth of beard, he changed into his only pair of dress slacks and his good brown sweater. After combing his thinning hair over the bald spot he stepped into the sitting room, where he was embarrassed to find that he was the only male without a coat and tie. Unfortunately, he hadn't brought either. The sweater would have to serve.

As soon as he came in, the room became as still as the woods. Obviously everyone knew who he was. Rose was back in her usual chair by the fireplace. "Ah, Louie!" she called out. "I want you to meet our guests."

He nodded. She thrust her sherry glass toward him, as if in a toast. "Folks, this is Special Deputy Sheriff Louis B. Davenport. Starting on my left here, Louie, we have Dr. and Mrs. Walter D'Arcy; he's a retired diplomat from New Haven. Then Harriett Quinlan, a librarian from New York City. The bright young couple over there is Jim and Cathy Baker, and that's their little girl Debby. This is their first visit to Spruce Island—they're from Cleveland. On your left is Alice Barnstable, who owns a bookstore in Philadelphia. She's also Mrs. D'Arcy's sister. On the sofa we have Miss Manhart and Miss Black, from Baltimore, and last, but certainly not least, is Frank Parkening, an insurance executive from Hartford, Connecticut." There were noddings and mumbles of greeting. She rolled her eyes. "The Thornhills haven't arrived yet, apparently."

"They're always late," Miss Manhart pointed out helpfully. Though she appeared to be in her eighties, the tiny woman enjoyed shiny, raven-black hair.

"Yes, they're late for everything," Miss Black agreed. Her hair, by contrast, was a dull off-white.

"Louie, do you want to say anything before we go in to dinner?"

He wanted to say: "Do you have a laxative?" But what he managed to come up with was: "Thank you, Mrs. Kelly." He glanced around at the guests, who were staring back at him. All the detectives he had known seemed to relish such a moment, when they were in total command, the center of attention. Davenport, however, had never enjoyed public speaking, nor was he much better in private. He took a deep breath and tried to relax. "As all of you know, I'm sure, one of your fellow guests was killed in a fall from a nearby cliff early this morning. We don't know yet what happened, but the threatening note found in his room suggests it was no accident. I understand that most of you are here for the month of July, or at least until the middle of the month, so there should be no hardship in my request that none of you leave the island for a few days. If any of you were planning a side trip, please check with me first."

"What about the islanders, Sheriff?" someone screeched. "You going to keep *everyone* on the island?" The woman's eyelids fluttered rapidly, like a pair of frenetic moths.

"At this point the most likely suspect is someone who knew him fairly well, Miss Barnstable," he replied. "Did Mr. Fairfax have any friends on the island that you know of?"

"No, or anywhere else," she snorted.

"Why aren't you wearing a badge, Monsieur Da-ven-porrrt?" D'Arcy demanded loudly. He seemed to find the whole exercise amusing.

"Well, Dr. D'Arcy, I'm not a deputy sheriff but a "special" deputy—a detective. We don't wear badges."

"How do we know you're who you say you are?" Frank Parkening was obese, with a voice like molasses.

Davenport whipped out his wallet and flashed his credentials around the room. "I think that's all I have to say for now, folks, except that I would like to speak with each of you briefly before you retire to your rooms tonight. Oh, and perhaps you would all be kind enough to give me a sample of your handwriting. We could take care of that now, on your way in to dinner. I see there's a pad and a pencil on the desk over there. Ms. Barnstable, you're closest. Would you mind beginning?"

She was casually dressed in a frowsy dress with unmatching ratty sweater. Her shoulder-length hair was gray and lifeless, but her eyes were not. She tamped out a cigarette. He gazed at it longingly. "Well, what do you want—my life story?"

Davenport smiled. "That won't be necessary. Just write—let's see—just print, YOU'RE GOING TO DIE. And your name."

"I would think this in bad taste under most circumstances, sheriff. But..." With a pronounced scowl, she followed his instructions, ending with her signature in a strong hand.

Each of the guests shuffled up to scrawl the requested name and message. As Misses Manhart and Black were signing in shaky scripts, a girl appeared at the door to announce that dinner was ready. Davenport glanced at the various handwriting samples before stuffing them into a pocket and following everyone into the dining room.

Nobody Knows Nuttin'

Davenport was seated with the two spinsters and Harriett Quinlan, the somewhat less elderly librarian, who fit the stereotype nicely. She was tall and very thin, with snow-white hair tied back in a bun. Her glasses were so thick that her eyes became almost owlish, and her shoes were sturdy. The two older women looked as though they would be blown away by a strong breeze.

He noted with interest that the other diners were murmuring among themselves, glancing his way from time to time, much as he would have expected from a group of curious, though innocent, onlookers. No one seemed particularly nervous, self-conscious, or fearful. No one avoided his gaze except for Baker, who seemed to ignore everyone. Davenport tried to listen to the mixed conversations. Many a case had been solved by overhearing some seemingly innocuous comment.

He spread a little butter on a Saltine. The women all did the same. "Miss Manhart, I wonder if you would mind telling me where you were between five and seven this morning."

She looked him directly in the eye. "Why, in bed, of course. Where were you?"

Davenport's lips played with a smile. "So was I. Miss Black?"

She stole a glance at Miss Manhart. "I was in bed, too, Mr. D," she murmured.

"Miss Quinlan?"

"I was birdwatching."

"Oh?" he replied triumphantly. "In the fog?"

She spoke in a brisk, clipped manner. "One can hear perfectly well in the fog, Louis."

He concealed a smile. "I see. And where did you do this—uh—birdlistening?"

"In the meadow."

"What meadow?"

"The one right in front of the house. You'll see it when the weather clears."

"How far did you go?"

"Not far. Just down to the beach."

"Did you meet anyone while you were out? Or see or hear anything unusual?"

"No, no one. Except Joey, of course. He was getting in some wood before it started raining."

"Who's Joey?"

"Joey Small. The handyman. The only thing I heard, besides the birds, was the drone of a fishing boat in the cove."

"But you couldn't see it."

"No."

The young girl who had opened the door earlier began to bring plates of food. Davenport was pleased to discover that they contained scallops sauteed in garlic butter, boiled red potatoes, and string beans amandine. He wondered vaguely how much this was costing the sheriff's office. Having had nothing to eat since the blueberry pie, he shoveled in a few scallops and gazed at his dinner companions, watching with some amusement as Miss Manhart carefully scraped her green beans onto Miss Black's plate, and took the latter's potatoes. Surely an act repeated thousands of times in the past, a moment of unabashed intimacy between two very old friends, though Miss Black watched the potatoes go somewhat wistfully, he thought. Were these three gentle women capable of committing a murder? Certainly. So were the young couple with the little girl. And, of course, Ms. Barnstable, who complained loudly about the food, the seating arrangements, and the wet firewood.

At this point a middle-aged couple barged in. Arguing vociferously, they took their places with the D'Arcys. It was difficult to tell them apart, except for the mustache worn by Mrs. Thornhill. Kelly, the dog, slunk out of the room. The argument continued, D'Arcy trying vainly to pacify first one, then the other. Finally they stopped bickering and devoured everything on their plates without a word. Could they have done in Fred Fairfax? Definitely.

Miss Quinlan asked the special deputy whether he was a birder, and when he answered in the negative, proceeded to enlighten him in some detail about the subject. "Did you know, for example," she asked him, her eyes huge behind her lenses, "that geese have been seen flying as high as 30,000 feet? Or that the wandering albatross migrates clear around the world? That birds live everywhere on Earth, from the Antarctic to the Sahara? That..."

Davenport filed everything away in his memory banks.

After dinner he managed to speak with each of the guests before they left the dining room. No one, other than Miss Quinlan, admitted to being up early that morning, or to having seen or heard anything unusual. In fact, no one seemed to believe that a murder had been committed. There had been no altercations (except between the Thornhills), no gnashing jealousies, no apparent motive of any kind.

"Fred must have just wandered off the trail," D'Arcy suggested authoritatively, as if that ended the matter. The huge smile appeared to be frozen onto a long, narrow face filled with long, narrow teeth.

"What about the note?" Davenport asked the retired diplomat.

"Anyone could have written that," the latter responded haughtily.

"Does that include you, Dr. D'Arcy?"

"Monsieur Da-ven-porrrt," the latter explained patiently, "if I killed everyone I didn't like I'd have drowned in blood a long time ago." But neither he, nor anyone else, could provide an ironclad alibi.

Davenport returned to the sitting room, where he found everyone except Parkening, who had gone back to his room to rest, discussing whether the fireworks display was on or off. Miss Quinlan trotted to the kitchen to find out. She came back to report that, due to the inclement weather, it was off.

The Thornhills and the D'Arcys retired to "the Cape Cod," the latter's small cottage at the corner of the Big House, to play bridge, leaving his dinner companions to finish a noisy game of Scrabble. Davenport stepped into the kitchen to talk with the staff. To his surprise the handyman was sitting with Rose, at a little table by the window, gulping a large glass of milk. Along the far wall a dishwasher hummed.

"Louie, this is Joey. He helps around the cottages. Cuts wood, does all the plumbing and repair work."

"Hello, Joey." Davenport apologized again for borrowing the twine. Joey pouted. His blondish hair had been wetted down and neatly combed.

"Joey never says much," Rose pointed out. He realized she had done this so he would go easy on the young man, who was clearly uncomfortable with strangers.

Davenport took the hint. "You find those keys?" he asked her.

"It's only 8:15, Louie. Nobody goes to bed at 8:15."

"Please don't forget. And I haven't seen a sample of your handwriting yet. Just routine. You understand."

Without a word she scribbled YOU'RE GOING TO DIE on a pad identical to the one on the sitting room desk, ripped off the sheet and thrust it at him. He studied it for a moment before slipping it into his pocket. "Joey?"

The dull eyes stared back at him.

"Would you mind doing me a favor and writing your name on that pad, there?"

He looked uncertainly at Rose and, when she nodded, took the pencil, painstakingly constructed a "JOEY SMALL" in large block letters. He handed the pad to Davenport, who tore off the page and added it to the others. "Thank you, Joey. Rose, where's the girl?"

"You mean Marge? She went home for the night. You can talk to her tomorrow if you need to. But she doesn't know anything about the—about what happened."

"Thank you. I will. And Lisa—where's she?"

"Out somewhere."

"Didn't you tell her I wanted to speak to her?"

"She's a grown woman, Louie. I can't do a thing with her. Has a mind of her own, like her father."

"I'll see her tomorrow, then."

"You can try."

"And about the address and phone number of Mrs. Fairfax—"

"All right, all right—I'll see if I can find it." She stomped out of the kitchen, Davenport trailing along behind. He thought he heard a snort from Joey.

The keys were the old-fashioned kind, complete with a skeleton key that opened all the locks. Reluctantly, Rose turned the latter over to him along with the address and telephone number, in Boston, of Mrs. Frederick Fairfax.

Clutching their keys, the remaining guests drifted back to their rooms or cottages. Davenport was left alone with Rose, who fell into her favorite chair and poured herself a glass of sherry. He asked her how long Joey had been with her.

"All his life."

"You mean he started working here as a boy?"

"He's my nephew. His father was killed in a boating accident. His mother never recovered. She was in a mental institution for a while, but they didn't do her much good. Now she lives with my other brother and his wife in Portland. Herb's an engineer. Built the city's new sewage system. Marge is an artist and I don't know what else. She's been all over the world. Hired on as a cook on a freighter once. Haven't seen them in years. Funny how things turn out, isn't it?" She took a sip of sherry before getting up and kicking the logs in the fireplace. The flames roared up immediately.

They sat quietly for a while. Davenport felt himself being hypnotized by the blazing firewood, which he could have gazed at contentedly for the rest of his life. Fire and the sea: they were never boring. Perhaps because they were both so dangerous.

But Special Deputy Sheriff Louis B. Davenport was not here to watch boats sail or logs burn. "I'll be right back," he announced, and hustled to his room. In a minute he came back with an ink pad and paper. "Just routine," he explained. "We know your fingerprints are on the note. We need to identify them in order to see if anyone else's are on there, too." After taking the impressions (her countenance was hard but her hands surprisingly soft) he thanked her for the best dinner he had had in some time, said goodnight, and returned to his room.

"Breakfast is at eight," she snapped. "After that we throw everything out."

Davenport smiled, closed the door, and began to undress before remembering that there was no shower or tub in the bathroom and he had forgotten to ask where to find one. He shrugged, closed the chintz curtains, and retrieved his threadbare pajamas from the bottom drawer of the bureau.

Lying in bed wishing his bowels would move, he ran the day's events through the cracks and crevices of his mind. So far he hadn't uncovered a single clue pertaining to the death of Fred Fairfax. As his late friend and colleague was prone to remark, "Worst kind of situation—nobody knows nuttin'." The case reminded him of another which took place under similar circumstances, though at a lake resort rather than a remote island. Simple matter of jealousy between two of the guests, but when his suspicion was aroused by certain inconsistencies in times and places, the killer's mind snapped and he nearly nailed Davenport by firing a shot through a window into his room.

He got up and, with considerable effort, managed to push his bed over to the corner. Certain that his incipient hernia was about to give way, he stuffed an unlit cigarette into his mouth, locked the door, and climbed back into bed.

The floodlight coming through the curtains cast a pale, ghostly luminescence in the room, making everything, even the flowers, seem colorless, distant, unreal. He could hear the sea splashing gently against the shore; he got up again and peered out the window. The fog had begun to lift and he could dimly see the meadow. For a long time he watched the single light of a boat creep across the cove. It was beautiful, peaceful. He could feel himself and his large intestine slowly, slowly relaxing.

A New Assistant

Davenport was yawning on the ferry dock at 7:15 with the personal effects of the decedent, as well as a large manila envelope containing the fingerprint and handwriting samples. The fog had returned but was not as dense as before, and the clouds seemed to be brightening by the minute.

All the vehicles going to the mainland had already been loaded on, including a rusty station wagon transporting the body of the late Fred Fairfax enclosed in a reusable spruce box. The crew wandered around the stern, waiting for last-minute arrivals. Davenport handed him the packages. "Remember me?"

"Yes, I believe I do. Mr. Sleepyhead." He glanced at the captain high above and chuckled.

"Who's driving the wagon?"

"Pete said somebody from the sheriff's office would pick it up on the other side."

"Dr. Houseman told you that?"

"That's what I said."

"Okay." Davenport held out the packages. "Give these to the deputy over there, will you?"

The crew wiped his hands on his pants. "That the dead guy's stuff?"

"Just some clothes and his personal things."

"You can put it in there," he said, indicating the makeshift hearse.

With a shrug, Davenport stepped onto the Island Haven, tossed everything into the passenger seat, and slammed the door. "Who's got the ignition key?"

"Don't worry," the captain shouted through an open window. "They'll get it." A great sluice of tobacco juice squirted from the wheelhouse and down to the water. The engine started up like a lion roaring.

Davenport jumped off the boat and watched as it disappeared into the mist. Next to a shed filled with twine he spotted a pay phone and called the sheriff's office. Oscar Peterson, the night man, was still on. He told the young deputy about the body, the packages, everything he knew so far. Asked him to get someone to contact Mrs. Fairfax and to call him at Porpoise Bay Cottages if she had any useful information. "By the way, Ossie, there aren't any pictures. I forgot my camera."

"Sheriff's gonna love that, Lou."

By the time he found his way back to the cottages the early-morning fog had burned off. He paused at the front door of the house and looked out over the meadow to the bay, blue and sparkling in the sunlight. The field was another sea of yellow and orange and white. The air was clean and fresh, like lettuce. He felt wonderful. No one could possibly die on a day like this.... He bounded into the dining room, where he found everyone except the D'Arcys, who never took breakfast, and the Thornhills, who were late. There were no seat assignments. He joined the Bakers, the attractive young couple with the baby. The toddler picked up a spoon and began to bang on the highchair. Her mother gave her a swig of orange juice. The banging resumed. She was temporarily quieted with a mouthful of cereal. A potential murderer? Undoubtedly.

Cathy Baker was a nurse, wide-eyed and friendly, her curly brown hair cut short. The picture of youthful innocence, he thought. Davenport asked about her background, unsurprised when she responded with, "There's nothing much to tell," as had almost everyone he had ever interviewed. But he managed to learn that she had obtained her nursing degree at a Big Ten university, where she had met her husband. "It was in the library," she recalled happily. "Every time I sat down to read I would find him sitting next to me. I thought it was a strange coincidence until I realized he was just too shy to say anything." She smiled and patted her husband's hand. His nearly invisible blond eyebrows rose and fell several times.

Baker continued to spoon in the oatmeal with rapid-fire movements. Every few seconds he pushed his plastic-rimmed, fiftyish-style glasses back up his nose. His shirt pocket was stuffed with pens and doodads lined up like birds on a wire. When he chewed, a muscle bulged in his jaw. On it rode a piece of toilet paper glued there by a dot of dried blood.

"Jim," Mrs. Baker informed him, "is a molecular biologist studying DNA replication and cell division in the slime mold."

"What's a slime mold?" Davenport queried, primarily to get the young man's attention.

A light came on in Baker's eyes. He dispatched the last of the oatmeal, pushed up his glasses, and began his standard lecture. By the time he had finished, Davenport had learned more than he wanted to know about this peculiar organism, which sometimes behaved as if it were a plant and other times like an animal, that in the vegetative state it is syncytial, i.e. the nuclei are not segregated by cell walls, so they divide synchronously. "This means that a large amount of material may be studied at any given point in the mitotic cycle without resorting to artificial means of synchronization. Ergo," he concluded, "the slime mold is the best organism available for identifying the factors which control nuclear division. If those factors could be identified, it should be a simple matter to figure out what regulates this process in both normal and cancer cells." Davenport filed this in his memory banks without comment.

Like his wife, Jim Baker had grown up in the midwest (though he knew nothing about football or basketball). He went to graduate school on a fellowship and met Cathy in the library. They had been married four years.

Lisa appeared with plates of bacon and eggs and whole wheat toast.

"No waitress today?"

"That's only for lunch and dinner. It gets more complicated then." Before Davenport could ask to speak with her later on, she hurried back into the kitchen.

"How'd you happen to come here?"

Baker gouged out the yolk of his egg with a piece of toast and retreated into some inner world. His wife answered the question. "It was purely by accident. We were on vacation, driving up Highway One, and ended up in Milbridge. When we saw the ferry we got on to see where it went." She glanced fondly at Baker. "He does things like that sometimes." She gave the child a bit of toast. "And we ended up here."

Davenport realized she was defending her husband, not wanting him to think Baker a total nerd. Would she lie for him, too? Of course. He asked Baker a question, realized he wasn't listening, and repeated it for his wife. "Does he do unexpected things very often?"

"Not *that* often. Otherwise it wouldn't be unexpected."

"Does he do them for the thrill of it, do you think?"

"I wouldn't put it that way. I think he just likes to break out of the routine occasionally. That's why he's such a good scientist—he comes up with ideas nobody else would think of."

At this point Davenport accidentally bit his tongue. He wondered whether it was bleeding, whether he had cut into a vein, what the long-term effect might be. He surreptitiously inserted his napkin deep into his mouth, retrieved it, found a bit of egg clinging to it, but, fortunately, no blood.

Chewing carefully on a warm piece of buttered toast he observed, "All the other rooms are occupied by people who have been coming here for years. How did you manage to find a vacancy?"

"I think one of the regulars died just before we got here."

"You mean Fairfax?"

"No. Someone else."

"Really? Who?"

"We didn't know him. You'll have to ask Rose."

"What do you do, Mrs. Baker? Besides being a nurse and mother? Any hobbies?"

"Not really. I read a lot."

"What sort of things do you read?"

"Murder mysteries, mostly. I read one about every day. There are lots of them on the shelves in the sitting room if you're interested."

"Yes, I noticed that."

"My favorite author is Agatha Christie."

"A lot of people would agree with you."

"Have you read *And Then There Were None*?"

"No, I haven't."

"It takes place on an island. There might be a clue in there for you."

"Maybe I'll read it."

"If you ever need anyone to talk over your ideas with, just let me know."

"Thanks. I'll keep that in mind."

"I've just started writing a novel myself."

"Really? What's it about?"

"About the island. I'm still taking notes."

"What are you going to call it?"

"*Murder on Spruce Island.*"

Baker came back to life. He scratched his head, leaving a meadow of cowlicks behind, and gazed penetratingly at Davenport. "Are we finished? I'd like to get into the woods and look for some slime molds. Did you know their favorite food is oatmeal?" His eyebrows did several more pushups.

The spoon started banging on the high chair. "Can't you shut that kid up?" Alice Barnstable wailed from across the room.

Porpoise Bay Cottages

Davenport walked Rose to the parking lot, defined by a few scattered particles of gravel. The sun was bright, but not hot, and the air redolent of spruce and the sea. Overhead, a small plane droned.

He spotted the stick figure of Miss Quinlan at the bottom of the meadow, her face lifted toward the sky. The dog ran down the path in her direction. Rose said, "Kelly always goes with anyone she finds walking on the trails."

"Did she go with Fairfax yesterday morning?"

"I don't know. You'll have to ask *her*."

Or his killer, thought Davenport.

The place was a farm a century ago, with the cottages serving various essential functions. Including the Big House there were five buildings in all, every one cedar-shingled, gray with age, and overgrown with ivy. To their right, as they faced the cove, the Cape Cod was nestled in a copse of birch and spruce. "The D'Arcys are in there," Rose reminded him. "Over to your left is the Blacksmith Shop. Edith Manhart and Callie Black are there. Just below them, in the Farmhouse, are Frank Parkening and the Thornhills. Farther up the trail is the Lodge, where Alice Barnstable stays. She comes for the whole summer, you know."

"Parkening stays with the Thornhills?"

"Yes. In separate quarters, of course. Like Miss Quinlan and the Bakers upstairs in the Big House. There used to be a barn right here, where the parking lot is. That's gone now," she lamented.

"Did it have a name, too?" he joked.

"The Barn."

Davenport nodded solemnly. "Rose—who was here last July in the Bakers' room?"

"Oh, that was the Topats. He died only last week. They had just arrived, actually. Such a shame. Jane had come into some money. She was a great-niece of one of the oil companies. Well, not the company itself, but you know what I mean. He got sick just before they left the island last summer. When Pete told him he had cancer, he cried like a baby. Not Les Topat—Pete. He always does that. So did I. It was a terrible thing. They were birders, you know, even worse than Harriett. Brought telescopes, cameras, books, and I don't know what all. They discovered one bird that hadn't been seen on the island in a century. Hardly ever remembered to come back for lunch. Les was an artist, too, though he wasn't very good at it. Did some nice watercolors and pencil sketches, though. Like the one of my husband in the sitting room. And the one of the bay in the Blacksmith Shop. You should go over and take a look at it some time."

"What happened to Mr. Topat? I mean, was he buried here?"

"His urn is in the house, on the shelf with some of his favorite books. Jane said he wanted it that way."

"He must've loved this place."

"Yes. Yes, he did. So did she. She gave us some money in his name to fix up the Big House. The places always need work, you know. Right now the roof on the Farmhouse could use some repairs."

"What about Alice Barnstable? Does she love the place?"

She wagged her head back and forth. "Don't worry about her bark. That's just the way she is. It's her bite I'd watch out for!"

"Did she ever bite anyone to death?"

"Not that I know of. But I wouldn't be surprised. Alice was married once, you know. To a college professor who never liked the island. Never liked *her*, for that matter. I think he married her for her looks, as well as her money. She was quite stunning in her day. Don't know what she saw in him, but they stuck together for quite a while, despite everything."

"Anything between her and Fairfax?"

"Alice and Fred? That would be a ridiculous concept."

"Why?"

"He was as obnoxious as Mort."

"Mort's her ex-husband?"

"That's right."

"Maybe she's attracted to obnoxious people." Davenport pointed to the path disappearing into the woods between the Farmhouse and the Blacksmith Shop. "I'd like to take a look at the cliff where Fairfax fell. Do you have time to walk that way?"

"Not right now. Got to do some shopping for Sunday dinner. That's at one o'clock, you know. Just sandwiches for supper tonight."

Davenport glanced up at the single-engine airplane, which seemed to be hovering overhead. Suddenly it stalled and dropped out of the sky, recovering just above the treetops. He shuddered. "The grocery stores are open on Sunday?"

"Not one. But Cousin Henry always opens up for me. I'm one of his best customers, you know."

"How about this afternoon? Can you drive me around the island? I don't have a very good idea of the layout here."

A mysterious smile crept onto her face. "I've got a better idea. You ever been up in a small plane?"

"Not a small one, exactly."

"It's a tradition. Harold T. Henderson takes all my guests for a tour of the island on their first visit. Went away a few years back to learn to fly. That's all he ever wanted to do. Never had much interest in the sea. His father was disappointed at first, but he got over it. H. T. always hopes somebody is going to take flying lessons from him. No one ever does, of course. You want to go up with him this afternoon, Louie?"

Davenport, who was afraid to climb a ladder, hesitated. But he didn't want to seem wimpy, not to this attractive woman who seemed unafraid of anything. "Well—sure. Okay. Why not?" He bared his teeth in a false grin, wondered whether he might have a piece of bacon stuck between them.

"Right after dinner okay with you? I'll give him a call."

He nodded miserably, but it seemed to be out of his hands. "Now I just follow this path down to the cliffs, right?" he managed to ask.

"Yes, only it's more up than down, and it's not a 'path,' it's the Red Trail. You'll see the marks as you go along—splashes of red paint on some of the trees and rocks. So that you don't get lost, you know. Well, toodle-oo." She climbed into a bright red pickup truck and started it before yelling: "I called Janet Blue. Richard's out feelin' in his weirs today. He'll talk to you tomorrow."

"He's what?"

"Checking his fish traps for herring," she said, with exaggerated distinctness.

"Oh."

In another moment she was speeding up the gravel driveway. He thought he heard her shout: "H. T.'s a good pilot when he's sober!"

The Scene of the Crime

Davenport threaded his way between the Farmhouse and the Blacksmith Shop and entered the woods. The aroma of warm spruce trees, muted the day before by fog, enticed him like a freshly-baked pie. It made him think of past Christmases at the orphanage, his excitement at the prospect of having something his own, even if it was only socks or a T-shirt. His ex-wife, on the other hand, always insisted on a sterile artificial tree—odorless, pink, devoid of olfactory memory.

A bright yellow bird appeared out of nowhere, flew across the trail in front of him, and disappeared into the thicket. From just above the treetops swooshed the heavy beat of a raven's wings, swimming hard against the warming air. A squirrel stared at him from a low-hanging bough. It was small, wiry, defiant, and seemed to be chattering, "Go awaaaaaay. You don't belong heeeeere."

Thirty yards up the trail he spotted the Lodge, where Alice Barnstable spent her summers. Her "lawn" consisted of a rusty hand pump surrounded by a patch of bare earth. The cottage itself was enveloped by spruces. Not a ray of sunlight came through except, perhaps, at midday. From it came a mooselike whoop: "Sheriiiifff!"

Davenport slid to a halt. Ms. Barnstable came running out her door. Whether it was the front or back he couldn't tell. "Where you headed?" she bellowed. "The cliffs?"

"That's right," he sighed.

"Hold on a minute!" She disappeared inside the house and came back wearing a floppy hat and poking the ground with a good-sized stick. "I was going for a walk anyway," she announced as she joined him on the trail.

"Fine. I don't know my way around yet. Besides," he said, "I'd enjoy the comp—"

But she was already six steps ahead of him, her mighty calf muscles rippling. He hurried to catch up.

"Nice day," he observed. She ignored him again. "I say, NICE DAY!"

"Clever of you to notice!" she yelled back, without turning around.

He trotted up beside her. "Is it like this most of the time?"

She picked up the pace. "Nope. Most of the time it's rainy and foggy. Then there are the insects. Trillions of 'em. I don't know why anyone would come to this godforsaken place."

"Maybe some people like rain and fog. It's rather pleasant in its own—"

"Nobody likes those goddamn blackflies."

"They seem to be about gone."

"And now the mosquitoes have arrived."

"Just for a while."

"Then it'll be time to go back to work. Anyway, I didn't come out here to discuss the weather and the bugs. There's something I thought I ought to tell you."

"What's that?"

"I know who killed Fred Fairfax."

Davenport stopped briefly, then ran to catch up again. "Really? Who?"

"Walt."

"Dr. D'Arcy? Why didn't you tell me that last night?"

"I wasn't born yesterday. I didn't want him to hear me."

"How do you know it was him?"

"I heard him early yesterday morning walking past the Lodge with Fred. You've talked to Walt, haven't you, Sheriff? He has a very distinctive voice. Like a foghorn with a cold. They were arguing about something."

"What?"

"I couldn't make it out."

"What time was that?"

"Six. Six-fifteen."

Davenport was becoming short of breath. Alice Barnstable, however, forged relentlessly ahead. "What motive do you attribute to the murder?" he panted.

"There are only two real motives, Sheriff. Jealousy and greed. Don't you ever read mystery novels?"

"Not many."

"Ah. It would be a busman's holiday, wouldn't it?" She snorted.

"More a matter of finding time. Which motive applies to Dr. D'Arcy?"

"Both."

At last they came to a plateau. "How so?" wheezed Davenport.

"In the first place, he was jealous of the attention Fred was giving to Pat."

"You mean Mrs. D'Arcy."

"That's what I said."

"Was it reciprocated?"

"How the hell should *I* know?"

"She's your sister, isn't she?"

"Yes, but we don't talk much."

"Why not?"

"It's a long story."

"Did he ever make a pass at *you*?"

"If he had I would have killed him."

"*Did* you kill him?"

"Like I said, he never bothered me."

"What about other women?"

"There were rumors about some of the islanders. That may be the main reason he came here. That and the target practice."

"Target practice?"

"Fred loved to shoot things. Claimed he was aiming at tree trunks and so on. But sometimes a bird or squirrel would get in the way. A deer once or twice."

"How well did Dr. D'Arcy know Mr. Fairfax?"

"They were college roommates. Along with Frank Parkening."

"What about the greed part?"

"My guess is that Walt wants a bigger chunk of the Project for himself."

"Project?"

Her eyes fluttered violently. "You haven't heard about the Project?"

"No."

"What do you interrogate your suspects about—the deodorant they use? It's the biggest thing that ever hit the island. Or most other places, probably."

"Tell me about it."

"Something like half of Spruce Island is owned by a Swiss family. All the virgin forest in the middle of the island. They want to sell."

"And who's buying?"

"A consortium. Just about everybody who comes to Porpoise Bay Cottages is in on the deal."

"Who else besides the D'Arcys?"

"Frank, the Thornhills. Even the ladies are in on it."

"Which ladies?"

"Manhart and Black."

"They pretty well-off, are they, Ms. Barnstable?"

"Evidently, Sheriff. Edith was a famous stage and silent screen actress at one time. That's about all I can tell you."

And actors are very good at telling lies and hiding their feelings, he reminded himself. "What about you? Do you have a piece of the action?"

"Me? I'm just poor relation. Couldn't afford a rock on the beach."

"How much money is involved?"

"For half of Spruce Island? We've got to be talking about millions, Sheriff."

"The guests here have that kind of money?"

"No, but they can get it. Fred was a banker, or didn't you know? His bank was going to be the chief financier."

"What does the consortium plan to do with all that land?"

"Why, build a theme park, of course."

"What's the theme?"

"Would you believe 'APTGAFIA'?"

"'APT— What?"

"APTGAFIA. 'A Place To Get Away From It All.' They want to build a conservatory, an aviary—you know, the whole flora and fauna thing. With a big hotel and a gourmet restaurant and all the rest."

"What do the islanders think of this?"

"About what you'd expect."

They were looking out over the bay. The Red Trail wiggled its way along the clifftop, but not so close that anyone could accidentally slip off.

He crept close to the edge and pounded a small red flag into the rocky soil. It was a sheer drop of at least three hundred feet to the rocks below. A person falling from that height wouldn't stand a chance. He backed quickly away.

"Still think he just fell, Sheriff?"

"Doesn't seem likely. Unless he wasn't paying attention. Maybe he was thinking about Mrs. D'Arcy or the theme park and wasn't watching where he was going."

"But the trail is worn bare along here and clearly marked. You'd have to want to leave it deliberately to stray that far away."

"Maybe he was just looking over the edge and slipped."

"In the fog?"

Davenport nodded. "Anything else you want to tell me?"

"I told you who killed him, Sheriff. Isn't that enough?"

"Quite enough. Incidentally, Ms. Barnstable. I'm not the sheriff. I'm a special deputy."

"I know that, Sheriff. I just wanted to see how long it would take to get your goat. It didn't take very long—your goat is pretty easy to get."

He stared at her. That was exactly what his ex-wife had told him too many times to remember.

A Bird's-eye View

Davenport looked hard for a sign directing him to the Spruce Island airport. He signaled a fellow traveler to stop, but the man only stared at him and drove on by. Just as the road was curving past Ferguson's Cove he spotted a rutted lane off to the left and decided to follow it. He had bounced only a few yards when the muffler was ripped from the exhaust pipe. The Plymouth roared in anger and dismay.

He had been seated for the early Sunday dinner with Alice Barnstable and the D'Arcys, who discussed politics throughout the meal. This was a subject that didn't interest Davenport in the slightest, not even when D'Arcy labeled Clinton a "womanizer," and his sister-in-law responded with a whinnying attack on Bush's mental capabilities.

He had finally caught up with Lisa Kelly, Rose's daughter and heir-apparent to Porpoise Bay Cottages. The energetic, chain-smoking young woman was of little help, however, in providing clues about what had happened to Fred Fairfax. He broached the subject of Fairfax's alleged affairs, inquiring delicately whether the man had ever come on to her. The look of abject disgust was answer enough, though he wasn't sure it was a reaction to the idea or to the question itself. As soon as the brief interview was finished she was careening up the driveway, off to wherever she spent her free time.

Nor was Marge, the waitress, able to provide any useful information. The shy girl of sixteen hadn't seen or heard anything unusual the previous morning. But she lived miles away and didn't come to work at the Big House until eleven o'clock. Did she know of anyone who might want to kill Mr. Fairfax? No. Anything she could think of that might help in his investigation? No. Nobody knew nuttin'.

The weedy lane widened to a clearing. The airport turned out to be a grass strip no more than 1500 feet long, a snake-like series of shallow hills and valleys. Along the edges fishermen dried their nets. At one end stood a forest of spruce. The other fell into the sea. The terminal was an old tool shed, adjacent to which stood the hangar: a pair of steel rings for tieing down Spruce Island's commercial fleet, an old Cessna 172. It was there that Davenport found the pilot, and vice versa. It was too late to turn around.

Harold T. Henderson stood only five feet five, but had the build of a tackle. Yet he was quick, never stood still, never seemed to stop talking in a high-pitched, staccato voice. Davenport, after climbing into the passenger seat, could hear him droning on and on outside the plane as he wiggled the various parts of the wing and tail. The special deputy sheriff jumped when the wheel in front of him spun left or right, lunged forward or back, as if it had a mind of its own. Finally Henderson hopped into the cockpit and started the engine, from which a cloud of blue smoke exploded. Davenport, dripping perspiration, cleared his throat and grabbed onto his seat. The plane started to roll.

Henderson taxied the aircraft, bouncing like an army jeep, toward the sea. Davenport gripped his seat tighter and tighter as they came closer and closer to the edge of the cliff. With nothing but empty space ahead they careened into a U-turn and proceeded to bump their way back toward the woods. On and on and on they rolled, lifting off and bouncing back and lifting off again toward the looming trees, climbing steeply just over their tops. "Flew right into them once or twice," Henderson shouted over the din. "Ended upside-down the second time. Lost a couple of teeth." He pointed to some wires in his mouth. Davenport swallowed hard and watched the forest drop away. He reached for a cigarette, sucked on it a couple of times. It nauseated him and he stuffed it back into the pack.

"This here's the altimeter," yelled the pilot. "See? Eight hundred, eight-fifty? See that?" Davenport shouted in the affirmative. A left turn and they were out over the water, which sparkled brightly in the afternoon sun. Proceeding south, along the main road, Henderson pointed out the village of Nor'east Head behind them, Centerville ahead, and Fog Cove on the distant southern shore. Cormorant Rock with its photogenic lighthouse appeared on their left. Looking down past the motionless wheel of the ancient aircraft Davenport thought he could make out the doctor's blue house on the near side of Centerville, and behind him, to the right, the Big House and two or three of the cottages. He imagined Rose holding court in front of the fireplace, a glass of sherry in her hand.

"This is the attitude indicator," Henderson screeched. "See what happens when we bank steeply left or right? See what happens? See that?" Davenport hung on. "And the rate of climb indicator there: watch what happens when we go into a sharp dive, then climb out. Got that?" Davenport felt the bottom of the plane drop away, followed immediately by the irresistible force of gravity kicking him in the seat of his pants. His stomach sent him a nasty message.

They proceeded along the coast past Seal Beach, where a few colorful people were sunbathing. Henderson pointed out Gull Island, Sand Harbor, Dog's Tail and Fog Cove as they slid around to the right. All of that paled in comparison to the vastness of the dense spruce forest at the center of the island, dwarfing everything else. "The Flukes up ahead," said the pilot. "See the whale's tail? North of that is Eagle Point, and then you can see the cliffs from there running all the way up to Porpoise Bay. Those little shacks on the beach ahead of us are for the dulsers."

"Dulsers?" Davenport shouted feebly.

"Dulse harvesters. Haven't you ever had any dulse? Can't leave the island without trying a mouthful of dulse. And that's Ferguson's Cove over on your right behind the airport—see it?" Davenport nodded and began to relax a little. The tour was almost over; they were turning toward the narrow landing strip.

But Henderson had another idea. "Nothing like flying, do you agree?"

Davenport heartily agreed, glad to be done with it.

"It's your airplane!"

"Huh?"

"Take the yoke—you're flying now!"

"Uh—but—"

"Go ahead! It won't bite you!"

Davenport's hands tightened on the wheel.

"Don't strangle it. Just tight enough so it doesn't get away from you. That's right. That's right. Now turn it a little to the left. See what happens? Now a little to the right. Get it? Now pull back a little. Good. Now forward. See that? Couldn't be simpler, do you agree?"

Davenport nodded. He was, in fact, beginning to enjoy himself. The sense of isolation, of control, of being completely in charge of his fate. He even managed a feeble smile, though he could feel the hairs rising from the back of his neck.

"Now for some *real* fun!" yelled Henderson. "My airplane!" He grabbed the yoke, thrust the throttle forward, and pulled into a slow, circular climb. Davenport's eyes glued themselves to the altimeter. Two thousand, twenty-five hundred, three thousand, four thousand, five, six. More than a mile high and still circling lazily over Spruce Island, now only a green patch in the big blue sea. To the west he could make out the hazy coast of Maine and beyond. To the east only air and water. The pilot pulled back the throttle and the plane began to slow down. A tug on the wheel and the nose lifted. Slower, slower. Henderson pointed toward the airspeed indicator. Fifty-five, fifty, forty-five. The only sound was the whine of a stall-warning device. It was a peculiarly peaceful sensation, almost like floating on air. Davenport began to relax again, ever so little.

Suddenly the nose of the Cessna dropped violently and the world began to spin around with unbelievable speed. Certain that he was going to die, Davenport's hands flew to the roof, his eyes as big as dinner plates. Spin, spin, spin, and finally the aircraft straightened out and began to pull up. He felt around frantically for what passed for an airsickness bag: an empty ice cream carton. "Blueberry ripple," he noticed grimly as he calmly screwed off the top and filled it with the chicken he had just eaten, the tomatoes with sour cream, the rice, and the blueberry pie à la mode, in reverse order, more or less.

Henderson roared with laughter. "Now, that wasn't so bad, was it?" he shouted. "Let's do it again!" And the nose of the plane lifted once more toward the heavens.

Happy Hour

Pat D'Arcy slowly opened the door to Davenport's tapping and almost fell down getting out of his way. She motioned toward a wicker sofa flattened against a wall. "Won't you have a seat?" she offered meekly. Her pure silver hair was a nest of coiffed wire, her makeup a patina of dried paint. Barely able to take his eyes off the jewelry she wore everywhere, he squeaked down onto a lumpy cushion, banging his knee on a glass coffee table riding the back of what appeared to be a wooden porpoise.

The Cape Cod was a small cottage furnished in modern Victorian, with flowered wallpaper and matching curtains. In the center of the living room stood a rusty pot-bellied stove, dull and cold. A handwritten appeal was tacked to the wall behind it: INTELLECTUALS UNITE!

He could hear D'Arcy in the kitchen noisily stirring cocktails. When the last tinkle had died, the diplomat, wearing a dark, neatly pressed blazer and huge, frozen grin, burst into the room. "Well, Monsieur Da-ven-porrrt, did you enjoy the tour?"

Davenport stared at the long, narrow teeth. "Every minute of it," he replied wanly, still queasy more than two hours after barely clearing the top of the cliff, bouncing at last to solid ground, and skidding to a halt just short of the trees.

D'Arcy nodded happily. "Of course you know by now that all our new guests must pass this initiation rite. Oliver Twist?"

"Huh?"

"Olive or a twist of lemon, Monsieur?"

"Oh. Olive, I guess." He wondered whether D'Arcy smiled in his sleep.

His host fiddled with the jar, in which, to Davenport's chagrin, floated a swarm of black particles resembling termites. He was about to ask for the lemon when a mottled olive and several of the tiny creatures dropped into his glass. D'Arcy pointed out the pictures on the walls—caricatures of several of the guests scissored from black paper by the late Mr. Topat. Davenport recognized Parkening's great bulk, but the others looked almost identical.

"So, Monsieur, how did you get from Boston to Machias, if I may be so bold?"

Davenport stuttered, "I needed a change of scene. And it's a stepping stone toward retirement." D'Arcy nodded absentmindedly and handed him the drink. He stared at it unhappily, reached for a cigarette, changed his mind. "You're a diplomat, is that right, Dr. D'Arcy?"

"Welllll," the latter grinned. "I'm retired now. Cheers!" D'Arcy dumped half a martini into his grinning maw.

Davenport lifted his glass, but didn't drink. He was waiting for the termites to settle. "What do you do now? Any hobbies?"

"Bridge. Deck tennis. History. Right now I'm working on my memoirs."

Davenport considered possible ways of addressing this tall, dignified public servant, toying with "your excellency" and "your grace," finally settling for something less formal. "Any idea who might have wanted Fred Fairfax dead, sir?"

"Not a one."

Davenport politely inquired whether D'Arcy might have been with Fairfax the morning he died, and studied the horsy countenance for subtle changes in demeanor. "That's a serious accusation, Monsieur Da-ven-porrrt."

"Is it true?"

The deep voice softened a decibel or two, in what passed, perhaps, for a whisper. "Not a word of it," he croaked.

Mrs. D'Arcy's head whirled toward Davenport. "It was Alice who told you that, wasn't it?" A hint of color had risen to her face. "Pay no attention to her," she pouted. "She lies like a rug."

"Now Pat," D'Arcy grinned, touching his wife's cheek with the back of his hand, "she's not as bad as all that."

"She's always been jealous of me. Even when we were little girls." She picked some lint off her stylish wool skirt.

"You're still my little girl," he reassured her with a brisk tug at her chin.

If he were smiling at her, thought Davenport, how would she know? "Did Mr. Fairfax ever make any kind of romantic approach toward you, Mrs. D'Arcy?"

Her head whipped around again. She cried, "Certainly not! If anyone was trysting with Fred it was Alice!"

Trysting? thought Davenport. How very quaint. And many, many murders are committed by very quaint people. Moreover, he reasoned, the lady protesteth quite strongly....

"I hadn't planned to tell you this, Monsieur," grinned D'Arcy, "but I heard someone who sounded very much like Alice outside with Fairfax early yesterday morning."

Davenport lifted his left eyebrow. "Why hadn't you planned to tell me? Are you sure it was her?"

"No, I'm not. That's why I didn't tell you."

"Wouldn't you recognize your sister-in-law's voice if you heard it?"

"It sounded like her," the diplomat patiently repeated. "The point is, I didn't *see* her." He took his wife's hand. She gazed puppylike into his rheumy eyes.

Davenport grunted and filed this information for later consideration. Either Alice Barnstable or Walter D'Arcy was lying, he surmised. Or possibly both. "What about the Project, Dr. D'Arcy? Did you stand to gain by Fred Fairfax's death?"

"Not in the slightest. In fact, it complicates things."

"Would anyone else profit from his demise that you know of?"

"His wife, I suppose. You'd have to take a look at his will to know for certain."

"Thank you. I'll do that." Special Deputy Sheriff Davenport took a generous sip of his drink. It hit the bottom of his empty stomach like the flame of a blowtorch.

D'Arcy proffered a plate of crackers decorated with boli of smoked herring glued to suspicious-looking smears of cream cheese. "Horse doover?" he grinned.

THE OLD LIGHTHOUSE

Davenport was starved. Just as he opened wide for a spoonful of creamed mushroom soup, however, his dinner companions, the Thornhills, roared into the dining room, bickering about the endless minutiae of their lives. Thornhill, ignoring Davenport entirely, stuffed a cracker into his mouth and began to chew it furiously while continuing his side of the argument. A bit of the Saltine flew into Davenport's bowl. Mrs. Thornhill added a fleck of spittle. Hoping they were both free of infectious disease, he spooned out the cracker crumb and scarfed down the soup, followed by a pollock salad sandwich and two huge wedges of chocolate cake.

During all this he managed to ascertain that the Thornhills had been married more than thirty years, had produced four sons, and had quarreled their way around the country three or four times, stopping for a week or two at the D'Arcys' home in New Haven on each trip.

With the hope of finding something they could agree on, Davenport asked about the rest of their family. The discourse began amicably enough, even misty-eyed, but by the time the coffee cups were refilled they were accusing each other of responsibility for the way their offspring had turned out. The three oldest had moved to various corners of the world and they rarely saw any of them. The fourth had married and settled on Spruce Island, though he never paid them a visit when they came in the summer. In fact, he was a member of the island's volunteer fire department, and in charge of the evening's Fourth of July's fireworks display, postponed from yesterday. With his wife glaring at him, Thornhill invited Davenport to join them later for the occasion.

After they and the D'Arcys had gone off to play bridge, Davenport wandered around the dining room inspecting the blue willow china (his ex-wife had managed to teach him a few things about the material world), the freshly-painted wainscoting, the photograph of the late Jack Kelly hanging next to an ancient pendulum clock. He studied the picture (the model, apparently, for Topat's sketch): a handsome man wearing a cap and scarf, perhaps on his way to or from a sailing trip. The mischievous smile generated a hint of a dimple in his left cheek, and a scar the shape of a crescent moon decorated his chin. Someone had lovingly stitched "Cap'n Jack" on the cap.

He strolled into the sitting room where Ms. Barnstable, Miss Quigley, and the elderly ladies had congregated for an evening of Scrabble. The fire was languishing and Rose's chair was empty. After a moment of indecision he tossed a spruce log onto the glowing coals, which were instantly extinguished. He cleared his throat and wandered on, checking out some of the volumes stuffed in no particular order into the built-in shelves. Eliot. Thackeray. Dickens. He passed quickly by the urn containing the late Mr. Topat. Some day we'll all be perched on a shelf, he mused, or scattered to the winds. Pausing at the bay window, which was crowded with porpoises of various sizes and materials, he stared at the wildflower arrangement centered in the midst of the graceful figures. When he looked closely he discovered subtleties he had never before observed. Patterns within designs within patterns, a never-ending vortex that made his head swim. He gazed out toward the peaceful cove. "No such word!" someone screeched.

Kelly, the dog, was making her way up the path in the meadow to the Big House. Do you know who killed Fred Fairfax? he wondered. Was it Walter D'Arcy? Or Alice Barnstable? Perhaps one of the Thornhills was planning to do away with the other, and murdered Fairfax as a decoy to throw any investigation off the scent? A technique not unheard of in the vast annals of crime....

Rose appeared and kicked the log that Davenport had tossed into the fireplace. The fire blazed up. "Oh!" cried Miss Manhart, a sentiment echoed by Miss Black, as Harriett Quigley clicked down a seven-letter word. "Shit!" bellowed Barnstable.

On a shelf to the right of the bay window Davenport found a jigsaw puzzle called "The Old Lighthouse." He took it down and, clearing a space on the big desk, spread out the pieces. Paul Thornhill banged into the room, cracked his knuckles, and muttered, "Ready for some fireworks, Loose?"

A Display of Pyrotechnics

The Thornhills yammered all the way to the Centerville ball diamond about the Project and the windfall it would provide for everyone, including the islanders. "Can't understand these people," Thornhill lamented. "They don't seem to realize what we're trying to do for them. Their property values would triple the minute word got out." Davenport stared at the golf ball-sized cyst on the back of his neck, which looked as though it could burst at any moment.

"I told you before," growled his wife. "The people here are Neanderthals. Like you!"

"What does that make you, you *primate*!"

"Who's a primate, you . . . you—"

Davenport interrupted to inquire about their relationship with Fred Fairfax.

"Well, Loose, we first met Fred when we started coming here."

"How long ago was that?"

"Well, let me see." He gingerly scratched the cyst, then more vigorously all around it. "Almost twenty years, I guess."

"Eighteen years," Mrs. Thornhill corrected.

"Did you know him in Boston, too?"

"We met him at the bank just before we first came here. That's how we heard about Spruce Island."

"How well did you get along with him?"

"I could never break into the "musketeer" circle, but we were on good terms. Fred was our investment counselor and brought us in on the Project."

"What about the other guests? Anybody have a grudge against Mr. Fairfax?"

"Not that we know of. In fact, everyone stood to gain a pile of money on their investments."

65

"Did either of you hear anything on the morning he was killed?"

"Not me."

"How *could* you, the way you snore?"

"*Me?* You should hear her, Loose. Sounds like a pig in a trough."

Thornhill parked on the stony shoulder behind a quarter-mile string of cars, and they crunched their way to the crowded stands facing the ball diamond.

Even though it was nearly dusk, Davenport could see all eyes turn to them as they approached the homemade bleachers. One or two of the parents pointed at him and whispered something to the children. Some of the kids ran up to him, giggled, and ran away again. One of them, a boy of about eleven, shouted, "You don't belong here, Mister!" A few of the adults in the stands chuckled.

"What happened—miss the boat?" yelled another.

"All right, boys, that's enough," admonished one of the adults, a tall, distinguished-looking gentleman with silvery blond hair. He looked familiar—perhaps he was a relative of one of the patients he had run across in the doctor's office.

"They don't like outsiders much, do they?" he mumbled to Thornhill.

"No, they don't. And you can come here for twenty years, and you're *still* an outsider."

The crescent moon hung low in the western sky like a giant D'Arcy smile. Davenport spotted the grizzled physician and the captain and crew of the ferry. None of them showed any sign of recognition as he picked his way to the top row and took a seat next to the Thornhills. Only the Bakers, who had brought Joey, the handyman, waved at them.

"Look, Maryellen, there he is!" Thornhill pointed toward the outfield.

"Looks good, doesn't he?" she replied, waving frantically.

"It's no use. He doesn't see you. And if he did, he'd pretend he didn't."

"Remember how he almost burned down the house?"

Thornhill chuckled. "He always loved to play with matches, didn't he?"

The dark figure struck a light and ran for his life. A dim trail climbed into the sky and erupted in a shower of color. Davenport regarded the glowing faces of the spectators, both children and adults—the smiles, the "oohs" after the beautiful bursts, the sudden laughter following the ear-ringing booms. He remembered taking his own daughters to see the fireworks when they were little. Like their mother, they didn't like them much. He noted that the Bakers' daughter squealed with pleasure at every bang and whistle.

The display was over much too soon. There was a smattering of applause and the audience dispersed within minutes of the spectacular windup, like seeds on the wind. The Thornhills were already halfway to their car when he spotted them, and he had to run to catch up. He wondered whether the little pain he felt in his chest was the first sign of an imminent heart attack.

"What was Mr. Fairfax like?" Davenport asked as they piled into the car.

"He used to go out on the beach and shoot seagulls," replied Thornhill, gunning the motor impatiently as he waited for a space in the traffic. "Or any other bird he saw—gannets, cormorants, you name it." Maybe the gulls killed him, thought Davenport. There were similar cases where dogs and other animals, who had taken all they could stand, had turned on their abusers.

"And squirrels and things in the woods," added his wife. "I used to hate to go on the trails when he was around." Could he have been pushed off the cliff by a posse of squirrels? Davenport pondered further. Or butted over by a vengeful deer?

"Maryellen, you twit, he wouldn't shoot you. More's the pity," he added under his breath. A bucketful of gravel sprayed onto someone's lawn as Thornhill roared into the road.

"Who's a twit?" shouted Mrs. Thornhill.

"What kind of gun did he have? Do you know what happened to it?"

"No idea, Loose. He kept it in his room."

"WHO'S A TWIT?"

"There was no gun in Fairfax's room."

"Then somebody must've taken it."

"*You're* the twit, you big lummox."

Except for the occasional insult, the three of them drove in relative silence until they were almost to the parking lot, when Thornhill observed, "He did a good job, didn't he?"

"Yes, he did," murmured his wife. "He always does."

When the engine stopped, Davenport stepped out of the car into a heaven of stars. Except for the floodlight illuminating the paths between the cottages, the spectacle was undiluted by the fires of civilization, undimmed by smoke or haze. Even his granddaughters' terminology was inadequate. It was the first time he had clearly seen the Milky Way meandering from horizon to horizon.

Thornhill, noticing him gazing at the night sky, reared back his head. "What are you looking at, Loose? I don't see anything but stars." He strode off toward the Farmhouse, his wife trailing along behind.

As Davenport approached the Big House he heard Thornhill complain, "What's that smell?"

"Probably your own breath blowing back in your face, you numbskull."
"Who's a numbskull? Apologize!"
"All right! I apologize!"
"For what?"
"For marrying a numbskull like you!"

A brief moment of silence was followed by a vociferous shriek. Fingering his .38, Davenport wheeled and headed for the Farmhouse. Mrs. Thornhill was running around in little circles, whining and wailing, her husband yelling for her to stop making so much noise.

"What's the problem, folks?" he called out.
"Somebody put a dead seagull in the kitchen, Loose!"
"Poor thing," sobbed his wife.
"She likes gulls," Thornhill explained with a shrug.

At Death's Door

Davenport was chasing someone without a face along the top of the cliffs. But someone else was chasing *him*, and he could barely move. It was as though he were slogging through molasses. His pursuer overtook him in extreme slow motion. He was certain he was doomed. At that moment they all reached the edge of the cliff. Davenport tried to stop himself but it was too late. He skidded in the slippery syrup, noting, as he plunged over the precipice, that the man he was chasing had disappeared. Just before he hit the beach his tormentor, a dead seagull, smashed against the huge cyst on the back of his neck.

He awoke with a jump, got up panting and palpitating, and poured some water from the pitcher into the bowl. One day older, another day closer to death, he reminded himself. He inspected and brushed his teeth, combed his hair back over the bald spot, and went in to breakfast.

Frank Parkening, his table companion, hardly touched anything. His face was pallid as a scallop; bags of grapefruits hung from his eyes and jowls. "Haven't been feeling too well after Fred's demise," he confided. Parkening was the slowest-talking man he had ever heard. It was like being back in the dream he had awakened from only a quarter-hour earlier. He remembered the gull in the kitchen of the Farmhouse. It was obviously a warning, but was it for Parkening or the Thornhills?

Davenport speeded up his own delivery in an unconscious attempt to prod the man into higher gear. "Why is that, Mr. Parkening? Were you a good friend of his? Are you going to eat that toast?"

The grapefruits under Parkening's eyes weighed down his lower lids, revealing dark pools of blood underneath. "A friend of Fred Fairfax?" he reflected alliteratively, his mouth gaping like that of a fish out of water. "That's a contradiction in terms." His fat forehead gleamed with oil and sweat. Suddenly his hand went to his chest. Alarmed, Davenport cried, "What's the matter?"

Parkening wagged his head and wheezed, thickly, "Heart trouble. Doctor says I shouldn't get too excited."

Little chance of that, thought Davenport, though he sympathized with Parkening's concern. "In that case, I hope you'll tell me immediately if you get a note similar to the one that was found in Mr. Fairfax's room. There's little danger if we take proper precautions."

"Not with my luck," Parkening wailed pitifully. "I'm next—I know it!"

"Do you have any thoughts on who might have wanted to kill him?"

"Not really," drawled Parkening through a filter of mucus. "In fact, we all stand to lose if the Project is delayed."

Davenport studied the sallow, paunchy face, the yellow, cat-like eyes swimming in blood. "Tell me about yourself, Mr. Parkening." He began to count the veins in the man's oversized nose.

"What's there to tell? I'm a self-made millionaire many times over. Impressed?"

"Not particularly."

"Why not?"

"Because no matter how much money you acquire, it's never enough."

"You're disgustingly honest, Davenport, I'll say that for you. An astute observation."

"Are you an honest man yourself, Mr. Parkening?"

"I wouldn't trust myself for a second."

"Did you kill Fred Fairfax?"

"No."

"Should I believe that answer?"

"Not necessarily." To Davenport's dismay, Parkening took a tentative bite of the toast. Munching slowly, he seemed to think aloud: "Why would I have killed Fred? He was the best financial advisor I ever had. I don't know what I'm going to do without him."

"How well did you know him? Personally, I mean."

"Quite well. We were roommates in college. He and I and Walt."

"Would you know whether there have been any recent incidents between him and Dr. D'Arcy? Anything that might lead to his demise?"

Parkening chuckled carefully, so as not to exert himself. "Fred didn't have any friends. But his clients were very loyal."

"What about lady friends?"

"That's a different matter."

Davenport surveyed the quivering jowls and recalled a similar case in which a jilted lover killed a corporate vice-president, only to fall for the CEO. When she was discarded again she did away with him, too. An open and shut case. Unfortunately, the murderess died while awaiting trial. Of a heart attack....

Parkening grimaced and checked his pulse. Breathing noisily, he murmured, "If you'll excuse me, I'm going to lie down for a while." Wearily he rose from the table and shuffled from the dining room, his rumpled suit clinging to his damp body.

Davenport barely managed to wait until he had gone before grabbing the food remaining on his plate.

The Lady Butterfield

Richard Blue gazed out the wheelhouse window. He was in his eighties, wiry, hardscrabble-skinned, and less talkative than the captain and crew of the Island Haven.

Davenport sat uncomfortably on the gunnel. It was windy and the sea wasn't as smooth as he had thought. He wished he hadn't eaten two breakfasts. A flock of gulls circled overhead, the feet drawn up against their tails, for all the world like landing gear. Their heads swiveled back and forth, as if searching for potential victims. He fished for a Maalox tablet.

Across the bay steamed a number of vessels like the "Blue Pastures," all shining in the sun, trailing snow-white wakes in the emerald water. He searched for an ice cream container and, finding none, staggered to the bow and climbed into the cabin to look for one. Ahead, the water roiled violently. Davenport groaned. "What's that—a rip tide?" he asked, to distract himself from the nausea.

Blue came alive, his thick white hair swishing around his head as he turned to Davenport. "Nossir, them's little fish bein' chased by bigger fish. It's a fish eat fish world, you know."

"What's that funny-looking boat over there?"

"That's a pumper. Pumps the fish out of the weirs, like that one over there, the 'Staff o' Life.'" An afterthought: "It's low tide now or all you'd see was the tops of them stakes."

Davenport peered at a circular structure enclosed by nylon netting dripping with seaweed. An opening at one end of the contraption faced the beach.

"What's a 'wear'?"

"Looks like a heart with an arrow in it, don't it? All right. Now the herrin' feed along the shore there," he said, pointing. "Then they come to a wall of twine and turn out to sea, along the arrow. Once they get into the weir they swim around and around, but they never find their way back out again. They seem to have a one-track mind, you might say, like a lot of people." He gazed at Davenport with steady black eyes.

"Heron?"

"Mostly herrin', yes, sometimes a mackerel or two. Occasionally a tuna. Once in a while a porpoise will get in. Maybe even a whale."

Davenport studied the man's face, which would make a fine handbag, he surmised, or a sturdy pair of shoes. "You catch whales in these things?"

"Not very often. When we do, we have to lower the nets and let 'em out. Had a mother and baby humpback in this one last fall. Mother got out. Young'un couldn't get over the twine. When we finally got 'im out he made a beeline for his mom. She was waitin' a couple miles out." The snowy hair swished back and forth. "'Twas quite a sight." Blue took off his cap and scratched his salty head. "One of these fine days, if you have time, you can come along and watch us seine 'The Blue Blood.'"

"Thanks. I might do that."

Blue broke into a wry smile, certain that Davenport wouldn't be back. He turned toward the shore. "Right up there, Deppity. That's where I spotted 'im."

Davenport focused his eyes on the bottom of the cliff. "Were you closer in? That's a fair distance from here. And it was foggy, wasn't it? How did you know it was a man?"

"Color."

Davenport's left eyebrow flew up. "His color??"

"When you're out on the water you notice anything unusual. Fog was pretty thick on Saturday, but it lifted a little as I came around here, and I saw a little red and blue on the rocks. Wasn't there before. I got out my glasses and took a good look."

Davenport strained to spot the little flag he had planted high above the rocks and confirm the location. "What did you do when you found him?"

"I radioed 'er in. Then I dropped anchor and took the dory onto the beach. Brought him down and rowed back out to the boat."

"You carried a man all the way across the beach?"

"He wasn't too heavy. Kinda scrawny-like. I figured he musta been from away."

"You didn't recognize him?"

"Can't say as I did."

"Then you took him to the doctor."

"Ayup. Right after breakfast."

Davenport gazed at the faraway shore, the cliff rising majestically above it. He shook his head.

"Ever hear the story of the 'Lady Butterfield'?"

Davenport burped sourly. "No."

The captain of the Blue Pastures proceeded to relate the tale of a vessel wrecked just offshore in a wintry gale a century earlier. "Two of the crew managed to swim to shore and climb halfway up that very cliff you see there—barefooted, mind you, in the dead of winter." He paused in the narrative to take a call from his wife, who wondered when he'd be home for dinner.

"Well, sir," he went on, "somebody at Porpoise Bay saw the disaster and made his way back to Nor'east Head for help. My granddaddy, Otis Blue, happened to be up there, and he got in his sleigh and came as far as he could—there wasn't any road out past the bay at the time—and he walked along the top of the cliff, where the Red Trail is now, until he spotted the two men hangin' down below. He climbed down that cliff to the sailors and carried them up on his back, one at a time, and got them to town before they froze to death. Quite a story, eh?" He pulled a pipe from a jacket pocket and lit up in obvious pleasure.

That was the last word spoken until they returned to the dock at Nor'east Head. The wind had not abated and neither had Davenport's nausea. After trying fruitlessly to keep himself level by leaning left and then right, he hung on and grimly felt his gorge rise and fall, rise and fall, with the waves.

Davenport Finds a Clue

Davenport watched admiringly as Joey swung his mallet and firmly struck a steel wedge. The spruce log split into perfect halves with an ear-piercing ringggggg. Then quarters, and eighths, and onto the pile of firewood. A big man, strong enough to throw someone off a cliff, he deduced. But, alas, what motive could a mentally challenged person have for doing in one of the guests? Unless, of course, he had taken orders from someone else....

The nameless flowers waved cheerfully as he followed Kelly down the path toward the beach. Unidentified birds whistled and warbled a variety of unfamiliar tunes, and the air smelled like the sea itself, whose gemlike surface was dotted with white gulls and colorful boats.

The shoreline was littered with broken molluscs, and even a dead seagull, maybe one that Fairfax had shot. Here and there he came across long, slippery strands of purplish seaweed, entangled like the intestines of some strange sea creature.

To his surprise the beach wasn't sandy, as it had looked from the Big House and Blue's boat, but was covered with stones the size of bowling balls. There's always a down side, he groaned. The dog, his four paws working harmoniously, had no difficulty treading the rocks. Davenport's two feet made their way haphazardly toward the spot where Fred Fairfax had fallen to his death. It was even worse where the tide had just gone out, leaving the greenish rocks slippery and treacherous. Crusty organisms competed for toeholds with the rockweeds and tiny snail-like creatures, waiting for the lifegiving ocean to return. Pieces of driftwood lay along the highwater mark like the bleached bones of grotesque animals, twisted into a variety of fantastic shapes.

To his left the land rose abruptly. High above, among the trees, Davenport spotted Baker, bent over and oblivious, searching for slime molds, he presumed. Carefully negotiating the wiggly rocks, he eventually found himself at the bottom of the tall cliffs, from whose walls a few scrubby spruces clung desperately to life. At the top waved the little red flag he had planted earlier, and he struggled toward the base of the cliff below it. Kelly, her snout covered with sand and dirt, set out on a quest of her own.

He watched a gull lift off from the beach, drop a clam onto the rocks below, and swoop down to claim its prize. Something about that event brought back misty memories of childhood, of walking barefoot along another beach, the pebbles gouging his tiny soles like knives. The pain in his feet had made him want to cry, but he had to keep up or he would be left behind. But where was the beach? Where were they going? And who was he trying to keep up with?

Half an hour after leaving the Big House he reached the spot where Blue had found the body of Fred Fairfax. With a stick bleached white by the ocean he poked among the rocks for evidence, and was almost instantly rewarded with a swatch of clothing that looked very much like the torn shirt the body of Fred Fairfax was wearing in Houseman's "morgue." A picture of the battered corpse flashed into his head. With the stick he gingerly picked up the shirt fragment.

The bloody cloth had been rolled into a ball. He unraveled it and, to his amazement, found a matchbox inside. Gently he pushed open the little drawer, expecting to find only soggy matches. Instead, there was a folded slip of paper like the one on which the threatening note had been written, miraculously dry. Carefully he unfolded it. Scrawled in a hand different from any of the samples he had taken earlier was a single word: PARKENING.

Fairfax had fingered Parkening! The man with the bad heart, the man nobody would suspect. He had greed for a motive, and opportunity as well. He could be faking his medical condition. Or hired an accomplice....

Kelly was nowhere to be seen. Hoping to avoid another difficult trip over impossible rocks, Davenport tried vainly to claw his way up the cliff. Wishing he had saved his energy, he finally began to retrace his steps along the beach toward the cottages. He hadn't gone more than a few yards, however, when his ankle twisted and slipped between two of the rocks. Roaring with pain, he gingerly extracted his foot and, using the piece of driftwood as a makeshift cane, hobbled back to the Big House.

Fearing that Rose would insist on calling the doctor, he made his way stiffly into the kitchen. No one was there. Relieved, he phoned the sheriff's office, only to learn from Olive, Tate's receptionist and secretary, that she had called him earlier: the sheriff wanted to speak with him—didn't they have answering machines over there? But now he was out on the campaign trail and wouldn't be back until evening. With the smoky voice came an image of Olive's thick lips and huge bosom.

"I'm going to send another note for handwriting analysis," he told her, "and a piece of bloody cloth. Please have him call me as soon as he gets back." With the help of the driftwood he hobbled back to his room, where he downed two buffered aspirin and climbed onto the bed. But he was unable to sleep. His ankle hurt and something about the matchbox note bothered him. How had Fairfax written the note, stuffed it into a matchbox, and rolled it up inside a shirt fragment, all with a broken neck?

The Coroner's Report

Davenport slept straight through dinner. Groggily he hobbled through the empty house and into the kitchen hoping for at least a sandwich and glass of milk. Lisa and Margery didn't seem surprised to see him, assuming, he supposed, that he had been out somewhere investigating the death of Fred Fairfax. Nor did they appear to notice his injury when he limped over to the wooden table and dropped into a chair. The teenager remarked that he had "found a great walking stick."

"Looks like a petrified snake," added Lisa, fiddling with the silverware drawer. In front of him she set a plate of fried clams and a sea-blue mug of coffee. His injury temporarily forgotten, he helped himself to a mouthful of seafood.

Marge began to hum a country tune. As always, the kitchen was warm and fragrant. Davenport, chewing voraciously, leaned back and closed his eyes. Somewhere a bird crooned a sweet, plaintive song. When the girls finished cleaning up they disappeared out the back door, Lisa calling out, "G'night, Louie." Suddenly feeling very much alone, he drowned his melancholy in the coffee and poured himself another cup.

The phone rang. He waited for a moment, hoping Rose would come in and answer it. Finally he grabbed the receiver. "Hello!"

"Lou, boy! Got 'er solved yet?"

"Not yet, Loch," he sighed. "What have you got for me?"

"Only about a minute, Lou; that's all I seem to have these days." Davenport heard a chuckle and papers rustling. "And a preliminary report from the doc. Your pal Fairfax didn't die from the fall."

"You mean he was dead when he went over the cliff."

"Brilliant. When I go to the House you'll be taking my place for sure."

Davenport tried to ignore the sarcasm. "What killed him?"

"Can't say. Don't have any photos," he added pointedly. Anyway, we need the rest of the test results. All we know is that it probably wasn't a suicide. Unless he drank himself to death—his blood alcohol was 0.22."

"How long was he dead before he was brought in?"

"Don't know that yet, either."

"Can't you speed this up a little?"

"You know these things take time, Lou. Learn to be patient, boy—you'll live longer!"

"Thanks for the advice. Anything else?"

"We got hold of Mrs. Fairfax. She could barely contain her glee that her husband had died."

"Think she hired someone to do it?"

"Nah. Just didn't like the guy very much. She was a lot younger than him. You know the first thing she did when she found out she was a widow?"

"Nope."

"Got rid of every one of the dogs. He had six or eight of them. Hounds."

"Yeah, he was an avid hunter, apparently. Did she know of any enemies Fairfax might've had on Spruce Island?"

"Nobody in particular. She doesn't much care whether we find out what happened or not. Kept calling it a 'lucky accident.'"

"Lucky?"

"For her. By the bye, it's still officially an accident until we know otherwise. We don't want the state boys coming in and getting all the credit."

"What about the clothing and the handwriting samples?"

"Nothing. None of the handwriting checks out. You sure you got everybody?"

"Everyone staying at Porpoise Bay Cottages. And the staff."

"Well, it was written by somebody else, then."

"And the fingerprints?"

"Mrs. Kelly's were all over everything, including the threatening note. Nobody else's were on there, though. Except—uh—yours, of course."

Davenport cleared his throat. "Copy that. By the way. I visited the site where the body was found."

"Anything turn up?"

"Found a piece of clothing and a matchbox. Inside the box was a piece of note paper with the name 'Parkening.'"

"So?"

"So maybe Fairfax was trying to tell us something."

"Or maybe not."

"Then maybe someone else is trying to tell us something. If Fairfax was dead when he went over the cliff.... I'll send it over on the next boat, anyway. Maybe you can figure out who wrote it." Davenport discerned the unmistakable whoosh of a large yawn. Before Tate passed out completely he added, "Do me a favor, Loch. See what you can find out about Parkening and the other people staying here. Umm—let's see—there's a Dr. Walter D'Arcy, who's not a real doctor, and his wife Patricia, from New Haven, Connecticut, and her sister Alice Barnstable, from Philadelphia. And a Paul and Maryellen Thornhill, from Boston; an elderly pair from Baltimore named Edith Manhart and Callie Black. And a couple calling themselves Jim and Cathy Baker, supposedly from Cleveland. A Harriett Quinlan from New York."

Another yawn.

"Now about this guy Frank Parkening: he's supposedly from Hartford. Claims he's got a heart condition. Maybe he's faking it."

"C'mon, Lou. You know how hard it is to get hold of a man's medical records, even for a murder suspect. *Is* he a suspect?"

"Everyone is a suspect. Maybe you can get the Hartford police to talk to his business associates and so on. See if there's a history—" He heard a distinct chortle.

"I'm meeting her for dinner tomorrow night."

"Huh? Meeting who?"

"Mrs. Fairfax."

"But she's in Boston, isn't she?"

"She's meeting me halfway. In Portland. Hurry and wrap this thing up, will you, Lou? I need you back here."

"What about my vacation?"

"Make it a nice one. But not too long. Say a good word for me on the island!"

A Late Visitor

To Davenport's relief the living room was still deserted. Giving in to the pain and pressure, he farted loudly. It was only then that he noticed someone slouched down in the sofa facing the fireplace. He hoped it wasn't Rose.

"That you, Davenport?"

"Oh, hello, Mr. Parkening. I—uh—I didn't see you there." He dropped into the comfortable chair next to the south windows, where he made a show of studying the flower garden.

"That's Jack's chair, you know. Rose doesn't like other people to sit in it."

"Oh, sorry," he mumbled. He glanced briefly toward Rose's inviting armchair, with the ever-present bottle of sherry on the table beside it, before joining Parkening on the sofa. "I'm glad you're here, Mr. Parkening." He lifted the newly-discovered evidence from his sweater pocket and held it up. "What do you make of this?"

Parkening's hand reached out in extreme slow motion to take the note. Davenport jerked it back. "I'd rather you didn't touch it, sir. Just take a look."

The hand slowly retreated into the fleshy lap, like the head of a turtle. Parkening studied the paper forever before rasping, "Where did you get this?"

"It was lying next to where Mr. Fairfax's body was found."

Parkening's hand drifted up and picked at his fat forehead. "Oh, God, I'm next!" With a groan he pushed himself to his feet.

"No, wait—"

"I've got to lie down," Parkening gurgled. He made his way agonizingly to the front door.

Nobody could look that bad, thought Davenport. It had to be an act.

After Parkening had gone he pocketed the note and gazed at the smoldering fire. He still didn't know, after all, whether Fairfax had been murdered, or whether he had simply died on the trail where someone had found him and, for some bizarre reason, tossed him onto the beach. Or whether someone killed him accidentally and then pushed him off the cliff, perhaps in a vain attempt to get rid of the evidence. Or whether he had staggered to the edge of the cliff, died there, and somehow stumbled over on his own.

He got up, and with the utmost care shifted the logs in the fireplace. The fire went out. He tossed in another, which significantly increased the production of thick blue smoke but not of flame. He tried kicking it, but succeeded only in re-injuring his sprained ankle. Hobbling around the sitting room and groaning miserably, he fished a cigarette from the ancient pack and jammed it into his mouth.

After the pain had subsided he retrieved "The Old Lighthouse" and limped to the card table, where a Scrabble game had been left unfinished. "UKELELE crossed with "FLIVVER" and, below that, "ICEBOX" with "BOBTAIL." Returning the board and all the letters to their box, he scattered the puzzle pieces onto the table. While he was turning them over the ladies came into the room. Both were wearing old-fashioned print dresses and thin white socks.

"Hello, Miss Manhart, Miss Black," he said pleasantly.

"Mr. D!" whined Miss Manhart. "How could you?"

"Yes, Mr. D—how could you?" echoed Miss Black.

"Huh? What?"

"You put away our game!"

"Yes, you put away—"

"Oh, I *am* sorry, ladies. I didn't know you were still playing."

"I'm going to give you a piece of advice, Mr. D," Miss Manhart said firmly. She paused, trying to find the proper words. "Sometimes a lady needs to go to the powder room," she finally blurted.

"Yes. Sometimes a lady needs to go to the powder room," seconded Miss Black.

"Look, I'll tell you what. I saw where all the letters were. Why don't I just set it up again for you?"

"You remember where they were? And the letters we had on our holders?"

Davenport was already sliding the puzzle pieces back into the box. They watched in profound amazement as he rearranged all the squares perfectly. "Thank you, Mr. D," said Miss Manhart as she took her seat.

"Yes, thank you, Mr. D."

"Your turn, Callie."

Davenport returned the puzzle to the shelf and strolled back into the dining room, wondering whether there was any leftover dessert. From the kitchen he heard the sound of a man's laughter. It didn't sound like Joey's.

He stuffed the unlit cigarette back into the pack and unconsciously checked to make sure he had his revolver. Treading softly, he squeaked his way across the dining room and gently opened the swinging door, an inch at a time. A tall, silver-blond man was just going out the back door. From the back he looked like the authoritative figure Davenport had seen at the fireworks display.

"C'mon in, Louie. Cup of tea?"

He pushed the door open. "Sure. Why not?"

She poured him one and cut him a piece of cobbler. "Finding any clues?"

"Not many. Do you mind if I ask who was here a minute ago?"

"Oh, you mean Rog. He's the mayor of Nor'east Head. And the whole island at the moment. It rotates between the Council of Mayors of the three villages. Wonderful man. Give you the shirt off his back. Wife died a few years ago. She was an amazing woman. Made the best jams and jellies in the state of Maine. Nobody knows her secret. She took it with her. Fact, she kept to herself most of the time. Started when their son ran off and never came back. He was no good. Everybody knew it but her. Drinkin' and carryin' on. Fathered half-a-dozen kids. Handsome devil, though, like his father. They say each generation rebels against the previous one—you believe that? Anyway, he was as bad as Rog is good. I'll tell you about Rog. He's the kind of man who makes sure that nobody he knows goes hungry. Leaves stuff on the doorstep. Anonymously, you know. But everybody knows who's left it. He's retired now. Not that old, either. Retired early, so to speak, if you can call what they did to him retiring. They phased out his job. Happens all the time on the mainland, I suppose, but not often around here." She stopped for a breath, took a sip of tea.

Through a mouthful of pastry Davenport mumbled, "Who phased out his job?"

Rose stared at him. "It wasn't Fairfax, if that's what you're thinking. Nossir, it was the government. You know—*cost*cutting. *Down*sizing. Some day they'll do away with taxes altogether. Let everyone fend for themselves. I only hope I don't live long enough to see it."

You may not, the way things are going, thought Davenport. "Tell me what you know about Frank Parkening. Does he really have a heart problem?"

"He's been complaining about his heart for as long as I've known him."

"How long is that?"

"About thirty years."

"Do you think he could be faking it?"

"If he is, he's done a good job of it."

"What else can you tell me?"

"Well, he was never the same after his wife died. I never knew her well. It was a long time ago. He's had problems with depression over the years, but he's been better this summer, I think. Up until now, anyway. President of a life insurance company in Connecticut, lives alone. I suppose what you want to know is whether he's rich and who gets the money when he dies? Well, he *is* rich and he's got a daughter somewhere. Never met her, though. She's a sculptor, I think. Or maybe a photographer. Lives out west somewhere. Utah, or one of those places."

"Did Parkening stand to gain anything by Fairfax's death?"

"Oh, I don't know, Louie. Why don't you ask *him?*" She stood up and stretched. "Well, tomorrow's another day. I'm going to bed. Turn the lights off when you're finished, will you?"

"Yes, I will. Good night, Rose." Nobody knows nuttin', he reminded himself. He swallowed the tea, doused the lights, and followed her path into the sitting room, where he noticed a small flame still jiggling in the fireplace. He was debating whether to sit down and enjoy it when it went out. His fate decided, he continued on to his room.

Having slept half the evening, he lay awake listening to the sounds of the night—a toilet flushing, something rattling, bed springs squeaking and squeaking upstairs. For a moment he thought of his ex-wife's nipples, and all the others he'd seen, every pair different, like eyes. The eyes of the reproductive system, he understood groggily. And Rose has beautiful eyes! But the last conscious thought he had was: this is *my* room, this is *my* bed . . . .

BIRDWATCHING

Early next morning, when the sun was shining yellow-green and casting long shadows in the woods, Davenport, slit-eyed and gaping, accompanied Harriett Quinlan down the dewy path to Porpoise Bay Beach. Though he was still limping, the foot felt better and he barely needed the driftwood cane for support.

Kelly bounded along in front of them, scouting the narrow path in the meadow, disappearing from time to time into the tall grass to check out a suspicious odor. The gray bun clinging to the back of Miss Quinlan's head bounced with each step, revealing the strap of her binoculars wrapped tightly around her thin, pale neck. Before they had gone far he heard her mumble something that sounded like "Why show sorrow?"

"What's that, Miss Quinlan?"

She turned halfway toward him, her long plaid skirt whirling around the still well-formed calves. "I said, there's a white-throated sparrow." Her voice was gleeful and full of excitement.

He shaded his eyes with his hand. "Where?"

"Oh, you can't *see* it. But can't you hear it in the alders down by the shore singing 'Old Sam Peabody, Peabody, Peabody'?"

Davenport listened carefully. He could hear a number of tweets and burbles, but nothing that stood out above the general din.

"There!"

"Oh, yes. Yes. I hear it. Old Sam Peabody, huh?"

"Of course in Canada it sings something else."

"Really? Don't they speak English in Canada?"

"You're putting me on, aren't you, Louis? In Canada, it sings, 'Oh sweet Canada, Canada, Canada!' Oh, look! There's a fawn!" she cried, pointing toward the woods to their left.

Davenport shaded his eyes again, but the little deer was already gone. "How did you happen to come here, Miss Quinlan?"

"An aunt of mine was one of the original group to come every summer. Spinsters, all of them. Another was the aunt of Pat D'Arcy and Alice Barnstable. The youngest of the group was Edith Manhart. She's the last survivor."

"How did Rose get the cottages?"

"The aunts gave it to her."

"Why?"

"She managed the cottages for them every summer when she wasn't teaching. Did all the cooking and cleaning. They paid her for it, but I guess they figured that wasn't enough."

"What does she teach?"

"First grade."

"What about Fairfax and Parkening? How are they related to the 'founders' of Porpoise Bay Cottages?"

"They're not. They were both college roommates of Walt D'Arcy. They used to spend the whole month of July talking about stocks and investments and that sort of thing. Very boring. None of them could tell a crow from a bluejay. It's like people who spend their vacations in some exotic spot playing golf or tennis. You can do that anywhere." She stopped abruptly and peered through the binoculars.

Davenport nearly ran into her. "You live in New York City most of the year, isn't that right, Miss Quinlan? You don't see many birds there, do you?"

"Are you kidding? The city's full of them. And not just in Central Park, either. There are even a few peregrine falcons."

"Really? And what do they find to eat in New York?"

"Pigeons, Louis. It's a bird eat bird city."

After pausing to pick a few tiny wild strawberries, surely the sweetest he had ever tasted, they continued toward the beach. Now he could hear white-throated sparrows everywhere. Harriett Quinlan halted again. "That's a Swainson's thrush."

"Huh? A what?"

"Swainson's thrush. There! That rising arpeggio—da da dee da *dee* da *DEE* da—hear it?" She whipped the binoculars in front of her thick glasses. "There it is! Hear it? Unless it's Joey."

"Joey?"

"He does bird songs. But I think that's a real thrush."

He listened hard. It came again. He turned to her. She nodded and smiled. "Swenson's thrush," he murmured.

"No, no, no—*Swain*son's thrush. *SWAIN*son's." She teased the field glasses from her head and handed them to him.

He aimed them toward the tree she was pointing at. Not only couldn't he find the bird, he couldn't even find the tree. "Beautiful," he said, passing them back to her.

"Oh, listen—the winter wren. Sang all last summer and never found a mate. Isn't it lovely?"

Within an hour he had learned the songs of several other species, including the red-eyed vireo, the yellowthroat, the nuthatch and the veery, which sounded like Miss Constantine laughing. All distinctive calls, none of which he had ever noticed before, but which were now stored in his memory banks. "I know *that* bird," Davenport sneered as a gull squawked overhead. "A seagull."

"In the first place, Louis, it's a herring gull, not a 'seagull.' In the second, don't feel so superior. Long after we humans have killed ourselves off, the world will still be full of gulls."

Davenport nodded uncomfortably.

They reached the beach, filled with the bowling balls which made walking uncomfortable and played havoc with falling bodies. It was high tide, however, and not far to the water. "That flock near the shore over there are eiders. They're quite common around here."

"Eiders," he mumbled.

"Yes, and see those black birds out on that big rock? With the long necks, spreading their wings to dry in the sun? Those are cormorants."

"Cormorants."

"Look! Porpoises!"

Davenport gazed at the sleek figures bounding in and out of the water, proceeding porpoisefully, he presumed, to some distant destination across the cove.

She pointed the glasses in a different direction. "Those little birds flying over the water are puffins. See how hard they flap their wings? They're really more for swimming underwater than for flying."

"Puffins."

"Some people call them 'sea parrots.'"

Just then another black and white bird flew out of the woods, skimmed along the surface of the water, grabbed a herring in its talons, and circled back over the forest, screeching victoriously, the fish flopping in its iron grip. "An osprey, Louis. Remind you of anything?"

"Uh, a peregrine falcon nabbing a pigeon?"

"I was thinking of Fred's killer," she sobbed, and ran back up the path toward the Big House.

He watched her go. She travels surprisingly fast for a septugenerian, he thought. A woman capable of surprising things. And one of the most compelling motives for murder, he knew, was outraged vanity.

The Big Banana

Over breakfast Davenport enjoyed a similar, though more colorful, history of the cottage ladies from Alice Barnstable. While she went on with stories about the aunts' walking all the way to Fog Cove for a picnic lunch, getting caught in a dory during a hurricane, etc., he surreptitiously studied Miss Quinlan, who was enthusiastically describing, for the Bakers, the migration pattern of the Red Knot. When Ms. Barnstable paused to sink her mulish teeth into a piece of toast he asked her, sotto voce, what she knew about a possible relationship between Fred Fairfax and Harriett Quinlan. Her reply was an osprey-like screech. He decided to wait until later to question her about other liaisons between the guests at Porpoise Bay Cottages.

While he crammed in the bacon and eggs, she offered to give him a ground-level tour of the island. He wiped the lard from his lips and nodded assent. When he had consumed the last crust of jam-slavered toast, but before he could ask for a third cup of coffee, she jumped up from the table, shouting, "Let's go!" Within minutes they were bounding up the long gravelly lane in an enormous yellow station wagon, Davenport's greasy hand clutching the passenger strap like the reins of a bronco. "The natives call this 'the Big Banana,'" she hooted, whisking a bit of dust from the dashboard.

At the top of the lane she turned left and roared off toward Nor'east Head. The vast vehicle, in serious need of steering and alignment adjustments, swerved back and forth across the road, bounced up and down on the worn shocks and springs. It was worse than Blue's boat. His breakfast stalked around his stomach like a caged animal looking for a way out. Moreover, an obnoxious odor permeated the car. He wondered whether they were being poisoned by fumes from a defective exhaust until he realized it might be himself—he hadn't had a shower in three days. He casually sniffed an armpit, which did nothing to settle his stomach.

Farther down the road they could see the houses of Nor'east Head, a church or two, a service station, and, behind it all, the sea. "A nice little village, don't you think, Sheriff?" she asked rhetorically. They came to the fork and swung left into town past Henry Sanders' grocery, the post office, and the hardware store before turning around at the pier, where Davenport got a good look at the old lighthouse, a perfect replica of the picture on the puzzle box.

They passed a playground identified as "Caitlin's Park." "Who's 'Caitlin'?" Davenport inquired.

"A girl who was killed by a car a few years ago. It was driven by some idiot from the mainland."

He was sorry he had asked.

As they drove along the coast toward Centerville, drivers and pedestrians alike stared into the dull yellow wagon. Maybe one of them is Fred Fairfax's killer, he reflected. In any case they certainly looked capable of the job.

They lurched past a stand of pastel-colored smokehouses, a few of which were in operation. "Used to be a big business here, smoked herring. Not so much anymore."

Davenport gazed dreamily at the wisps drifting upward from the little sheds, where rows of gulls glared at them from the roofs. "Why not?"

"What's that, Sheriff?"

"Why not so much anymore?"

"People's tastes change. Most of it nowadays is shipped overseas."

"Where do they get the smoke?"

"They burn big chunks of spruce or driftwood. Slowly. Takes about six weeks for the whole process."

"A time-consuming operation."

"Spruce Islanders don't worry too much about consuming time. There's no rat race here."

He was thinking much the same thing. The villages, the people, the way of life seemed like something from an earlier era. "What's that road there heading away from the sea?"

"That's the one to the other side of the island. Goes through the heart of the spruce forest where the theme park will be built."

"What's on the other side of the island?"

"Speak up, Sheriff—can't hear a thing out of my right ear."

"What's on the other side of the island?" Davenport shouted. "The west side."

"Just woods and cliffs. And Dulse Cove, of course. You've tried the dulse, haven't you, Sheriff? It takes a little getting used to, but it grows on you after a while."

At Centerville Davenport spotted the doctor's office. Now he saw there was a little mortuary next door. "Good location for it, don't you think?" Barnstable observed. She pointed out the school, the bank, the drug and liquor stores. A car was being towed into Gannet Banner's garage by a cheerful-looking attendant, who glanced briefly toward the Big Banana. The smile disappeared.

Just south of town, on a high hill overlooking the Atlantic, stood a cemetery. "Only graveyard on the island," she informed him. "Everybody ends up here." Approaching Fog Cove they spotted the Island Haven off to the south on her 9:30 trip back from the mainland and, in the village itself, the lumber yard and gift shop. Davenport noted with satisfaction that each of the towns boasted its own service station, run by brothers Petrel, Gannet, and Cormorant Banner, respectively. All were stuffed with broken cars and trucks, and each had its group of joking kibitzers standing by. "Is it my imagination, Ms. Barnstable, or are people happier here than other places?"

"Wouldn't you be, Sheriff?" she barked. "They live on an island isolated from the problems the rest of the world seems to be overwhelmed with. There are no poisonous insects or plants, no large carnivorous animals. It's cooler here than on the mainland, warmer in winter. They're healthy and prosperous. No one is rich and no one is poor. There are few outsiders, and then only for a couple of months in the summer. If that's not enough, what would it take to make you happy?"

Davenport was delighted to learn that there was nothing vicious or poisonous on the island. "Then why don't you live here all year round?" he countered.

"I'm a masochist," she replied.

All down the island children played baseball, swung from trees, dared one another to jump from a log pile. But all such activities ceased when the wagon lumbered by. Elsewhere, men and women were laying out batches of dulse to dry in the bright sun, lawns were being mowed, logs split, window frames painted, clothes hung out.

"I noticed that the people here look a lot alike. Why is that, Ms. Barnstable?"

"There are basically three families on Spruce Island, sheriff: the Blues, the Hendersons, and the Banners. I don't mean there's a lot of inbreeding, but everyone is distantly related in some way. The founders came here a long time ago and never left. Except for the Indians, of course. They were already here. The Blues were the original natives. Short for 'Bluefoot.' They used to make blueberry wine."

"What do the islanders think of the summer visitors?"

"They tolerate us, Sheriff. They have to hear your name about fifty times before they can remember it, and even then they ignore you. As I say, they tolerate us, but that's about all." One of them, in fact, gave the Big Banana a finger as they passed by.

"Did they tolerate Fred Fairfax, Ms. Barnstable?"

"Barely."

Davenport offered to buy lunch "if there's anyplace to eat in Nor'east Head."

"What for?" she snorted. "We have to pay for lunch at Porpoise Bay. Might as well eat it." As they rumbled down the lane she added, "By the way, Sheriff, have you tried Joey's shower bower?"

A New Theory

Davenport had just enough time before lunch for a sponge bath in his room. Since he was running out of clean underwear, he put on the ones he had just taken off and rushed to the dining room.

The Bakers joined him at the corner table, where the toddler immediately banged his shoulder with a spoon. He asked her mother how the novel was coming.

"Great!" she replied breathlessly. "I know who all the suspects are!"

"Really? Who?"

"All the guests at Porpoise Bay Cottages."

"Uh-huh. And who dunnit?"

"Haven't figured that out yet. But I've got a theory."

"You do? I'd like to hear it."

"I don't think it was one of the guests who killed Mr. Fairfax. I think it was someone else."

"You mean an islander?"

"Maybe. Or someone from the mainland."

"Why couldn't it have been one of the guests?"

"They all had too much to lose."

Davenport glanced at Baker, who was busy scribbling something on a scrap of paper he had pulled from his pen-lined pocket. "What, for example?"

"Money. He was everybody's broker. He made them all rich. Or richer."

"How do you know Fairfax didn't just have an accident?"

"If you thought that, you wouldn't be here, would you?"

Davenport suppressed a smile. "Interesting theory. If you figure out who killed him, you'll let me know before you make an arrest, won't you?"

"You're making fun of me, aren't you, Deputy Davenport?"

"Not at all. In fact, I need all the help I can get. If you see or hear anything that might be useful, please tell me immediately."

"I certainly will," she beamed.

Lisa arrived with steaming plates of clams. "After lunch," she whispered to Davenport, "I'll show you where the shower is."

But when the meal was over Lisa was not in the kitchen. "She ran to the drug store, Louie," Rose told him. "Anything I can do for you?"

"No. No, thanks. Tell her I'm outside."

"Good idea."

He wandered out the kitchen door and around to the front of the Big House, where he spotted Mrs. D'Arcy bending over in the meadow. The hairs on the back of his neck flew up: he wondered whether she was sick—or poisoned. His stomach began to feel queasy. When she straightened up he realized she had merely been staring at something on the ground. "Find what you're looking for, Mrs. D'Arcy?"

Her head jerked toward him and her hands came up to frame her pale face. "Oh, Mr. Davenport, you frightened me." A necklace and several rings glistened in the sun.

"I'm sorry." He strode down the path toward her. "I was wondering what you were looking at."

"Just a little patch of viper's bugloss," she confessed.

"Nasty name. What is it—an insect?"

"Oh, no, Mr. Davenport," she stammered. "It's a beautiful blue flower, though some people might call it a weed. It's in the eye of the beholder, I suppose."

"And what are those other flowers? Or would you call them weeds?"

Mrs. D'Arcy seemed to gain confidence, apparently pleased that anyone would ask her anything. "That's orange hawkweed. Also known as Indian paintbrush. But the yellow ones aren't yellow hawkweeds. They're called mouse-ear hawkweed. See how the petals look like little ears? There are lots of flowers farther down, if you're interested."

"Sure."

She trotted off toward the bay, Davenport trailing behind. By midafternoon she had filled his head with the names and characteristics of more than two dozen floral species—yarrows and selfheals, meadowsweets and cinquefoils, and that was only in this particular meadow, and only in early July. "At other locations and other times of year the picture would be entirely different," she declared triumphantly. The songs of Swainson's thrushes and white-throated sparrows bombarded his ears. "You should come back next June. The lilacs in Nor'east Head and the lupine around Fog Cove are spectacular that time of year."

"Where's Dr. D'Arcy?" he asked as they strode back toward the house.

"He went over to see Frank about something. You know—business."

"Tell me, Mrs. D'Arcy: what was Mr. Parkening's relationship with Mr. Fairfax?"

"They were college roommates. We've all gotten together every summer since then. Except for the latest Mrs. Fairfax. She doesn't like it here. And Frank's wife died many years ago, you know. Lovely woman."

"Yes, I heard about that. But what I wanted to know was: do you know of any reason Frank Parkening would want to—uh—cause harm to Fred Fairfax?"

Mrs. D'Arcy turned even whiter than usual. "Oh, Mr. Davenport. What a terrible thought."

"Yes, I suppose it is," he agreed, declining to point out that *someone* had had such a thought. "Can you think of anyone else who might've had some kind of grudge against Mr. Fairfax?"

A little color returned to her cheeks and, for the first time, she looked him in the eye. "If you're thinking of my husband, Mr. Davenport, he didn't do it." Then she added, more sheepishly, "Paul Thornhill had a fight with Fred the night before he died."

"You mean a fistfight?"

"Oh, no. An argument. But it sounded pretty heated."

"Why didn't you tell me this before?"

"You never asked me."

"Where were they?"

"Out in the meadow somewhere. It was after dark. Walter was already asleep. I was too, but the noise woke me up."

"Are you sure it was them?"

"No, not really. They were down close to the shore. But it sounded like them."

Lisa called from the Big House: "Louie!"

"Enjoy your shower, Mr. Davenport."

THE SHOWER BOWER

Almost relaxed for the first time in days, and anticipating the upcoming dinner, Davenport headed for "Joey's Bower," an outdoor contraption constructed of chicken wire and ivy and fed by a black plastic pipe running down the hill from a distant well.

"You're lucky the sun is out, Mr. D," Miss Manhart called from the porch of the Blacksmith Shop.

"And blackfly season is over," added Miss Black.

"You'd be doing some fine dancing otherwise."

"Some fine dancing, Mr. D." The ladies giggled and hurried inside.

The alfresco stall consisted of a platform built from wooden slats, and a shower head made from the spout of a sprinkling can and fixed with a simple shutoff valve to control the flow. He tossed the towel and robe, borrowed from Rose's late husband, onto an old wooden chair and, wondering whether anyone could see him through the ivy, or might walk in, he cleared his throat loudly and stepped onto the platform. But the sun-heated water was surprisingly warm, and he forgot his concerns. As was his habit, he began by urinating, thinking as he did so how much his wife hated for him to piss in the shower. Or to leave the toilet lid up. Or the cap off the toothpaste. So many rules, so little time. A momentary pain in his abdomen caused him to reflect that he was probably coming down with a bladder or kidney infection. Then he thought about the Hitchcock movie, *Psycho*.

The water began to feel progressively cooler and, suddenly, ice-cold. Captivated by the flute-like voice of a wood thrush, he turned it off and reached for the towel. At that moment the thunderclap of a rifle jerked him around. The bullet zinged over his head and splintered the wooden slat above the shower head. Squeaking "Holy shit!" he instinctively threw himself to the ground. All he heard now was the cry of the summer wren and his own labored breathing. In the space of a split second he wondered what it would feel like to get a bullet in the back of his head, how he should've let the phone ring and gone to visit his grandchildren, what his corpse would look like lying in Houseman's cellar. Covered by bits of mud and twigs he crawled to the chair and grabbed the robe, his heart pumping hard. Cautiously he peeked out of the bower and caught a glimpse of a red flannel shirt disappearing into the trees. He didn't give chase, though he took a few steps for appearances' sake. Stupidly, he had left his gun in his room. Complacency killed the cat, he reminded himself.

The guests were popping out of the cottages with surprise and fear on their faces. They seemed relieved when he stepped out of the shower. "What's the trouble, Louis?" Miss Quinlan shouted.

"Anybody see anyone who doesn't belong here?" he yelled back. Sticks and stones cruelly attacked his tender feet.

No one had seen anything. However, the gun certainly hadn't been fired by Miss Quinlan or Cathy Baker or the ladies.

"Go back to your rooms. Keep your doors locked. I'll have further instructions before dinner."

Just then Parkening staggered from the Farmhouse and eased slowly to the ground, as if he had been deflated. He, too, was wearing a robe. Davenport stepped gingerly toward him. The man was fumbling around in a side pocket. "Pills..."

Davenport knelt beside him and found the vial. He popped one of the tiny pellets under Parkening's tongue.

"Thank you," he blubbered. "Thank you." In another moment he was trying unsuccessfully to climb to his swollen feet.

Davenport helped him up. "Did you see anything, Mr. Parkening? Did you see where the shot came from?"

"No," he gasped. "No, I didn't. But I saw someone in a red shirt running through the woods behind the Farmhouse. I was just heading for the shower. Oh, my God, Davenport, someone is trying to kill me!"

Hard Evidence

Still smudged with dirt and flecked with grass, Davenport retrieved his last clean set of underwear. He dressed quickly, grabbed his revolver, and returned to the scene. On a spruce branch there appeared to be the remains of a chalked "X" where the missile had gone into the shower, as if someone had marked a target. Peculiar, he thought, unless—

He calculated the angle of trajectory and, using his stride as a yardstick, paced to where he figured the bullet would have hit the ground. A few minutes' searching revealed a telltale rip in the earth, and a little digging in the rocky soil with the skeleton key produced the bullet, which appeared to be from a .22-caliber rifle. Elated by this bit of good luck, he rubbed off the dirt, flipped it into the air, whirled once, caught it with a flourish, and slipped it into his pocket.

Grinning broadly, he returned to the house, bagged the specimen, and tossed it into an envelope preaddressed to the sheriff's office.

Victoriously he marched into the kitchen and placed a call to Machias. "He's out campaigning, Lou, but I'll see he gets the message," Olive promised him.

"Okay, Ollie. Say—maybe we could take in a movie when I get back . . . ."

"We'll see," she demurred. He visualized the full lips and bust, whiffed the orangey perfume.

When he hung up he found Lisa gazing unsmilingly at him. She took a draw on her cigarette. He unconsciously reached for his ancient, half-empty pack, and almost asked her for a light. "I'm going to want to speak to the guests before dinner," he sighed.

She shrugged. "Go ahead. But dinner's at six."

Davenport checked his watch: five-thirty already, if it hadn't stopped again. He returned to his room, carefully combed his hair back over his bald spot, slipped on his nice sweater, and strode into the sitting room to await the other guests. He noticed that the fire needed attention, gave it a confident jolt with his foot, watched it blaze up for a moment before fizzling out.

The guests drifted in one or two at a time. Davenport returned their mumbled greetings but refused to answer questions until everyone had arrived. At a few minutes before six Rose came through the door and, after nudging the fire into blazing glory, took her usual chair. She poured herself a glass of sherry.

"Where are the Thornhills?"

"They'll be here shortly, Louie," she assured him. "You go ahead. I'll fill them in."

He glared at the front door. "All right." He turned to face his audience. "Ladies and gentlemen, as you know there was a bullet fired into the shower a short while ago. Fortunately, no one was injured. Mr. Parkening and I both caught a glimpse of the gunman. If there was any doubt before, I believe now that someone is trying to cause deadly harm to one of you."

"It was meant for me," wailed Parkening.

"Maybe, maybe not. In any case, this changes the situation radically. From now on I suggest that all of you stay close to someone else at all times; better yet, in groups of three or more. And to let me know where you're going and who you will be with. I'll leave a signup sheet on the desk over there in case I'm not here." He looked over his audience. "Mrs. Kelly, I wonder if it would be possible to put Ms. Barnstable in with someone else until we get this matter cleared up."

"Hold it right there, Sheriff! I like the Lodge, and I'm staying where I am!"

"That's your right, but I strongly advise against it."

"What *we'd* like to know, Mr. D, is what you're going to do about this."

"Yes, Mr. D. What are you going to do about this?"

"We're doing all we can, ladies. The sheriff's office is investigating everything related to Mr. Fairfax's death, and now we have a bullet. But we need your co-operation. All I'm asking is that you take reasonable precautions for the time being. Lock your doors at night, don't go out alone, and report where you're going and who you're with at all times."

"It's no use," Parkening moaned. "Someone's going to kill me!"

"Please try to stay calm, Mr. Parkening. We'll try to see that that doesn't happen. Dr. and Mrs. D'Arcy, would you please tell us where you were at about 4:30?"

"We were at the liquor store, Monsieur."

"Anybody see you there?"

"Only the clerk."

"Would he remember you?"

"He should. He's been there for the last fifteen years. He might not know our names, but surely he would recognize us."

"Do you know *his* name, Dr. D'Arcy?"

"No."

"And you, Ms. Barnstable?"

Her eyelids fluttered briefly. "I think it's George."

"I meant, where were you at 4:30 this afternoon?"

"Hiking on the Red Trail."

"Anybody see you?"

"Only a couple of tourists. An old couple from Indiana. Retired schoolteachers."

"Would you recognize them if you saw them?"

"Sure. They've been coming here longer than I have."

"Mr. Baker, how about you?"

Baker's eyes came into focus. "Well, I was looking for spores."

"Spores?"

"You know—slime mold spores."

"In the woods?"

"Yes."

"See anyone run by?"

"No. I was over by the airport."

"Find any?"

"Yes, I did. Some bright red ones that I haven't identified yet. I'll go get them." He started for the door.

"Never mind. I'll take your word for that. Rose, do you know where Joey was at 4:30?"

"I sent him off to the hardware store at about four o'clock. He was back by five."

"What did you send him for?"

"Some roofing nails. Why, Louie? Do you think he's planning to shingle somebody to death?"

"Does Joey drive?"

"He took his bicycle."

Marjorie Jordan opened the door to the dining room. At that moment the Thornhills barged into the sitting room. Thornhill wasn't wearing a tie. "If Loose doesn't have to wear one," he proclaimed, "then neither do I."

"Mr. Thornhill—where were you at 4:30 this afternoon?"

"Collecting shells down on the beach at Fog Cove."

"Did anyone see you there?"

His wife piped up, "No, but we saw the mayor of the island on the way back."

"Did he see you?"

"I think so, Loose. Fact is, we almost ran into him. What's this all about?"

"Somebody's trying to kill me!"

"Now, Mr. Parkening, there's no reason to believe that."

"When I'm feeling better I'm going home," he whined limply.

Dinner was a simultaneously quiet and noisy affair, the silverware clanking against plates with an unearthly ring. Everyone stole surreptitious glances at everyone else, misinterpreting a return glance as a threat. Even the Baker baby seemed wary and uncomfortable, staring bug-eyed and silent around the room. When Parkening got up to leave, all the guests bolted toward the door like so many lemmings, leaving half-eaten desserts, partially-consumed cups of coffee. Davenport reluctantly followed them into the sitting room.

Baker suddenly rushed upstairs. Everyone stared at Davenport, who was as puzzled as they were. In a few seconds he came bounding down bearing the spores he had collected earlier. While Davenport studied the bag of little red dots, Cathy corroborated the times of departure and arrival, her husband's excitement on returning with the bountiful harvest, which reminded Davenport of the acne he had suffered as a teenager.

Baker enthusiastically explained that under the right conditions of moisture and nutrition the spores would germinate into tiny ameba-like creatures that would eventually become the large, colorful syncytia with the synchronously-dividing nuclei so useful for studies of mitosis and differentiation. "Maybe this is a new species," he exclaimed. "What do you think of *Physarum bakerii?*"

Davenport grunted and stuffed the information into his mental files. The baby squealed the whole time, as did Alice Barnstable.

In the kitchen, Joey, too, was able to produce an alibi, and a bag of roofing nails as well. "What do you plan to do with those, Joey?"

"Put some shingles on the top of the Farmhouse." He chomped down on a tangled web of dulse.

"Thank you, Joey."

"That's okay."

After dismissing the handyman, Davenport placed a few phone calls. First the Seaview Bed and Breakfast in Fog Cove, whose tenants had run across Alice Barnstable on the Red Trail at "4:15ish." The retired teacher remembered him, inquired how he liked the island.

"Very much," he replied, without mentioning the killer running around loose, a definite negative. "I can see why you keep coming back."

"It grows on you, doesn't it?" There was a brief pause; he heard whispers and mumbles, and then she came back on. "Would you care to come for tea tomorrow?"

"Thank you. Maybe some other time." He thought he heard someone growl, "I told you he wouldn't come."

Next, the manager of the liquor store, George Banner, who vaguely remembered the D'Arcys' buying a bottle of gin, but couldn't swear about the time.

And finally the mayor of Spruce Island, who laughed when he was reminded that someone had almost run into him in Centerville between 4:30 and 5:00. "Oh yes, Louis," he added. "Everybody on the island watches out for the Thornhills. His driving skills are legend."

Davenport didn't bother asking how the mayor knew his name; obviously Rose had filled him in. "Okay if I come and see you sometime tomorrow morning?"

"Sure. Come to the pier about eight."

"Uh, which—"

But the mayor had hung up. Davenport wandered back to the deserted sitting room, where he paced back and forth, back and forth, in front of the fireplace. Every one of the guests at Porpoise Bay Cottages had an alibi for the time of the shooting. Which meant that someone else had done it. An accomplice, hired to throw him off the scent? Or maybe the killer was an islander. Even Spruce Island must have its share of crazies, loners perhaps, strong, good with a gun, someone who enjoyed pushing people over cliffs, picking them off in showers.

Absentmindedly he took a book from one of the shelves between the fireplace and the front door: *And Then There Were None*, one of those recommended by Cathy Baker. Standing, he perused the first page. He dropped down on the sofa and read the second and third. When he finally looked up, the grandfather clock was striking eleven and the judge was shot in the head. Only four little Indians to go! He reached for a raggedy cigarette, stared hard at it, pushed it back into the wrinkled pack.

In the kitchen he found a dish of tiny wild strawberries and ate them hungrily, rinsed out the dish and put it where he supposed it belonged. Then he wanted a cigarette more than ever. He returned to the sofa, gazed at the smoldering fire for a few minutes, glanced at his watch, shrugged, opened the book and turned the page.

The Mayor of Spruce Island

"Going somewhere, Louie?" Rose yelled through the kitchen door.

"Thought I would—why?"

"Mind dropping this off at the dump?" She indicated four large plastic bags of trash.

"I'm going the other way," he protested.

"Well, Mr. Special Deputy Sheriff, everybody's going the other way. But somebody's got to go to the dump."

Faced with this incontrovertible logic, he loaded his trunk with the smelly refuse and started up the driveway.

"By the way," she yelled, "there's another mystery for you to solve. Somebody ate the strawberries we were saving for cake icing."

In the dump's circular drive he was greeted by dozens of squawking gulls, who waited until he was upon them before leaving the ground, playing a game, perhaps, daring him to try to run them over.

He emptied the trunk, tossing out a few items of his own—an old shoe, a rusty screwdriver—and climbed back into the Plymouth. With its feeble horn he tried vainly to warn the gulls settling on the driveway ahead of him. They ignored him until the last minute, then cursed him for rousting them again.

Passing Caitlin's Park he heard something clunk against the side of the car. He braked to a halt and jumped out. A group of pre-adolescent boys stood beside the road. "All right—which one of you threw the ball?"

A half-dozen innocent faces stared back as if he were speaking a foreign language. At last one of the players lifted his hand. Davenport was about to start in on his standard "Next time you're going to jail!" speech when a second one raised an arm. Then a third. In another second the rest of the arms shot up. He was left with his alternate warning: "I'll be watching out next time," and climbed back into the injured Plymouth with as much dignity as he could muster.

He found Mayor Banner just where he said he would be, fiddling with some ropes on Fisherman's Pier. He was tall, muscular, ruggedly handsome, his wavy silver-blond hair combed straight back. In his early sixties, perhaps. Davenport introduced himself and was met with a steady gaze and strong handshake. "You're Tate's deputy, right?"

"You know the sheriff?"

"He was here once with his wife. Didn't like the place."

Davenport declined to mention that Tate didn't have a wife. "He told me it rained the whole time."

"It does that sometimes."

"This your boat?"

"Yep."

"You a fisherman?" Davenport inquired.

"Nope. I was a lighthouse keeper. Cormorant Rock. Retired now. All of us are retired. They automated all the lights. Bad mistake. They'll find that out one of these days. I still go out to the Rock once in a while. Make sure everything's shipshape. Kinda miss the smell of paint and diesel oil. You want to go?"

"Thanks. I'll take a raincheck on that. You know why I'm here?"

"You mean on the wharf? Or on the island?"

"The island."

"Heard somebody fell off a cliff the other day."

"That's right. Name was Fairfax. Did you know him?"

"Not personally. Prob'ly seen him around. All you people from the mainland look pretty much alike to me."

Davenport gazed into the unblinking blue eyes before turning away, toward the quay. Boats and buoys, floats and nets intertwined in a rainbow of color. It looked almost unreal, as if it were a huge painting. Gulls circled overhead, wailing, anticipating disaster. Another flock sat resting on the still water. Higher up, a small plane climbed, dipped, and spun. A wave of vertigo washed over him. He tried to swallow, got choked on his own spit.

The mayor pounded him on the back.

"Mr. Banner—" he squeaked.

"Rog."

Davenport coughed, cleared his throat. "Rog, there is reason to believe [*hack*] that Mr. Fairfax was murdered."

"That so?"

"Seems to be. And yesterday, someone took a shot at me while I was having a shower. With a rifle. I didn't get a good look at him, but he was wearing a red flannel shirt. Ran off into the woods. What I was wondering, the reason I came down here, was to ask you whether you have any idea who might've done that. For example, would you know how many of the residents here own a .22-caliber rifle?"

"And wear a red flannel shirt? You just described about half the people on Spruce Island."

"I figured as much. But I thought maybe you could help me narrow down the possibilities."

"Louis, I know everyone on this island. If anyone was out taking pot shots at our summer visitors, I'd know about it."

"Well, is there anyone who doesn't fit in with everyone else? Anyone who stays off by himself or doesn't talk to people much?"

The Mayor studied a pile of lobster buoys on the opposite pier. "A couple of people, but I don't think either one of them would be your man."

"Can you tell me where I might find them? I just want to talk to them."

Banner scratched his chin, then his head, and finally he lifted his face toward the sky and gave his Adam's apple a good going over. "You'll likely find Hermit at Dulse Cove. That's his name—Hermit. His mama had a wonderful sense of humor." He gazed fondly at the sea.

Davenport gazed, too. A gull sitting on the water suddenly vanished. The others lifted off, shook the water from their bodies, and flapped westward toward the dump. He blinked and looked again.

Banner said, "You saw the gull disappear?"

"Yes. What the hell happened to it?"

"A ballast fish prob'ly got it."

"Huh?"

"The sea's a dangerous place, Louis. You can be out on the water and it's clear and beautiful; next minute a storm comes up, you bash into a rock and you're on the bottom." He snapped his powerful fingers. "Just like that."

Davenport stared at the water, wondering what might happen the next minute.

The mayor chuckled. "Makes life interestin', don't you think?" The smile disappeared and he leaned toward Davenport as if to divulge a confidence. "Byron's an alcoholic. Course no one's perfect. He lives in the little house up the lane from here." He pointed with a crooked finger, one that had been injured somehow. "There it is—that little white one. But you're barkin' up the wrong road."

Davenport watched the plane spiral down over the airport and disappear behind the trees. He shuddered. "You say Byron's a drinker. Are there a lot of alcoholics on Spruce Island?"

"A few. Half the people here are drinkers, the other half teetotalers. The righteous half considers all the rest of us to be drunks, but of course there aren't any more here than anyplace else."

"How about drugs?"

"Not much. Some of the kids are smoking marijuana. Comes in from the mainland. You know how it is."

"Anyone with a criminal record you know of?"

"Nothing like that, Louis. Once in a while somebody breaks into the liquor store, or one of the groceries. Everybody knows who it is. We take care of it amongst ourselves. If somebody from away tries to interfere, he would find that we all stick together, pretty much."

Davenport thought of the boys at the playground. "What is there for a kid to do on an island like this?"

"Anything he wants, within reason, o' course."

Davenport studied the strong jaw, the spikes of gray stubble. "All right. I won't trouble you further. But if you think of anything that might help, give me a call, will you? I'm staying at Porpoise Bay Cottages."

"Yes," he said. "I know."

Dulse Cove

Byron's place was hardly bigger than his granddaughters' dollhouses, two small rooms at most. The yard was cluttered with buoys and nets, an old wooden lobster trap. Davenport realized finally that they were for decorative purposes.

He tapped softly on Byron's door. Hearing no response, he banged louder. Casually he peeped through the front window. The living room appeared tidy; no one was sprawled on the floor or the lumpy overstuffed chair. He tried the door. It was unlocked. He considered going in and taking a good look around, but thought better of it. If he screwed up this case, it would almost certainly be his last.

The house commanded an excellent view of the sea and the coastline down the island. In the distance he could see the Centerville smokehouses and, beyond that, Cemetery Hill. A few ships steamed here and there, seemingly haphazardly, in the bay. He decided to see what the other side of the island looked like.

The sun was bright and the drive along the coast made him feel strangely—there was no other word for it—happy. Except for the suspicious stares of the islanders who passed him in their pickup trucks, he felt at home here. Perhaps he had been born in a place like this....

He turned onto the road that wandered across the island to Dulse Cove. In a mile or so he spotted a little parking spot with a trail leading off to the right and a faded sign, "Blueberry Hill." He smiled, imagining a field of pies, of muffins, of jam and ice cream. He was just starting on a stack of blueberry pancakes with blueberry syrup when he found himself plunging down a steep, narrow road, which dropped off precipitously on one side. His grip instinctively tightened on the wheel.

A beautiful natural harbor came into view. The tide was low, and a few men were bent over in the surf, picking strands of red-brown seaweed and tossing them into large wicker baskets. Unlike the beach at Porpoise Bay the terrain was sandy.

On a boulder protruding from the water several cormorants dried their wings in the sun. A few seals played at the base of the rock. The air was rich with the life of the sea. Except for the gentle stirring of the waves it was absolutely still.

The nearest picker, sloshing in hip boots, didn't hear Davenport approaching. When he spoke, the man reared up and let out a whoop. "Holy jumpin' Christ, Cap'n. You nearly scared the life out of me."

Davenport begged his pardon. "I'm looking for a man named Hermit."

"Well you found him. You shouldn't ought to sneak up on people like that." The man looked like a cousin of Richard Blue.

Davenport apologized again. "Maybe you know why I'm here."

The dark eyes stared back at him. "Don't know nothin' of the sort." He went back to picking.

"Name's Davenport. I'm a special deputy sheriff from the mainland. Came to investigate a suspicious death."

"Who died?"

"Man named Fairfax."

"Never heard of 'im, Cap'n. Must be from away."

"You own a rifle?"

"Nope."

"Can you tell me where you were the day before yesterday at six in the morning?"

"Right here."

"And yesterday between 4:30 and 5:00 P.M.?"

Hermit removed his baseball cap and brushed back his coal-black hair. "Same place. I hardly ever leave here, 'ceptin' in the winters. Ask anybody."

"I'll do that." Davenport felt the stubble on his chin. He reminded himself to shave again before dinner. "Where do you sleep?"

"That's my shack. Up there." He pointed without looking toward the top of the beach. A strand of dulse hung from his wrist, as if he had risen from the bottom of the sea.

"How do you get groceries?"

"Bring just about everything I need in the spring."

"You must make pretty good money at this."

"Enough to keep me in rum and tobacco the rest of the year! But that ain't why I do it. I love to dulse. You ought to try it."

"Doesn't look like much fun to me."

"Take another look. It's quiet and peaceful. Nobody around to bother you. Just you and the sea and the birds. You pick for a couple of hours, then you can rest till the next low tide. And it's quite satisfying knowing you're doing something to benefit the world."

Davenport's left eyebrow came up. "You mean the dulse?"

"Healthiest stuff there is." He reached into a pocket, pulled out a handful of the dried seaweed, and stuffed it into his mouth. He offered a smaller batch to Davenport. "Ever try any? Finest kind!"

Davenport stared at the stiff brown strands. "Know anybody who would want to kill someone from away?"

"That would depend on what the stranger done."

"He might have been sleeping with one or two wives."

"That ain't nothin' to kill anybody for! Plenty of wives to go around!" Hermit guffawed and slapped his knee.

"That your real name? 'Hermit'?"

"Yep. But it ain't got nothin' to do with livin' by myself. My old mom thought I looked a little like a crab."

"You know something? You do!"

Hermit threw back his head and roared. "I know it! She was right as rain on that one! Go ahead—try my dulse. Just dried yesterday!"

Davenport took the half-dozen strands and pushed them into his mouth. Instantly he knew he had made a mistake. It seemed as if the entire ocean had been evaporated, and he had taken a mouthful of the salty residue. "T'anks," he waved, and strode away, pretending to study the beach.

Hermit called out, "See you at the Dulse Festival!"

When he reached the Plymouth, Davenport gagged once and coughed out the seaweed where Hermit couldn't see him. Spitting through the open window, he rattled, white-knuckled, up the steep narrow road back to civilization.

A Debt Repaid

Still nauseated when he reached Nor'east Head, Davenport wondered whether he had been poisoned. It was not unknown for detectives investigating a murder to fall victim to a cup of tea or innocent slice of cake. Had even happened to him once or twice when he was young, inexperienced, and still susceptible to a lovely lady's charms. But Hermit the dulser was far from beautiful and, in any case, would have had to be a magician to fool him that way.

Or perhaps it was stomach flu.

He popped a Maalox tablet and rattled up to Byron's little house, where he repeated the knocking, the casual peering through the curtainless window, the consideration of unauthorized entry. He wandered around to the back, where he found nothing but a garbage can and an old garden hose lying in the tall grass. Sorely tempted to take a peek into the green plastic container, he glanced around at the two or three nearby dwellings; curtains dropped simultaneously in all of them. Gazing unconcernedly toward the pier, he ambled back to the Plymouth and headed for the relative privacy of Porpoise Bay.

Approaching Caitlin's Park he spotted a familiar group of kids playing baseball. He slowed down and half-watched as a well-hit ball shot toward the road, two of the boys chasing after it. At that moment he noticed a truck careening toward him on a collision course with the faster of the two boys, the driver adjusting something on the dashboard, oblivious. Davenport pounded on the horn: not a squeak came out of it. In a split second his foot was on the accelerator and the Plymouth, after a moment's hesitation, responded. He swerved sharply to the left and onto the shoulder, sliding to a halt in front of the boy. The ball rolled under his car and the front wheels of the truck, whose driver, by now, had seen what was going on and came to a screeching stop. Arms raised in an attempt to protect himself from the sudden appearance of the Plymouth, the young Mantle banged into it and bounced off. It was the same kid who had informed him, at the fireworks display, that he didn't belong on Spruce Island. The boy was fighting hard not to cry, and losing.

A country tune blared from the truck. The driver came running up. "That was quick thinking, Louis. You all right, Bobby?"

Massaging an elbow, the boy got to his feet. He stared at Davenport and nodded slowly.

"How did you know my name?"

"I imagine everybody on the island knows your name by now. You want a ride home, Bob?"

The boy declined. "Well, you be careful next time." He took Davenport's hand into his callused paw and shook it hard. The special deputy sheriff managed not to wince. "I'm Perry Crane, Bobby's uncle. I won't forget this." Without another word he turned and headed back to the truck.

By now all the children had gathered around Davenport. He patted a couple of them on the shoulder. The sandy-haired outfielder, teary streaks lining his dusty face, started to speak.

"I'll tell you what a man once said to me in a similar situation," Davenport interrupted. "He said, 'That's all right, son. Maybe you can do the same for someone else some day.' Well, my little friend, it looks like this is the day."

Another Victim

What narrow, jagged paths our lives take, Davenport mused. A man dies, a drunkard doesn't answer his door, and so a little boy survives. Serendipity. We're all lucky to be alive.

Until he was eight or nine he had never thought much about the possibility of dying. Climbing to the top of the big maple tree on the scrubby front lawn of the orphanage didn't seem at all terrifying, even when he accepted his own challenge and scooted out to the end of a skinny branch high over the scrubby lawn. It never occurred to him that the limb might break, but suddenly he found himself plummeting down and down. He just managed to catch a lower branch and hang on tenuously, screaming for succor. A policeman who happened to be passing by climbed over the wrought-iron fence and made it to the tree just as young Louie lost his grip. He fell into the cop's arms, bowling him over and breaking his nose and glasses. When the man got up, he waved away the boy's tearful attempt to thank him. His only comment was, "That's all right, son. Maybe you can do the same for someone else some day." He hobbled off, and that was the last Louie ever saw of him.

The long-standing debt finally repaid, Special Deputy Sheriff Louis B. Davenport roared into the parking lot and, with a flourish, switched off the engine. The sky has never been so blue, he thought. Doesn't it ever rain here? He was hungry, too, ready to devour anything, if he wasn't already too late for lunch. Inhaling deeply the crisp air, he swaggered toward the Big House. Where are you, old Sam Peabody, Peabody, Peabody, you little bugger? In the sitting room he was greeted by Rose Kelly, who cried, "Louie! Where the devil have you been?"

"Huh? What's the matter?"

"Something's happened to Frank Parkening."

"What? What happened to Parkening?"

"He didn't show up for lunch."

"Well it's only—uh—" His watch had stopped. "Maybe he—"

"Frank's never been late for a meal in his life."

"Did you check his room?"

"That's what I'm tryin' to tell you. When he didn't show up, Margie went over to get him but he didn't answer his door, and it was locked. So I sent Joey over and he looked into Frank's window and saw him lyin' on the bed. He just came back. I told him to get a crowbar and break open the window."

"Maybe he was just sleeping."

"Joey didn't think so."

"Why didn't you use your skeleton key?"

"*You* have it, remember?"

Without answering, Davenport lumbered across the lawn to the Farmhouse. Rose was a few steps behind him, lamenting, "He told me after breakfast that someone was tapping on his window during the night. And he heard strange sounds outside his room, and the doorknob rattling."

He ran to the back of the Farmhouse. "Joey—never mind!" The handyman whirled around, dropped the uplifted crowbar just as it was about to strike, and backed away from the window with obvious disappointment.

They all trotted to the front of the cottage. "Why the hell isn't this door locked?" Davenport shouted rhetorically, and hurried through the little kitchen and sitting room, Rose and Joey following close behind. He turned left into a short hallway. "Which one is his room?"

She indicated the one on the right. He fiddled with the key, finally got the door open, and stumbled into the darkened room. Frank Parkening was lying on the bed, his pudgy hands clawing the sheets. His face was swollen and distinctly purple, like a giant plum with a protruding tongue. The lifeless eyes stared dully at the sloping ceiling. There but for the grace of God, thought Davenport. On the dresser fluttered a piece of paper. With a reasonably clean handkerchief he retrieved the note, a 4 x 6 sheet torn from a lined pad. In large, printed letters, it correctly predicted: YOU'RE GOING TO DIE. "Rose, you and Joey wait outside."

When they had gone he closed the door and examined Parkening's pockets, where he found the room key and nothing else of importance. Clutched in a hand, however, was another fragment of paper on which was scrawled the word: D'ARCY.

He examined the dresser drawers, finding only extra-large underwear and a folder containing a map of the Project with some legal papers outlining certain financial details. Strewn around the room were playthings of all kinds: an Erector set, Tinker Toys, Lincoln Logs. A track snaked across the floor; on it a miniature train chugged slowly through a tunnel and into a tiny village. He found the switch and turned it off.

Davenport had never had an electric train. He stared at it for a moment, turned it on again, and watched it chug its way around the countryside and back to the station. For several minutes he toyed with the switch, running the engine fast and slow, fast and slow. The sweet smell of ozone filled the bedroom. He turned up the juice. The train jumped the track and crashed into the closet door.

Rose and Joey were waiting for him under the grape arbor. "He's dead, isn't he?" she surmised.

His only response was, "Ask the guests to keep the cottages locked as well as their rooms, will you, Rose?"

"I'll suggest it, Louie, but I can't run around and check on them every five minutes."

They returned to the Big House, where he called the doctor and requested an ambulance or hearse. "I've got patients here, Louis. Just toss him in Rose's pickup and bring him on down."

After he had helped Joey load the heavy, sheet-draped body into the truck bed, he hurried back to the kitchen and dialed Tate, who was out of his office. Olive finally managed to reach the sheriff by radio, and he returned the call on his cellular phone.

"What's up, Lou?"

"Another one, Chief."

"Gawd! Somebody else take a tumble?"

"Nope. Might have been a heart attack. Or something made to look like one." He explained the Parkening situation, ending with: "It's a whole new ball game, Loch."

"What do you mean? You just said it was probably a heart attack."

Davenport could see the look of exasperation on the sheriff's tanned face. "I said it 'might have been.' But how do you explain the threatening note?"

"What are you suggesting, boy?"

"A financial motive, perhaps?"

"As good a one as any. Where's the body now?"

"I just sent it down to the doc. He'll have it on the first boat tomorrow, I imagine."

"You need any backup on this?"

"I don't think so, Loch. But could you get me some search warrants?"

"C'mon, Lou, you know I can't do that unless you have something to go on. You don't, do you?"

"Not much," Davenport admitted. "Just the notes. The odd thing is, they're not in the same handwriting. Let me know how they compare with the others you have."

"As soon as I can, ol' buddy."

"Anything yet on Fairfax?"

"Not yet," sighed the sheriff. "These things take time, you know."

"What about the blood on the shirt fragment I sent over?"

"Oh, yeah, I almost forgot about that. Maybe the people over there are being knocked off by angry birds."

"Huh?"

"It was seagull blood."

"No kidding!" Davenport paused to let that sink in. "You dig up any dirt on the other people here?"

"Still working on that, son. Only thing I have so far is Alice Barnstable. Claims to be poor even though she's loaded. But very tight-fisted."

"I suspected as much."

"By the bye . . . ."

"Yes?"

"Don't get into any arguments with her."

"Why not?"

"She was a champion debater in college."

"I'll try not to. Incidentally, see if you can find out anything about Parkening's will while you're at it."

"Thanks, Inspector—I hadn't thought of that. Gotta go, son. Tell those people not to panic. And Lou?"

"Yeah?"

"See if you can keep this from happening again, will you?"

"All I can do is advise them to stay together and not to do anything stupid."

"Another call's coming in. Enjoy your vacation. Put in a good word for me over there."

"My—?"

The sheriff hung up. Davenport, already lost in the grisly details of an earlier case, absentmindedly replaced the receiver. The killer had murdered a number of teenage girls all over Boston. The victims had been accosted while they were walking through one of the city parks, often carrying library books. They had all been strangled and hacked up with an ax. Surprisingly, sex was not a factor. The perpetrator turned out to be a middle-aged, married man who had lost a long-awaited promotion to a woman. Davenport had staked out every library in the city and finally found his misogynist killer.

He remembered that he had missed lunch. There were two refrigerators in the big kitchen; both had little porpoise magnets across the front holding recipes for pot pie and cupcakes with strawberry icing. He opened one of the doors and found a leftover chicken leg, which was soon a happy memory. He went for the breast. In a few minutes half a chicken had disappeared, leaving him holding the grisly evidence. He found a paper bag, threw the bones inside, and pushed them to the bottom of a large green garbage can. As he pulled his greasy fingers from the plastic container an idea occurred to him: could there be some other way into Parkening's room?

An Invitation

Davenport found Rose in the flower garden. He yawned, picked at an ear, and inquired casually about alternate routes into the guest rooms.

"Well, there's the window, but that's been frozen shut for years. Even Joey can't get it open."

"I was thinking about the floor."

"Not likely. There's no basement in the Farmhouse."

"What about a tunnel?"

"Nope, no tunnel."

"Would you know if there was one?"

"Of course I'd know—you think I'm blind?"

"All right, all right. Could you call the guests to the sitting room? I need to speak to them."

"What—again? Oh, all right." She dropped her trowel and started off toward the Blacksmith Shop. Davenport went in and checked the signout sheet. Not a single name on it.

Even the Thornhills showed up promptly, and without argument. No one else said anything, either. Only D'Arcy was smiling.

Davenport stood with his back to the crackling fireplace and watched the guests arrange themselves. When everyone was finally seated, he began. "Ladies and gentlemen, as you all know, Mr. Parkening, unfortunately, is no longer with us. At this point we don't know exactly what happened to him. He may have died from natural causes, just as Mr. Fairfax might have. What leads me to believe otherwise is that a threatening note was found in both men's rooms after their demise, as well as the dead bird in the kitchen of the Farmhouse. And the pot shot someone took at me in the shower yesterday. Also, Mr. Parkening appeared to hear noises outside his room and someone tapping on his window last night. I'm going to suggest to you that, until we learn otherwise, we consider this to be a double murder and take appropriate steps to insure that it doesn't happen again."

He noted that he had everyone's attention. "From now on I must insist that everyone in this room sign the pad indicating your whereabouts, and remain in the presence of at least one other person at all times, night and day. You too, Ms. Barnstable. This means that you are going to have to double up with someone until we can find out what's going on here. I would suggest you stay in the Blacksmith Shop with Miss Manhart and Miss Black, if that's agreeable with them."

She mumbled something foul, but, to his surprise, didn't argue the matter.

"Rose, I would like you to move into Lisa's room, or vice versa, if possible, or find a double room elsewhere. Dr. and Mrs. D'Arcy, you might consider moving into the Farmhouse with the Thornhills if that wouldn't inconvenience you too much."

"You mean into Frank's room?" cried Mrs. D'Arcy, her jewelry glistening in the firelight.

"Now, now, Pat," grinned D'Arcy. "Can you guarantee our safety if we do that, Monsieur?"

"No, but your risk, if any, should be greatly reduced."

Miss Manhart spoke up. "Mr. D, we're frightened. We'd be happy to have Alice move in with us if she's willing. But what are you doing to find the person who is responsible for all this?"

"Yes, Mr. D. What are you doing to—"

"We're doing all we can, ladies. I'm currently looking for someone on the island who would have both a motive and the opportunity to commit murder. In the meantime the sheriff's office and the coroner are doing everything possible to determine what caused the deaths and who the perpetrator might be."

"Loose, I still don't think anyone's been murdered here, but we're willing to cooperate if it will make everyone feel safer. But I want to ask you one question: are we free to leave the island and go home if we want?"

"I can't prevent you from doing that, Mr. Thornhill. Never could. But I would request that you advise me of your plans if you decide to do so. Now, as for you, Miss Quinlan—"

"Thank you, Louis, but I'm staying put."

"It's your funer—I mean, that's your decision. But if we take the proper precautions, there shouldn't be any more trouble."

"We're *all* happy to hear that, Louie," Rose offered drily.

"Are there any more questions?"

"Anyone for slime mold hunting this evening?" Baker inquired hopefully, his nearly invisible eyebrows rising and falling like inchworms.

There were no takers, except for his wife, who breathed, "I'd love to go."

"Take the kid with you," Barnstable suggested.

Lisa came in from the dining room. "Phone call for you, Louie. It's Mary Crane."

Davenport had not seen her smile before. It was quite beautiful, like her mother's. "Who's Mary Crane?"

"The mother of the boy whose life you saved today."

He headed for the kitchen. "Remember what I told you, folks."

"She already hung up," Lisa called after him.

He turned. "Well, what did she want?"

"She wanted you to come for supper tonight."

"What did you tell her?"

"Not to accept such an invitation would be a dire insult, Louie. I told her you'd be happy to come. If you want to weasel out of it, be my guest."

Dire? thought Davenport. "What time?"

"Suppertime on Spruce Island is five o'clock. You should be there at 4:45."

"Take Kelly with you, will you, Louie?" Rose implored. "She likes that old hound of theirs."

"Too bad," added her daughter, striding briskly toward the kitchen. "Wednesday is gourmet night."

A History of Spruce Island

Rattling back toward Nor'east Head, Davenport began to have second thoughts about accepting the Cranes' invitation, regardless of whose feelings might be hurt. But surely, he reasoned, none of the other guests could get into trouble during or immediately after dinner if they stayed together.

Someone in a passing truck gave him a finger. An index finger, he realized, not the middle one. He wondered whether Spuce Islanders had evolved their own peculiar insults. Another car passed, and another index finger rose from the steering wheel. Eyes that were once blank and suspicious, even hostile, now seemed bright and friendly. After the third wave he returned the gesture. It appeared he was no longer a pariah.

Following Rose's directions he pulled up in front of a large frame house, where he was greeted at the door by a muscular, fortyish man, who shook his hand for a very long time without saying a word. His eyes were blue-green, like the sea, and his face the color of concentrated sunlight. The steely grip finally relaxed.

Davenport was led into the sitting room, where eleven-year-old Bobby, his brother and sister, and the dog were waiting. The room was sparsely, though comfortably, furnished, with handmade rugs scattered around the hardwood floor. A small wood-burning stove stood in one corner. The ceiling was dominated by unfinished spruce beams. To his surprise, a pad of paper like those used for the threatening notes lay on a desk in another corner.

The hound began to bay as soon as they came into the room. "Quiet, Rusty!" Crane shouted. "He won't bother you, Louis. It's just that we surprised him. He's deaf as a post and has lost his smeller to boot." Nonetheless, the dog slowly rose and sniffed him thoroughly.

"How old is he?"

"Twenty-two."

"He's not doing too badly for twenty-two! I've got the Kellys' dog out in the car. Should I—"

"Carolyn, you and Dylan let Kelly out of Louis's car, will you?"

The girl leaped off the sofa and ran out with the smaller of the two boys and the ancient dog.

Crane cleared his throat. "Bobby, you have something you want to say?"

The boy stood up and carefully studied his feet. "You want to see my seashell collection?"

"Nahhh—that's not it," his father admonished.

"Thank you for saving my life," he said to the floor.

Davenport placed a finger under Bobby's chin and lifted it up. "Just remember what I told you."

Bobby nodded. "I will."

"The other boy is Dylan and the girl's name is Carolyn."

The latter, who had just come back into the room, was seven or eight and, like the others, red-haired and freckled. The smaller boy followed her in. They both smiled at him. Carolyn was missing a tooth and eager to give him all the details. She tilted her head to one side when she spoke. Davenport resisted the urge to wipe the spittle from his face.

When she had finished her story, Crane said, "She was sick last night, weren't you, Carolyn?"

The girl nodded. "I barfed," she reported cheerfully.

Davenport wiped the spittle from his face. Crane grabbed his arm and led him into the spacious kitchen. There he presented his wife, Mary, who tried to speak, but could not. On the other side of the room stood a second cooking stove, an old wood-burner. Sitting in front of it, peeling potatoes, was a woman who appeared to be as old as the dog. She was introduced as Grandma Nan, who was a hundred and six. She looked up, and he could see that she was blind. "Grandma Nan is the all-time champion potato peeler for the state of Maine. Won at the state fair forty-five years in a row until she retired. Still does it at the Dulse Festival."

Grandma Nan thrust out a bony hand, palm forward. Davenport wasn't certain how to take it. "She wants to feel your face," Dylan eagerly informed him.

He bent over to comply. After running her rough fingers over his eyes and nose and mouth she nodded silently and went back to peeling, leaving his nostrils filled with the pungent aroma of freshly-stripped spuds. He watched as the old woman went at another one. She didn't use a peeler, but a razor-sharp knife. With one continuous cut she made her way around and around the potato. They all watched quietly until the entire coat dropped intact into a carefully-placed bucket. She grinned toothlessly—he could see the remains of a strand of dulse on her tongue—and the next one came under the knife. Capable of murder? You bet!

"Grandma Nan was a midwife. Delivered most of the people on the island, I imagine. Everyone over ten, anyway."

While the women were preparing supper, the others wandered around the back yard, which encompassed a large vegetable garden. Beyond that a rainbow-colored field stretched downhill toward the spruce woods and the sparkling sea. A number of fruit trees were showing signs of production. The dogs romped in the orchard like puppies.

In the yard were the usual accouterments of growing children: bicycles lying where they had been left, a ball and glove, a pup tent. Near the house, spruce logs were lined up in neat, parallel rows, and next to them stood a tall stack of lobster traps arranged like bricks in a sturdy building.

"Beautiful place you have here, Mr. Crane."

"Don."

"Don. In fact, the whole island's beautiful. I've never seen anyplace like it."

"Yes, we're quite attached to it," Crane remarked.

"Isn't that an ovenbird, Dad?" Bobby wanted to know.

"No, son, that's a nuthatch."

"Oh, right."

Davenport watched the robin-size bird walk head-first down a birch tree. He filed away the information. "What are those little red berries in the woods over there?"

"Those are bunchberries. They're edible, if you ever find yourself lost in the woods. Best thing about them, though—when you see bunchberries, the blueberries can't be far behind."

Davenport squatted down, picked a few, and stuffed them into his mouth. He quickly spat them out again.

Crane and the boys laughed. "They're not so flavorful, though." From somewhere he pulled out a handful of dulse. "This will take the taste out of your mouth." Davenport's lip curled involuntarily as he accepted a couple of strands, bit off the end of one. The rest he surreptitiously pocketed.

They followed a narrow path through the field and into the woods, the dogs leading the way. The boys veered off into the trees. "Look, Dad—chanterelle!"

"So it is. Amazin' how they just seem to come up overnight, ain't it?" He offered one to Davenport, who politely declined. "Better take some of them back to your mother, Bobby."

When the boys had gathered a handful and run toward the house, Crane took the opportunity to speak. "Louis, I can never repay you for what you did for my son. But if there is ever anything we can do for you, just give us a holler. Anything at all."

"Well, there is one thing."

"You just name it."

"Maybe you know that I'm here to investigate the death of one of the guests at Porpoise Bay Cottages . . . ."

"Yes, I know." He scratched his stubbly chin. "Is that why you have those tics?"

Davenport started to pretend ignorance, but knew it would be futile. "A doctor I saw in Boston once told me it had to do with being abandoned as a child. On top of that, there was something that happened while I was on the force there."

"What was that?"

He didn't feel like going into it, but Crane's utter ingenuousness was hard to counter. "Well, my partner and I were investigating a murder case. We cornered the perpetrator in an abandoned house. It was a standoff. We were pointing our weapons at him, and him at us. I guess I should have shot him while I had the chance, but I didn't. He killed my partner and *then* I shot him. It's one of those things where you lie in bed at night wishing you could have it to do all over again."

"Maybe you made up for that today, Louis."

Davenport shrugged. "There was another death at the cottages this morning, did you know that?"

"Heard about it just before you came over."

"Who told you?"

"Lisa Kelly. Rose is my wife's second cousin. They're both Banners."

"Is that so? Anyhow, both of the victims, and most of the other guests, apparently, are in on a proposed development project for the island. Do you know about that, too?"

"Yes, I've heard something about it."

"What I was wondering is, do you know of anyone on the island who has a lot at stake in this? Someone who might suffer a loss or be hurt in some way by this development?"

"That would cover just about everybody who lives on Spruce Island, Louis."

And none of them know nuttin', Davenport reminded himself. "Tell me something about the island and the people who live here."

"That's quite a bit of territory, but I'll do my best. Right after supper. It's five now. We'd better be gettin' back in."

The meal passed with the usual family patter, punctuated by periodic shouts at the dog to lie down and stop drooling. It was obvious that he had been treated to countless table scraps in the past. Grandma Nan put away a huge mound of mashed potatoes and gravy, washed down with a mug of "Indian tea."

"What's Indian tea?" Davenport asked with genuine interest.

"An extract of burdock roots," replied Mary Crane. "And a few other things." He thought about asking for a cup of it.

"Tastes terrible," said Crane, reading his thoughts.

He was pleased to discover that no one put on any special airs and there was no attempt to involve him in every conversation. It was almost as if he were a long-lost relative, a member of the family, welcome to put in a few cents' worth, but under no pressure to do so. Bobby proudly mentioned that his face was sprouting a layer of peach fuzz. His sister wanted to know what that meant. "Means I'm turnin' into a man," said the boy.

"Or that you're turning into a peach!" countered Davenport, grinning like D'Arcy. Despite the recent lunch he pleased everyone by eating everything offered to him, including two huge wedges of warm rhubarb pie and a mound of homemade vanilla ice cream.

After supper everyone retreated to the sitting room, where the dogs immediately fell asleep in front of the stove, even though there was no fire in it. Grandma Nan was helped to a chair in the corner, where she commenced to knit the sleeve of a small wool sweater. Davenport was offered the best chair and a glass of blueberry wine, which he gratefully accepted.

When everyone was settled, Crane took a sip of wine and began his history of Spruce Island. Curiously, Davenport noted, the kids listened attentively, gazing at the ceiling, nodding from time to time, as if they had heard it all before and were comparing the present version to something in their memories.

"Spruce Island was settled by loyalists to the crown of England during the Revolution," he began. "These were the Hendersons. They shared the island with the Kennebec Indians, later known as the Bluefoot tribe, who helped them turn back rebel invasions from Machias." He looked straight at Davenport, who smiled uncomfortably. "All the Blues on the island are part Indian," he went on. "Later on, a family of Irish named Banner landed and settled here, too."

Davenport took a sip of wine, smacked his lips.

"The three family groups settled at the three choice harbor sites on the island, which are now Nor'east Head, Centerville, and Fog Cove. The Nor'east Head family was the Banners, the Centerville family was the Hendersons, and the Fog Cove family was the Blues. Of course other people came and went, but most of the people living on Spruce Island descended from these three family stocks. As far as we can tell, our own family is mostly Banners and Hendersons. I'm the Henderson, Mary's the Banner."

"But we're all part Blue, aren't we, Dad?"

"That's right, Bobby. Everyone here is part English, part Irish, and part Indian. Spruce Island eventually became American territory again, but we've pretty much kept to ourselves over the years. Sometimes somebody goes over to the mainland for schooling or work, but they usually come back to the island eventually.

"Spruce Islanders have made their livings for the last two hundred years from the sea. Most of us are fishermen or lobstermen or scallopers. Originally there was a thriving boat-building industry in Centerville and Fog Cove, and a sardine-packing company at Nor'east Head. A hundred years ago we supplied the whole world with millions of pounds of smoked herrin'. You can still see the smokehouses down below Centerville, and a few down around Fog Cove, and some of them are still in operation today. But most of us now are fishermen. I, myself, lobster and scallop. Maybe you'd like to go out on my boat sometime."

"I'd like that."

Crane smiled warmly. "The population of Spruce Island is about nine hundred, and hasn't changed much in the last century or so, ever since the heyday of the smoked herrin' industry. Art, down at the drug store, claims that every time somebody's born on the island, somebody else leaves. Har, har, har. He used to be on the radio, you know. But we don't want it to get much bigger because the island wouldn't support a whole lot more people. Besides, we like it just the way it is.

"I hope that answers your question."

Before Davenport could reply, Carolyn asked, "Are you married?" Her eyes were the color of emeralds.

He hesitated. "Well, I was once."

"What happened?"

He had been asked this question before by children, but the parents had always pointed out that such a query was considered impolite. No one spoke up, however.

"Well, it's a long story."

They waited. "My wife and I never really got along very well. One day she just left." He hoped that would do it.

"Any children?"

"Two daughters. Both of them are grown now."

"Grandchildren?"

"Two. Both girls."

"Do you see your family very often?"

"Not often enough."

There was a long silence. He wondered whether to change the subject. Bobby got up and pulled a photograph album from the desk. Without a word he handed it to Davenport, who opened the cover and began the entire picture history of the Crane family, beginning with Grandma Nan's wedding. There were photos of boats and lobstering, of picnics, of swimming and hikes and baseball games, birthdays and graduations. The children gathered around him to point out special features. It was as though he were a long-lost uncle.

This was followed by a tour of the entire house, highlighted by a shell collection worthy of a museum, and Bobby knew the names of all of them. Around his room were strewn books and puzzles and clothing; it was nothing like the rigid atmosphere of the orphanage or his house in Boston. Davenport would have given an organ to trade places with the bright, freckle-faced boy.

The rest of the evening was spent wandering on the shore. It was low tide, and Bobby pointed out the various mollusks clinging to the rocks. He splashed some water on the barnacles and showed Davenport how they opened their mouths and drank it in, to the dogs' unflagging interest. The sun began to set, and the scattered clouds were tinted with hues of blue and rose like none he had ever seen.

On the way back to the house he learned that Mary Crane, like Rose, was a teacher. In the winter months it was her husband who did most of the cooking. "He's a wonderful baker," she told him. "In fact, he baked the pies we had for supper tonight."

"He also make the wine?"

"That's right. Pretty handy with a hammer, too," she added proudly. "He built the house, you know."

He asked her how she had met her husband. She stared at him. It was a meaningless question—Spruce Islanders knew each other all their lives.

Crane came up. "Well, I guess we better go to bed so Louis can leave."

Suddenly a bat swooped down past Davenport's ear. He instinctively ducked, flailing his arms wildly. The Cranes all laughed. "Maybe you could be in the variety show this year, Louis. We can always use more comedy."

The whole family walked him to the Plymouth. Davenport opened the front door and Kelly jumped in. He carefully placed an entire rhubarb pie in the back seat and reluctantly climbed in himself. "Come back any time, Louis," Crane told him. "Consider yourself a member of the family."

As he roared away, the children all yelled, "G'bye, Uncle Louie! G'bye!" Davenport stuck his hand out the window and gave them all a finger.

A Face at the Window

Davenport carefully maneuvered the pie through the front door of the Big House and glanced around the sitting room to verify that the remaining guests were all still alive. Everyone seemed to be accounted for, huddled like a flock of gulls, waiting warily for something to happen. No one was playing bridge or Scrabble.

Thornhill cracked his knuckles. "Bringing coals to Newcastle, Loose?"

"My spouse, the comedian," observed his wife.

"Where can I put this?" Davenport asked Rose, who was holding forth in the comfort of her usual chair.

"Same place we kept the leftover chicken we were going to make into pot pies, Louie." She stood and held out her hands. "One of Cousin Don's? Looks wonderful." She disappeared into the dining room.

"Did you have a nice dinner, Mr. D?" Miss Manhart inquired.

"Yes, Mr. D, did you have a nice dinner?"

"Supper, ladies," snapped Alice Barnstable. "They call it supper in this godforsaken place. Dinner's at noon."

"Oh, that's right. I keep forgetting."

"I keep forgetting, too."

"Yes, thank you, it was wonderful. Now then—did anyone see or hear anything unusual while I was gone?"

The guests glanced at each other and shook their heads. Cathy Baker piped up: "I finished Chapter One of my novel!"

"That's terrific," said Davenport without enthusiasm. "I can't wait to read it."

"I left out some things about your background. Could I talk to you about that some time?"

"Well... Where's Miss Quinlan?"

Rose had returned from the kitchen. "She's already gone to bed, Louie. She's an early riser."

"And Joey?"

"In the Shed."

"Is that where he sleeps?"

"Only in the summer. In the winter he's in your room."

"And Lisa?"

She sighed. "In her own room, all year round."

"I mean, where is she now?"

"Out somewhere. I can't do a thing with her."

"Yes, I know. All right, ladies, if you're ready I'll escort you to your cottage. You, too, Ms. Barnstable."

"*Thank* you, Sheriff. Thank you *so* much."

"No—I didn't mean you weren't a—" He gave up, hopelessly outclassed. "I assume you've moved your things to the Blacksmith Shop."

She nodded with a scowl.

"Dr. and Mrs. D'Arcy, are you all set up in the Farmhouse with the Thornhills?"

"We are, indeed, Monsieur Da-ven-porrrt."

"Then we'll all go over together. The rest of you may feel free to go to your rooms at your convenience. I'll be back in a few minutes."

With his skeleton key Davenport unlocked the door to the Blacksmith Shop and led the women inside, through the sitting room and into the kitchen, where he flipped on the light. On the table lay a very dead gull.

The ladies shrieked. Gingerly he picked up the carcass and escorted it outside, where he hurled it deep into the woods.

Paul Thornhill was just going into the Farmhouse. "What the hell, Loose?"

"Nothing. Just a dead bird."

"Ooooooooohhh!" wailed his wife.

Davenport hurried back into the Shop, where he checked all the rooms, peered under the beds. "Everything's okay, ladies. Be sure to lock the door after I leave. Good night."

"But Mr. D—"

"Yes, Mr.—"

"Nothing to worry about. Just lock your doors. You'll be okay. Sleep well."

"Easy for you to say, Sheriff."

He repeated the process in the Farmhouse. No one was hiding under a bed or in a closet. "I'll see you in the morning, folks."

"Let's hope so, Loose."

"Bonne nuit, Monsieur."

By the time Davenport returned to the Big House the sitting room was empty. The sherry bottle had been put away and a few red coals glowed softly in the fireplace. He checked the dining room and kitchen, found the back door locked. The pie was in the refrigerator. He thought about having another piece, decided against it, popped a Maalox tablet instead.

He returned to the sitting room, dropped onto the Victorian sofa, and gazed at the ebbing fire. Three days he had been on Spruce Island without coming up with any real clues, except for a shred of evidence that the killer might possibly be an islander. If so, that narrowed the possibilities down to about nine hundred people. He considered putting on another log. Instead, he got out "The Old Lighthouse" and began to set it up. There was a tap on the window behind him.

Startled, Davenport ducked and instinctively reached for his .38. He whirled to find a middle-aged man pointing toward the front of the house and disappearing in that direction. Davenport holstered the revolver, but kept his hand on it as he opened the door. Standing outside, bright in the porchlight, was a man clad only in dirty jeans, a tattered orange T-shirt, worn-out running shoes, and a baseball cap, from which protruded long, stringy, blond hair.

Davenport recognized him: it was the guy coming out of the woods he had almost run over four days earlier when he was looking for Porpoise Bay Cottages. The man was weaving slowly from side to side. The middle finger of his right hand was stuck in a bottle of beer. "Are you the shurff from Machias?"

"Maybe. Who are you?"

"Byron. I heard you were lookin' for me."

"Oh, yes. Byron. Come on in."

"Thankee."

The man dusted off his jeans and wiped his feet vigorously on the little mat. His breath was worse than the geezer's from Indiana.

"On second thought, I'll come outside."

Byron backed away. Davenport studied the matted hair and greasy beard for clues. He headed for the parking lot. Byron followed alongside, weaving from side to side like a goose. "Byron, there may have been two murders here in the last few days. I was wondering if you might know anything about that."

"Wasn't me, Shurff." He raised his left arm as if taking an oath. "I swear it wasn't me."

"I didn't say it was. I heard you are out late sometimes and I thought you might have seen something that nobody else has."

"Nope, I haven't seen or heard a thing."

"Well, if you do see anything unusual, or if you remember something, will you let me know?"

"If I see anything unusual, you'll be the first to know, Shurff."

Davenport cleared his throat. "Where were you yesterday afternoon at 4:30?"

Byron thought hard. "I don't know, Shurff, and that's a fact."

Davenport handed him a five-dollar bill. "Thanks for coming, Byron. Remember: I'm depending on you."

With a wave of the bottle he declined the money. "That's all right, Shurff. My neighbors take pretty good care of me."

They reached the parking area. "Where's your car?"

"Don't have one."

"You mean you walked all the way out here?"

Byron nodded.

"I'll give you a lift back to town."

"That's all right. I usually walk most of the night anyway." He waved a hand in a circular motion, as if cleaning a window, and started up the long driveway.

Davenport watched him waddle away, the bottle swinging from his finger like a pendulum.

Back in the house he checked the dining room and kitchen again, peered into the refrigerator, fought off another urge to consume a hunk of Crane's pie, went to his room and locked the door. Unable to sleep, he sat down in the reading chair and reached for his cigarettes. He tapped one from the nearly-empty pack and stuck it in his mouth.

Still restless, he got up again, shuffled to the front window, and gazed toward the bay. The half-moon hovered over the woods, and the trees cast long, ominous shadows in the cold light. The Cape Cod was dark, apparently deserted. He stepped to the window facing the other cottages, where he thought he saw someone dart behind the Blacksmith Shop. He rubbed his eyes, stared at the cottage, but found no corroborating sign of movement. No lights were on, either there or in the adjacent Farmhouse. He sucked on the cigarette. Hard to believe, he thought, that someone might die on a peaceful night like this.

Just then he heard a scream. Then another, in a different voice. Waving his revolver, he discarded the cigarette and bolted for the front door. Lights came on in both cottages. He ran toward the commotion, quickly unlocked the door of the Blacksmith Shop, and banged inside. Feeling his way in the dim light, he called out: "Miss Manhart? Miss Black?"

Alice Barnstable appeared at the top of the staircase. "It's all right, Sheriff. Nobody's hurt. Come on up."

He found the ladies in their long flannel nightdresses sitting on their bed, their heads in their hands. Both were weeping. "Now, now," he said in his most soothing voice. "It's all over. Miss Manhart, what happened?"

"Oh, Mr. D, we heard Frank outside. He was calling to us."

"We heard Frank calling to us, Mr. D."

"Mr. Parkening's not here, ladies. He's down at the doctor's office."

"No, he's not. He was here. We heard him. Didn't we, Callie?"

Miss Black nodded. "We heard him, Mr. D."

"Did *you* hear anything, Ms. Barnstable?"

"No, I didn't, Sheriff. But I'm on the other side of the hallway."

"All right, ladies, calm yourselves. You probably had a bad dream."

Miss Manhart dried her eyes on a frilly handkerchief. "I've got to go to the bathroom," she cried.

"I do, too."

There was an awkward silence while the ladies helped each other down the stairs, calling out with one voice, "Would you care for a cup of tea, Mr. D?"

Before he could decline, another pair of shrieks came from below. He charged down the staircase, revolver drawn. A bat flew over his head. He ducked and instinctively swung at it with the gun. It flew up the stairs and disappeared. He heard a whoop from Alice Barnstable.

But the ladies were still wailing. Miss Manhart's wig had fallen off and lay at her feet. She was totally bald. On the kitchen table lay a 4 x 6 sheet of paper. He was certain it hadn't been there when he had rushed by only moments before. He read it without picking it up. It stated, flatly, YOU'RE GOING TO DIE. . . .

Davenport thought: Byron! He ran out of the building, past the bathrobed ghosts of the D'Arcys and the Thornhills and into the parking lot. The old Plymouth started easily in the cold, dry air, as if eager for the chase. At the top of the long driveway he switched off his lights and turned toward Nor'east Head, driving carefully in case Byron popped out of the woods somewhere. A few seconds later he saw in the distance, bathed in the cold light of the moon, an unmistakable figure waddling along the road toward town, the bottle still dangling from a middle finger. Davenport stopped the car, turned around, and rattled slowly back to Porpoise Bay Cottages.

APTGAFIA

Special Deputy Sheriff Louis B. Davenport rolled around in his bed until four o'clock in the morning with indigestion of mind and body. Sweating heavily, he listened for unusual sounds, watched the shadows on the curtains for signs of unexpected movement. He dearly wished he hadn't eaten half of the rhubarb pie, and wondered whether to stick his finger down his throat and get it over with. The same finger he had stupidly given the Cranes when he left, the wave reserved for meeting vehicles coming the other way, he now realized.

Someone was systematically doing away with the guests at Porpoise Bay Cottages. Not a stranger, who would have been noticed, but someone, apparently, who lived on the island. But who? And why? The only link between the victims seemed to be their long acquaintanceship, their annual migration to Porpoise Bay, and their involvement with the proposed Spruce Island Development Project, APTGAFIA. Who had so much to lose, if the Project went through, that he was driven to commit multiple murder? The property wasn't even owned by an islander, and it wasn't being used for anything. Foggily he reminded himself to call Tate in the morning, see if he could find out who the Swiss owner was, and who was in possession of the land surrounding the Project site.

The whole thing reminded him of an earlier case, one in which a paper company had built a factory right next to a retirement complex. One of the old gentlemen, worried about noise and pollution, something he thought he had finally escaped from, freaked out and killed half the board of directors at the groundbreaking ceremony.

But no one was planning to build a factory or pollute the island, and there were far worse things than a theme park. In other hands the land could be clear-cut or strip-mined. It had to be the work of a lunatic, he concluded, a serial killer, and a very clever one, as all of them were. Someone had it in for the summer inhabitants themselves. Would D'Arcy, the third college roommate, be the next to go? If so, why were the gull and the note left in the Blacksmith shop and not the Farmhouse or the Cape Cod? He finally drifted off with the haunting image in his mind of Byron waddling down the road, a beer bottle permanently attached to his middle finger.

He awoke with a start; someone was banging on his door. "Louie? It's Lisa. Are you coming in to breakfast or not?"

"Huh? What time is it? My watch stopped again."

She sung out: "The ladies have gone."

"Gone?" He hopped around the room and stumbled into his shorts. Where did they go?"

"Home. Took the first boat."

"They left the island?"

"That's what I said. You awake, Louie?"

Davenport stuffed his shirt into his trousers and unlocked the door. "But they were just here a few hours ago."

"And now they're not." She turned and headed toward the kitchen. "If you want any breakfast, you'd better get into the dining room. Place closes in five minutes."

He followed her in and took a seat with the D'Arcys, who had made a special effort to be present, though they weren't eating. Everyone, except for Harriett Quinlan, who had her nose in a bird book, sipped coffee and stared silently at Davenport as if waiting for some profound announcement or, at the least, a hint of optimism and good cheer. The only thing he managed to come up with was: "Anybody else find a note last night?" He took a shot of caffeine and glanced at the Thornhills, seated with Alice Barnstable, and the Bakers, at a table alone. They all shook their heads. The clock struck nine. He could hear the cries, squawks, and whoops of ravens in the spruce trees outside. It sounded as though they were sitting in the middle of a jungle.

"Dr. D'Arcy," he sighed, "why don't you tell me what you know about the Project. Who is this Swiss family that owns half the island and how do you know they're willing to sell their holdings?"

"I *don't* know," grinned D'Arcy. "Fred Fairfax was handling that part of the deal."

"And he was doing the whole thing through his bank?"

"That's right."

"Couldn't you get the name of the owner from the local registrar of deeds?" piped in his sister-in-law.

"Maybe so. Right now I'm trying to find out how much you all know about this thing."

"We don't know much about it, Monsieur. Except that Fred thought it looked like a good investment opportunity."

Thornhill said, "He mentioned to me once that the name was Braun, or something like that."

"Did he ever tell you why they were selling? Or what the asking price was?"

"The way I heard it, Loose, this 'Braun' guy was a wealthy industrialist, maybe the richest man in Switzerland or close to it. He was planning to build a castle and retire here, but apparently he died a couple of years back. I don't think there was an asking price. I think Fred was planning to run an offer up the flagpole and see if the family saluted it."

"Did he run it up?"

"Nope. He was planning to get all his investors lined up this summer. But he fell off the cliff before he could do that."

"The principal investors were to be Fairfax himself, Frank Parkening, the D'Arcy's here, and you and Mrs. Thornhill, is that right?"

"Plus the ladies," added D'Arcy.

"You wouldn't know it to look at them, Loose, but they're worth millions."

"How did they get all that money?"

"The same way most wealthy people do: they inherited it."

"Are you worth millions, Mr. Thornhill?"

"Well, I don't want to get into that right here. Let's just say that we're planning on holding up our end of the deal."

"And you, Dr. D'Arcy? Are you and Mrs. D'Arcy planning to hold up your share of the load?"

"Dollar for dollar, Monsieur Da-ven-porrrt."

"Even though Mr. Fairfax and Mr. Parkening are no longer behind the venture?"

"The ball is rolling," smiled D'Arcy. "Nothing can stop it now."

"Well, it looks like someone may be trying to, doesn't it? Miss Quinlan, are you involved in this scheme?"

"I don't want any part of it," she stated flatly. "It's too Republican for me."

"What's wrong with Republicans?" demanded Mrs. Thornhill, clanging her cup against her saucer. Kelly got up and left the room.

"Plenty! Everything!"

Mrs. Thornhill jumped up, red-faced. "I'll be in the sitting room. Are you coming, Paul?"

"Ah, relax. She didn't mean anything personal."

"Now, now," cajoled D'Arcy. "Let's all try to get along."

She sat down again, still fuming.

Davenport focused his attention on the newest guests. Baker was gazing at the ceiling and mumbling to himself, totally unaware of what was going on. "Don't look at *us*, Deputy," protested his wife. "We're spending most of our savings on this trip. We never even *heard* about the Project until we got here."

"What we want to know, Loose, is how you're planning on protecting us from this deranged killer, whoever he is."

"As I told you earlier, Mr. Thornhill, and all the rest of you, there's safety in numbers. The more the better. I would suggest, though, that your best bet would be to leave the island. If the killer is an islander, it would be very difficult for him to follow the lot of you."

"We're not leaving, Monsieur," D'Arcy responded pleasantly, as if asking for the sugar.

Baker had come out of his reverie and was staring at him. "What about you, Mr. Baker?"

"And miss all the excitement? Not a chance." His wife smiled at him warmly. His eyebrows did several quick pushups. The baby pounded his chair with a spoon.

"Can't you shut that kid up?" Alice Barnstable screeched.

Suddenly Mrs. D'Arcy cried, "They'll kill us! They'll kill us all! I know they will!"

"You shut up too, Pat!"

D'Arcy came around the table and wrapped an arm around his wife's shoulder. "Now, now. We've been in tougher scrapes than this. Remember Venezuela?"

"Oh, God," she moaned, "I thought all that was behind us."

"By the way, Dr. D'Arcy, do *you* know the name of the Swiss family that owns the parcel you're trying to buy?"

"No idea. You might be able to get the information from Fred's bank. But I suspect that what you'll get is the name of the owner's investment firm. The real owner may be difficult to track down. The Swiss are very careful about their privacy." He grinned broadly as if the whole thing were vastly amusing.

Blueberry Hill

Davenport examined himself in his shaving mirror, found a piece of bacon stuck in his teeth. He picked it out, sniffed his armpits. Too early in the day for a shower, he surmised, but he had no more clean underwear. He rolled on extra deodorant, combed his hair back over his bald spot, and returned to the sitting room.

"What are you going to do now, Sheriff?"

"I'm going for a hike, Ms. Barnstable."

Her eyelids fluttered violently. "A hike? At a time like this?"

"I want to see this land everyone seems so interested in."

"You'd better take someone with you, hadn't you, Loose? Whoever you're looking for took a shot at you, remember?"

"I'll take Kelly. She'll sniff out any trouble. By the way—where are the Bakers?"

"They went for a plane ride."

He reached for a Maalox tablet.

"Anyone for bridge?" grinned D'Arcy, rubbing his hands together briskly. "Deck tennis?"

You have to admire his courage, thought Davenport. Unless, of course, he's the one who...

Davenport and his passenger clamored their way up the long driveway and onto the road, the dog taking in the view. He took particular care with waves. Most of the men gave him a finger, but few of the women. He began to realize that the gesture was like a handshake, to be returned only if offered. But you had to be on your toes because there wasn't much time to react. Perhaps, he decided, it's better to give a finger just to be sure. Or might that be offensive to those who didn't want one?

He turned onto the road to Dulse Cove and into the massive spruce forest. They bounced along for a few minutes until Kelly began turning around in her seat and making little whining noises. Davenport looked ahead and spotted the pulloff next to the road and the small, faded sign indicating the path to Blueberry Hill. He decided to take a look.

As soon as he opened the door the dog bounded out of the car and ran up the unmarked trail, which was clear, if uneven. Roots rose up to trip him, and every so often a branch reached out and slapped his face. But as he forged deeper into the woods the wind died away completely, and the path became a soft carpet of spruce needles and small cones. Sometimes he would see Kelly bolt out of the woods, fly across the path, and disappear into the other side, as if hot on the trail of some invisible quarry. It was obvious they were slowly climbing. He began to breathe a little heavier and finally took off his shirt, though the forest was cool. He wished he had brought something to drink.

Occasionally he heard a familiar song, and he smiled in recognition. Along the way he noticed self-heal, orange hawkweed, daisies, and columbine. In a glade of bracken he spotted two trampled-down, circular beds, their occupants—deer, presumably—having only recently departed, leaving behind the pungent odor of warm ferns. But the most salient feature of the journey was the all-pervading, spicy aroma of spruce trees. He vaguely envied the birds and squirrels who lived there.

Up and up they climbed, the dog stopping from time to time to see what was taking him so long. In the eastern sky he spotted a small plane flying down the coast. Ahead he heard the rush of moving water, and they came across a narrow bridge and gurgling stream, where they drank their fill of the cold, clear water. It was only later that he wondered about bacterial contamination.

The forest became darker, and the sweet fragrance of spruce overwhelming. He passed strange, colorful mushrooms, some with bites taken out of them. Kelly bounded around a curve. In the distance he could see a dazzling brightness, a light at the end of the tunnel. When he came closer he saw that it was a clearing in the woods illuminated by a blast of sunlight, at the center of which the dog rolled joyously onto her back.

When he emerged from the trees a panoramic vista opened up around him. He could see the entire eastern coastline—all three towns, the main road, Cormorant Island with its barber-pole lighthouse. Off to the west were the cliffs and the sea and, in the distance, he could make out the town of Milbridge, draped in a web of fog, as if a giant spider were lurking just offshore. Above that was the nuclear power plant, and he could almost smell the huge paper mill at Nirvana defecating into the sea. To the south of the island he spotted the ferry passing by Sand Harbor, and to the north, next to Ferguson's Cove, the little island airport. To the left of that he thought he could detect smoke wisping from the chimney of the Big House. He discovered that he was surrounded on all sides by tiny, pink, unripe blueberries, millions of them. Soon the entire hill would be another sea of blue.

Kelly was already asleep in the sun. Davenport, exhausted, lay down beside her, where the new luxury hotel would be built, and dozed off. Overhead, the nose of the airplane lifted, then dropped violently and the plane began to spin and spin and spin . . . .

A Hike in the Woods

Davenport was awakened by the gentle splashing of raindrops on his face. Kelly sniffed around the periphery of the clearing, oblivious to the passing shower.

He picked a few handfuls of the pink berries to take back to Rose. Having nowhere else to put them, he stuffed them into his pants pocket. The rain picked up. He called to the dog, who ran down the path toward the car.

The narrow trail was dry, but the little parking lot was not, and the old, wet Plymouth wouldn't start. He waited, tried again, waited some more, tried again. The battery was dying. He pounded on the steering wheel and tried again. The battery was as dead as Fairfax and Parkening.

By the looks of the dirt road, no one had come along since the rain began. There were only two options: walk back to the main road or hike cross-country along the stream toward Porpoise Bay. It should be drier in the woods, he reasoned, and Kelly might well help him find the way.

At first it was pleasant trekking along the bubbly creek, the trees protecting him from the rain, which had slackened again to a sprinkle. Then it became harder going. The spruces weren't co-operating: their interlocking limbs, too limber to break, reached nearly to the ground in some places, making it impossible for him to proceed unless he crawled under them. They didn't stop Kelly, however, and she was soon out of sight. After many minutes on legs unused to such exercise, he gave up and decided to take the path of least resistance, wherever it might lead him. He knew he had to emerge from the forest somewhere.

Soon he could no longer hear the stream. The forest grew thicker and the branches multiplied. There was no sign of his hiking companion. He decided, finally, to return the way he had come. But all directions looked exactly the same.

A sparrow appeared on a branch in front of him. He stared at the bright, blinking eyes, the yellow "eyebrows," the striped head, the snowy throat. Slowly he lifted his hand, slowly, slowly, he proffered a finger.... The bird flew off.

If Kelly were already home Rose would probably send out a search party. But what if something had happened to the dog, or she was lost, too? In any case, there were plenty of bunchberries around to stave off hunger. He found the stream again and took a cold drink, forgetting to worry about *E. coli*.

There was a barely-audible noise. "Kelly?" The appeal was answered by more rustling. In the dark forest he could see nothing moving. He heard it again. Too big for a dog. A bear, perhaps? He drew his gun.

But Alice Barnstable had told him there were no large or dangerous animals on the island. Except for the people, of course! He began to creep away from the sound. The rustling seemed to follow him. He thrashed harder, pushed away limbs, dove under them where necessary, anything to get away from whoever was tailing him. Now he could actually hear his pursuer breathing—stentorian gulps of air. Caught in a trap, he turned toward the tormenter, pointed his gun, cried, "Alright, you! Come on out! I've got you covered!"

He waited. The forest was silent. Then he heard it again, this time from a different direction. He whirled and pointed the .38 toward the gentle crackling. It stopped. Except for the dripping of the rain and the Swainson's arpeggios there wasn't a sound. He thrashed as hard as he could through the trees, the limbs tearing at his face and hands and clothes, nearly putting out an eye on one or two occasions. At last he came to a tiny clearing and realized he was on a trail. Instinctively he crossed the path and took cover behind a giant spruce. He waited. A mosquito landed on his hand. He watched it swell up with his blood. Someone was approaching. He aimed the revolver, the one he had hesitated to fire in Boston, and slowly squeezed the trigger....

It was a deer, and a small one at that. Davenport exploded in laughter. The young doe stared at him for a moment, sniffed deeply, snorted, and ran back into the forest.

After recovering his breath, he proceeded down the trail, stopping every so often to listen for sounds of civilization, hearing nothing but the steady dripping of the trees. But the rain itself had ended, and the sun was coming out.

He followed the path to a clearing. No, a parking lot. *His* parking lot. The Plymouth was still there, along with a pickup truck. "Get lost, Louis?"

Mayor Banner inquired cheerfully. He climbed out and offered Davenport a wad of dulse, which he politely declined.

"No, just going for a little hike."

Banner stuffed the dulse into his mouth and nodded.

"Uh—car wouldn't start. And the dog ran off. I tried to find her."

The mayor grinned. "Well, she made it home. Rose was worried about you. H. T. reported seeing you here."

"The pilot? How did he know—"

"He noticed your car. Harold kinda keeps an eye on things for us. C'mon. I'll give you a ride."

Some Muddy Footprints

Even from the driveway Davenport could hear the wailing of Maryellen Thornhill. He jumped out of the mayor's pickup and hurried toward the front of the Big House. As he turned the corner he spotted Rose and all the rest hovering around the Cape Cod. Kelly ran to greet him.

"What happened?" he yelled.

"Well, Loose," Thornhill called out, "in your absence someone shot a hole in the cottage here. Luckily, none of us was inside."

"But there does seem to be a dead body in there, Monsieur Da-ven-porrrt."

"How do you know that, Dr. D'Arcy?"

"Take a whiff, *mon ami*."

Davenport noted that a window frame was splintered, apparently by a bullet. "No one was hurt?"

"No thanks to you, Sheriff."

"Did anyone see who fired the shot?"

"No one saw a thing, Loose. We were all in the sitting room waiting for dinner. But all of us heard it. That means none of us could have fired it, wouldn't you say?"

Nor did the mayor, Davenport thought, glumly. That leaves only 899 islanders and the odd visitor. "Does that include Rose and Lisa?"

"I was there too, Louie. Lisa and Margery were in the kitchen. What happened to you, anyway? You're all cut and bleeding."

"Where was Joey?"

"He was doing some painting in the Blacksmith Shop."

"Where is he now?"

"He didn't fire it, Sheriff, if that's what you're thinking."

"How do you know that, Ms. Barnstable?"

"I saw Joey come out of the Shop right after the shot was fired."
"But you didn't see anyone around the Cape Cod?"
"No, I didn't."

Davenport unlocked the door of the cottage and crept inside. The bullet had penetrated the frame and continued in an upward direction until it lodged near the top of the opposite wall. Evidently the shot was fired from somewhere in the meadow sloping down toward the bay. On the glass and porpoise coffee table lay a dead gull, and next to it a 4 x 6 note. He picked up the paper with his handkerchief, read the familiar message, folded it, and stuck it gingerly into his shirt pocket. The bird had been dead for some time. He studied the red rings around the eyes, the matching patch on the lower beak, the brownish feet, the ruffled feathers caked with wet sand. It seemed smaller than they looked in the dump, and much less ominous.

He found a kitchen ladder and, with his pocket knife, pried the missile out of the plaster. Another .22-caliber bullet like the one that had almost nailed him in the shower. He dropped it into his pocket alongside the note.

When he turned around he found everyone, including Rog Banner, huddled outside the cottage. They followed him closely as he locked the door and led them over to the Big House. Behind him Maryellen Thornhill sobbed for the dead gull. He escorted them into the dining room and bade them enjoy their dinner. "Save me something, will you, Rose?"

"Okay, Louie."

He reached into his pants pocket and handed her as much of the pink mush as he could pull out. "I thought you might make a pie out of this."

She smiled and shook her head. On his way out he heard her murmur to the mayor: "People from away—they have to learn everything one step at a time."

He found Joey in the Blacksmith Shop painting a windowsill. His upper lip was wet and he was sniffling. At first he thought the muscular handyman was crying, but, when he sneezed several times, Davenport realized he had a cold. He tried to stay on the other side of the room. "I won't bother you Joey. I was just wondering whether you had seen whoever it was that took a shot at the Cape Cod a while ago."

Joey stepped closer. "No, Mister. I was painting that window over there. I came out but I didn't see nobody, except for someone down by the beach."

Davenport backed up against the big fireplace screen. "Do you know who it was?"

Joey was face-to-face with him. "Nossir. I didn't know him."

The special deputy sheriff cupped his fist over his nose to filter out as many viruses as possible. "Did you see what he was wearing?"

Joey sneezed. "A red shirt."

Davenport retrieved his handkerchief and pretended to wipe his nose, which he kept covered as he sidled toward the door. "Anything else you can tell me?"

"No."

"All right, Joey. Would you remove the dead gull from the Cape Cod when you're through here?"

"Sure, Mister!" he replied. A little too eagerly, Davenport surmised.

He banged through the screen door, stuffed the handkerchief into his hip pocket, and returned to the scene of the crime. Expecting to find nothing, he nonetheless poked around the meadow at about the spot he estimated the shot had come from. To his surprise he discovered a distinct footprint! Jubilantly he jogged back to the Blacksmith Shop to ask Joey, through the screen, whether he had any plaster of Paris.

"Sure, Mister. I'll get it as soon as I finish this window and take the dead gull out of the Cape Cod."

"The dead gull can wait."

Dejectedly: "Okay, Mister."

Davenport waited impatiently while Joey finished painting, rinsed out his brush, and headed for the Shed to fetch plaster and water and an empty bucket. Together they walked to the meadow accompanied by the strange, double-note song of a veery. Davenport pointed to the ground. "Joey, do you think you could make a cast of this footprint?"

"Sure could!" he answered proudly, blowing his nose on the ground.

Davenport's stomach gurgled. "Good. Bring it to the Big House when it has set, will you?"

"Okay."

He entered the kitchen through the back door. Lisa glared at him, but made no objection when he strode to the phone. Marge was already clearing the dining room tables. His stomach growled more insistently than before.

"Mnello?"

"Loch? Davenport here."

"Lou, boy! I was just leaving. What's up?"

"Somebody shot a hole in one of the cottages here. Nobody hurt. Might be the same rifle that plugged the shower a couple of days ago. You got anything for me on Frank Parkening?"

"Not much. Mm, let's see. As far as we can make out, Parkening died of natural causes, and some of your guests are more or less who they claim to be, but not all."

"For example?"

"You're going to love this."

"Go ahead."

"In the first place, your Dr. D'Arcy isn't any kind of diplomat. Doesn't have a doctorate, either. He was an aide for a while. Spent some time in South America—uh, let's see—in Venezuela, but left when he got mixed up in some crazy investment scheme. Lives off his wife. She's pretty well fixed. Only one problem."

"What's that?"

"She has a history of mental illness."

"What kind?"

"Not that kind. Depression, mostly. Tried to kill herself once or twice."

"I'll keep that in mind. What else?"

"Well, Parkening was an insurance executive like he said, but he was also the only employee. Had his own little agency in Hartford."

"How did he get so rich?"

"Like D'Arcy, he married it. Wife died under mysterious circumstances, but he was never implicated."

"What about his heart?"

"That was legit. Probably what killed him. Course we have to wait for the lab tests to be sure."

"Did you find a will?"

"We're still looking for that."

"Anything else?"

"I saved the best for last."

"What?"

"The Thornhills have been involved in shady deals all their lives. Small-time con artists. Both have done some time, but they're clean now."

"Where'd their money come from?"

"What money? They're poor as church mice. Unless it's in a secret bank account or buried somewhere."

"Anything on the handwriting analysis?"

"I was coming to that. None of them match up with any of the samples. But the funny thing is that the threatening notes are all written in a different hand."

"I thought so. But I wanted another opinion. Anything else?"

"That's all she wrote. What about you—any leads?"

"Very few. I'll send the bullet and the latest note over on the next boat. And maybe a footprint."

"Whose footprint?"

"That's what *I'd* like to know."

"Any theories?"

"I think the perpetrator may be an islander. Otherwise we're looking at a hired killer."

"Motive?"

"Don't know yet. One possibility is that he doesn't want the consortium to buy half the island."

"Why not?"

"It's a mystery to me. From what I can tell it would be good for the economy." There was a clattering of dishes. Davenport signaled Lisa to be more quiet. She shrugged and made eating gestures. "But everyone at Porpoise Bay Cottages is scared. The ladies—I mean Miss Manhart and Miss Black—left this morning. Now the rest of them are demanding I give them police protection. I think I'm going to need that backup you mentioned."

"Can't do it, Lou. We've got a prison breakout and a missing girl and we need every man we've got. And there are certain other . . . obligations."

"I can't guarantee their safety, Loch."

"See if you can get them to leave."

"Easier said than done. Incidentally, the land they want to buy may be owned by a Swiss national. Can you get someone to try to track him down?"

"As soon as we get this mess over here straightened out. Hang in there, son." The phone clicked.

"Easy for you to say," Davenport murmured.

The Doctor Makes a House Call

Special Deputy Sheriff Louis B. Davenport stationed himself in front of the roaring fireplace. "I just spoke with the sheriff," he informed the guests assembled before him. "He recommends that everyone leave the island until we can get all this sorted out."

"When is he going to send reinforcements?" demanded D'Arcy.

With your wife's money, thought Davenport, you could buy your own bodyguards. "He can't. There's a prison break and a missing girl. He was hoping I would come back and help *him* out."

"You mean our lives are in your hands, Loose?"

"No. They're in your own hands. Just stay together, like I said before. Better yet, leave the island."

There were no takers.

"I finished Chapter Two. You want to take a look?"

Davenport threw up his hands, marched off to his room, found the bathrobe he had borrowed earlier and, remembering to pocket his revolver, hurried outside for a quick shower, taking care to scrutinize the woods for red shirts before disappearing into the bower. Afterward, he put on some clothes he hadn't worn for a while and returned to the sitting room. No one had moved.

Barnstable was holding forth on the subject of books and how few people read them any more, but no one seemed to be paying any attention. Davenport continued to the kitchen, where he was met by Lisa banging in through the swinging door. "It's Mom!" she cried. "Something's wrong with her!"

"What? What's wrong with your mother?"

"She's sick! I think she may have been poisoned!"

Davenport slithered past her and swung into the kitchen. Rose was lying on the floor, holding her stomach, groaning. Kelly was there too, licking her face. He knelt and gently took her hand. "Rose!" he shouted.

"No need to yell—I can hear you!" she gasped. "Call Pete. Terrible pain." She was pale as a ghost and perspiring heavily.

"Lisa!" he yelled, only to find that she was right beside him. "Phone the doctor! Fast!"

To his amazement she complied without a word. "Pete? It's Mom! She's having terrible pains in her stomach. Louie is here. What can we do?" Rose moaned again. He patted her hand. "All right," Lisa said into the phone, and hung up.

"What did he say?"

"He said to put her to bed. He's on his way."

"Help me, will you?"

Together they lifted Rose to her feet, half dragged her through the dining room past the pop-eyed guests and into the sitting room. Davenport asked Lisa, "Isn't there anything we can do until he gets here?" They helped her into her room and laid her gently on the bed. His eyes swept the little vestibule—the plain dresser, the table with a pink-flowered pitcher and bowl, her night stand with a thick book lying on it, a murder mystery—but there was no note.

"He said not to do anything until he sees her."

Rose was rolling back and forth. Davenport stared at her with fear and concern. This was not just another potential victim in the long string of cases he had been involved with over the years. In the short time he had known her... "Where the hell is the doctor?" he demanded.

As if he had heard the question, D'Arcy's penetrating voice filled the Big House: "Here he comes!" In another minute Houseman strode in and calmly requested that everyone leave the room. Lisa and Kelly, he added, could stay.

Davenport reluctantly obeyed, closing the door against a half-dozen worried onlookers, including himself. He was beginning to feel some stomach pain of his own. That's it, he thought. I'm doomed. "Is anyone else feeling sick?" No one was. Then he remembered that he had eaten hardly anything since breakfast. He returned to the kitchen.

He stared into the refrigerators trying to decide whether to take a chance on any of the food, finally settled for some cheese and smoked herring. As he pushed in the last mouthful, Joey came in through the back door waving something heavy and smiling toothily, as if he had been taking lessons from D'Arcy. "Here it is, Mister," he said, almost tripping as he hurried to show his artwork. "And I got rid of that dead gull." Just as he handed over the cast he sneezed, covering Davenport's face with another deadly spray.

"Thank you, Joey," he mumbled thickly, studying the already rock-hard plaster, which displayed an unusual pattern of wavy, parallel lines. "Good job."

Joey smiled even more broadly. "Is there anything else you need a picture of? I've got more plaster stuff."

"Not just now, but hang on to it. I may need another one later."

"Okay, Mister."

"That's all, Joey. You can go."

He seemed disappointed. "Where's Auntie Rose? I didn't have no supper yet."

"She's not feeling very well. I'll tell Lisa to get you something."

"Okay." He sat down at the little wooden table by the window and waited.

Davenport shoved open the swinging door and traipsed through the dining room. Lisa was sitting in her mother's chair talking with Houseman. The guests hovered around them. The old doctor was just closing his bag. "I gave her some Demerol. She'll be all right in the morning." His eyes were red, as if he had been crying.

"What was it, doc?" Davenport asked him.

"Not sure. Could be anything."

"Well, was she poisoned, or not?"

"Maybe. All we can do is get some samples of the stuff she ate and send it away. Take a while, though."

Davenport drummed his fingers on the sofa. "You get Parkening to the mainland okay?"

"Guess so."

"Figure out what killed him?"

"Looked like a simple case of heart failure to me. What've you got there, Louis? A dinosaur track?"

Davenport showed him the footprint. "Ever see anything like this?"

Houseman broke into a laugh.

"What's so funny?"

The grizzled physician turned around and lifted a foot, like a horse about to be shod. "Look familiar? Half the men on the island wear that type of shoe. Cousin Art got a good deal on 'em. Must've bought a thousand pairs."

"Who's Cousin Art?"

"Art Dazzledorf," said Lisa. "The druggist. But he sells shoes and clothes and about everything else."

"Just the same, there's only one pair that would exactly match this cast. Lisa, what would someone do if he wanted to get rid of a pair of shoes?"

"He'd probably throw them in the dump. Everything ends up there. Unless he didn't want anyone to find them. Then I suppose he'd bury them or throw them in a closet."

"Except it's pretty hard to bury anything around here, with this rocky ground," Thornhill put in. "You'd need a backhoe."

"I'll have a look at the dump. You're sure Rose is all right, doc?"

"Sleepin' like a baby," Houseman assured him.

"Thanks. I wouldn't want anything to happen to her."

"Me, neither. Well, I'd better go and get some of that cheese and smoked herring Rose swallowed."

A Stroll in the Dump

A few minutes later Davenport, still shaking, made his way to the parking lot.

"Louie!" Lisa called through the kitchen door. "Would you mind taking some stuff to the dump?"

He shrugged. What did it matter when his life was almost over anyway? "Kelly want to go, too?"

"She wants to stay with Mom."

"Figures." He loaded the back of the Banana car, which Alice Barnstable had reluctantly agreed to let him borrow. As he was pulling up the driveway he heard a screech: "Don't get it scratched—I've had it a long time!"

It was after nine o'clock, but the sky was still light, puffy with pink and orange clouds. There was little wind and the backlit trees looked soft and peaceful. Who would try to poison someone on a day like this? he asked himself. The answer came immediately: the person who did away with Fairfax and Parkening. But what motive? Maybe Rose, a near-victim herself, had some thoughts about that. He decided he had better have a long talk with her as soon as she was able.

Even the dump seemed to bask in a warm glow, the gulls and ravens perched on the back fringe and the surrounding trees, quiet for once, apparently sated. High above, others sailed in wide circles for the sheer joy of it.

A scrufty raccoon nosing its way into a plastic bag slunk off when Davenport slammed the door of the Big Banana. He stood for a moment at the edge of the crater gazing at the enormous mound of debris. A ragged teddy bear, sprawling comfortably on a torn kitchen chair, stared at him with its remaining eye. An old washing machine rested peacefully on its side after a long life of hard work. Barrels and tubs and motors and bags of household trash, each with a story of its own, filled his vista.

He focused his attention more rigorously, searching for shoes someone might have tossed away in the past few hours. There was one, halfway out, stuck between the webbing of a rusty lawn chair. And there was another. And another. Everywhere he looked there were shoes. Many of them, though worn, still had clear parallel grooves in the soles.

He tied his handkerchief around his face and plunged into the garbage. Wading slowly, grabbing up a shoe here, another there, he checked the bottoms for their wear patterns and dried mud before tossing them off to the side. A sharp metal object ripped his semi-clean pants but, fortunately, didn't break the skin. The wind came up behind him, and the smell became stronger. He picked up the pace, checking shoe after shoe until he came to one perched on top of a trash bag, spotlighted by the setting sun, as if placed there by some primitive artist. As he reached over to grab it, there was a rustling at his feet, and he glanced down to see a rat scurry away and disappear under the layers of junk stretching into the distance. "Holy shit!" he cried out, jerking his foot from the mire, then setting it down and lifting the other. Knees pumping high, he marched back to the front of the pit, his whole being focused on where his feet came down, in a hopeful attempt to avoid jagged metal and toothy animals. No longer aware of the aroma, he hauled himself onto the pitted driveway just as someone fired a shot through the windshield of the Big Banana. Wide-eyed, he hurled himself behind the wagon, fumbled for his revolver, and peered around the massive vehicle to see who was doing the shooting. A red flannel shirt disappeared into the woods and out of sight. Davenport fired in the direction of the fleeing shirt, managing only to plug a spruce tree. He leapt into the station wagon and, spinning gravel everywhere, roared out of the depths of hell toward Porpoise Bay Cottages. Peering intently through the spider-webbed windshield, he asked himself another question: was the bullet meant for him, or for Alice Barnstable? Or for the Banana itself? And who, besides she and Lisa, knew he was going to the dump?

After prying the missile form the back of the driver's seat, Davenport strode into the kitchen to place another call to Lochinvar Tate. "P.U., Louie, you stink!" Lisa observed matter-of-factly. "You've just got to shower more often!" The sheriff was unavailable and couldn't be reached. He left the message that yet another bullet would be on the first boat in the morning.

In the sitting room he found the unlikely pair of Barnstable and Quinlan, now roommates, playing Scrabble. As gently as possible he broke the news that the Big Banana had been shot. "God's teeth!" was all that Alice could growl before the two of them flew from the smell of sweat and refuse.

To calm himself he pulled out "The Old Lighthouse." But Topat's urn got his attention. He lowered the porcelain jar from the shelf and removed the lid, expecting to find ashes, perhaps some bone fragments, a tooth or two. Instead, a small diary protruded from the remains. He fished it out and carefully dusted it off.

Les Topat and his wife had been coming to Spruce Island every summer for decades. The ledger was a chronicle of meals, hikes, visitors, birds spotted or heard, games won and lost. He flipped through the years to the end, written a year ago, at the time the malignancy had been diagnosed, apparently. On the last page was a single black entry, in Topat's artistic hand: YOU'RE GOING TO DIE!

A Cup of Tea

Davenport awoke with a sneeze. His head ached, his throat hurt, his eyes wouldn't open all the way, his nose was full of something, and he still stunk. He got up and blew his nose. It filled again. He felt awful but was secretly happy: as long as he had a cold, he reasoned, he was less likely to catch any of the nastier viruses that might be floating around. The toothpaste tasted terrible. He tried to comb his hair but couldn't get it to stay down over the bald spot.

Dressed in his pajamas and borrowed robe, he stumbled into the dining room. "Good morning," he croaked. No one responded. All were surreptitiously testing their food on Kelly, who was surprised and delighted by the windfall.

He sat down at a table by himself and gazed at the photo of Rose's dashing ex-husband, who seemed to be everything that he was not. "Everybody all right?" he wheezed.

Glumly: "So far, Loose."

"Anybody had the orange juice?"

"We all had some, Louis. It seems all right."

He was just lifting the glass to his aching face when Lisa's head poked through the swinging door to announce that he had a phone call. He shambled into the kitchen.

"Somebody get that package down to the boat, Lisa?"

"I think so."

"Good. H'lo?"

"Uncle Louie?" a small voice responded. "Will you umpire our Little League game today?"

"Who's this?"

"Bobby."

"Oh. H'lo, Bobby." He reached into the pocket of the robe and pulled out his already-saturated handkerchief. "What can I do for you?" He snorted loudly into the gooey rag.

"I was wondering if you would umpire our Little League game this afternoon."

"I don't know, Bobby. I'm pretty busy today." But the words 'Uncle Louie' echoed pleasantly in his ringing ears. "What time?"

"It's not till six o'clock. Can you come?"

"I guess I could try."

"Gee, thanks, Uncle Louie. It's at Centerville. See you later!"

"Yeah." Davenport hung up the phone and asked Lisa how her mother was doing.

"Mom's okay, I guess." she assured him. "She just called from Henry's to see if she forgot anything."

"The grocer?" he honked into the handkerchief.

"That's what I said."

"Didn't the doc want her to rest today?"

"You know how she is—I can't do a thing with her."

He nodded understandingly and slumped back to the dining room, where everyone was thoughtfully sipping coffee. Kelly waited patiently by his chair.

"More trouble, Sheriff?"

"Not really, Ms. Barnstable."

Lisa reappeared as he was lifting his fork. "Another call, Louie."

He sighed again and sneezed his way into the kitchen to take the call from Tate.

"Louis! "I've got somethin' down here you might like."

"Who is this?"

"Gannet, down at the garage."

"Oh. My car ready?"

"Just needed a little adjustment in the carburetor."

"How much?"

"I fixed your horn while I was at it, and reconnected the muffler. Want me to order a new bumper?"

Davenport tried hard to open his eyes all the way, but the light was too bright and he closed them. "No, that's all right. How much do I owe you?"

"Don't know. Haven't added it all up yet."

"Okay. I'll be down in a little while."

He toddled back to the empty dining room, where Kelly was standing on the table, licking his plate. He coughed miserably and headed toward the sitting room.

"Another call, Louie. Kelly! Get down from there!"

"I'm not taking any more calls, Lisa. Except from the sheriff's office."

"It *is* the sheriff's office."

He made his way back to the phone. "Davenport."

"Lou? It's Olive."

"H'lo Olive. Sheriff in?"

"That's what I'm calling about. He's campaigning in Bangor today. Won't be back until tonight. Should I have him buzz you then?"

"There's no message from him?" He heard papers shuffling and imagined her small, plump hands at work.

"Not that I can find."

Davenport could feel something accumulating on the end of his nose. He tilted his head back so it wouldn't drip onto the table. "Who's in charge?"

"Manny, but he's out on the road."

"Okay. Tell the sheriff there was another shooting. The victim was a station wagon. No injuries. Except to the wagon."

"I'll tell him, Lou."

He raised his head another notch. "And tell him to call me as soon as possible."

"Okay. And Lou?"

He stared at the freshly-painted ceiling. "Yeah?"

"Take care of that cold."

Davenport cradled the receiver and reached for his handkerchief a second too late. He mopped the table with it before wiping his nose. Finding Lisa watching him, he tried to brush his unruly hair back over his bald spot. Now his arms ached.

"What you need is a cup of tea," she asserted. "I'll make you one."

Davenport sunk into a chair. "I don't feel very good," he confessed.

"No kidding," she said, putting on the kettle.

He watched as she scurried around for a mug and the tea. "Tell me about your father."

She lit a cigarette. Her eyes, he noted, were sky blue and penetrating, like the man in the photo. "He was an English teacher," she began, dreamily. "From away. It took a while before he was accepted here."

"How long did it take?"

"Forever, basically. You have to be born here to be a true islander."

"What if you come here as a baby?"

"Then you're a baby from away."

"So your father never belonged?"

"Well, it's not quite that simple. Dad was a wonderful teacher, and all his students loved him. He was eventually made an 'honorary' Spruce Islander. That doesn't happen very often."

"What about you? Are you a kind of hybrid?"

"No, I was born here, so I'm a genuine islander."

"What happened to your father?"

"Asthma."

"I'm sorry."

The kettle began to whistle. Lisa worked over a steaming mug for a few minutes and then handed it to him.

Davenport took a sip. He was certain his head had imploded. "Wow! What kind of tea is this?"

"We call it Indian tea. It'll cure anything."

"Tastes terrible, but I think I feel better already."

Rose, loaded down with groceries, struggled through the back door. "Louie! Find anything at the dump?"

He started to get up to help her, but realized he was already too late. "Only another bullet. How are you feeling today?"

"Much better. You don't sound too good, though."

"I gave him some Indian tea," Lisa told her.

Rose nodded. "That'll cure anything."

"Well, I'm off!" cried her daughter, who flew out the back door.

Davenport started to speak, gurgled, cleared his throat. "You need any help putting that stuff away?"

"Thanks, but I'd rather do it. Then I'll know where it is."

He watched her open various cabinets and refrigerators, admired her unhurried dexterity and strong legs.

"Your hair looks nice today, Louie."

He tried to brush it down.

"Jack had a bald spot, too. I became rather fond of it. It was like the sun coming up in the morning."

He decided to change the subject. "Rose, there's something I've got to ask you."

She stopped fiddling with the macaroni and turned toward him. "What's that, Louie?"

"Did you get a threatening note?"

She turned back to the counter. "No, I didn't."

He pondered this information, filed it away, retrieved something else. "Lisa is—what—thirty? Thirty-five? How come she isn't married yet?"

"Well, Louie, let's just say she's the modern type. She has boyfriends all over the place, but none she wants to live with on a permanent basis. Too particular, like her father. Besides," she grunted, reaching for the top shelf, "she loves the cottages. Especially the kitchen and the dining room. Always has."

"And what about you?"

"I love 'em, too."

"I mean, did you ever think about getting married again?"

She stared at him. "Anybody I'd be interested in is already taken, and the rest aren't worth having."

His nod was a mixture of relief and disappointment.

"Louie, I hate to be the one to tell you, but you need another shower."

"I don't have any clean clothes to put on. I was wondering about a laundromat."

"Never mind that," she said. "We'll find something for you."

THE CATALOG OF POISONS

Davenport felt better after a nap, and even better after a hot shower and lunch. Rose had found him a clean shirt and pants and some jockey shorts with little hearts on them.

On his way to the parking lot he spotted a sledge hammer and wedge lying shiny in the sun beside the huge pile of firewood. He looked around: no one was watching. Placing a log precariously on its end he tapped the wedge into the soft wood. When he thought it was solidly rooted he heaved the hammer back and over his head and went mightily for the bullseye. The next thing he knew the wedge was flying past his left ear, singing like a giant tuning fork. He broke into a cold sweat. From the Shed came the sound of laughter. Laying the hammer where he found it, he tucked in his shirttails and hurried to the Big Banana.

Despite the cracked windshield, the trip down the island became a test of his newfound proficiency with the finger wave. By his own count, there were nineteen chances to respond (or not) and he was certain he was correct on all but a few. There was some question, however, in the matter of two or three cars in a row: do you leave the finger up or flash several quick ones? He also seized the opportunity to try the sideways nod, a not infrequent response to a wave, but only by the men. By the time he got to Centerville he was becoming confident of that as well, though he had developed a persistent crick in his neck.

The garage was packed with cars waiting their turns, like the patients in the doctor's office. He pulled in beside the Plymouth and killed the engine. Inside the dark building a group of men were huddled together, laughing loudly but speaking in soft voices. He waited a few minutes, memorizing license plates on the junk cars crammed into a corner of the lot. Finally he went inside. Gannet Banner emerged from the center of the group. "Afternoon, Louis," he said, pleasantly. "She's all ready." The others offered unexpected greetings. He returned a sideways nod.

"Got something else for you," said Davenport, squinting as they strolled from the shadows into the sunlight.

"What happened to the Banana?" the tow-headed mechanic asked him. He offered Davenport some dulse, which he pocketed with thanks. "Hunting accident?"

"Might be, except that it isn't hunting season."

"Depends on what you're hunting for, I'd say." Banner stuffed a wad of the dulse into his mouth, exposing widely-spaced front teeth. "How soon does she need it?"

"As soon as possible."

"Figured as much. Have to order a new windshield and seat back, though. Should get 'em tomorrow."

Davenport climbed into his car. "Fine. I'll tell Ms. Barnstable." He turned the engine over; it responded immediately. "Thanks, Gannet," he said. "See you later."

"Didn't you forget something, Louis?"

"What?"

"The bill."

"Oh. How much is it?"

"Oh, I don't know. A dollar-fifty ought to cover it."

Davenport reached for his wallet. It was gone. "Somebody must've stolen my billfold," he whined.

"Not likely, Louis. Prob'ly left it back at Cousin Rose's."

"Can I owe you?"

"No hurry. Just drop it by next time you get a chance."

While in Centerville, Davenport decided to visit the drug store. Despite its small size it stocked piles of clothing, racks of snacks, shelves of toiletries, and hundreds of shoes like the ones worn by the elusive rifleman, as well as stacks of pads of the type the threatening notes had been written on. "You the druggist?" he inquired of the man making little marks in a ledger.

"Hello, Louis," Dazzledorf responded without looking up. He appeared to be at least in his eighties. His hair was the color of fresh snow but his eyebrows were bright orange and hung over his eyes like little paintbrushes. A Henderson, Davenport deduced.

"How'd you know who I am, Mr. Dazzledorf?"

"Art. I 'spect everybody on the island knows who you are."

"Does everybody know that Rose Kelly might have been poisoned last evening?"

"Prob'ly."

"Do you have any idea what a person on the island might poison another person with?"

"Damn near anything."

"What could he get in the pharmacy, for example?"

Dazzledorf opened a drawer and handed Davenport the catalog of restricted substances. "Cyanide, strychnine, arsenic, and all the rest," he summarized. "Plus a lot of less common toxins. 'Course you'd have to have a damn good reason before I'd give any of 'em to you."

Davenport flipped through the pages and considered what it might feel like to swallow a spoonful of one of the listed substances. "This where Doctor Houseman gets his drugs?"

"Nope. He has his own sources. Course his patients come here with their prescriptions. Pete carries mostly samples of this and that."

Davenport handed back the catalog. "Have you sold any of these in the past few days?"

"Well, let me see...." He bent over the ledger and his eyes disappeared again behind the orange paintbrushes. "Nope, nobody has picked up anything lately. Course they could've gotten it earlier. Or somewhere else. On the mainland, for example." When Davenport didn't respond, he added, "Fact is, anything can be toxic if given in high enough doses. Even water."

"Water?"

"You can drown if you drink enough water," he chortled. "Didn't you know that, Louis?"

"What do you have that would give you a bellyache?"

"Almost anything. As I say, it depends on the dose."

"You mean a big enough dose will do it?"

"No, a small enough dose. A big dose of any of the usual poisons would prob'ly act so fast you wouldn't know what hit you."

"So if Rose swallowed something poisonous, but it only gave her a stomachache, it would have to be a relatively small dose?"

"That's what I said."

"Is it possible that somebody might have been trying to scare her?"

"Damn near anything is possible in life, wouldn't you say, Louis?"

"I guess I would agree with that. Thank you, Art."

"Hear the one about the guy from away who came in here with a cough?"

"No."

"Stranger came in the other day with a cough. My grandson was here, too—you'll see him at the Dulse Festival. I gave him something, he swallowed it and left. The boy said, 'What did you give him that laxative for? He had a cough, not constipation.' I said, 'Look at him out there. He's *afraid* to cough!'" The druggist roared with laughter. "See you at the Festival tomorrow!"

"I don't know. I'll try to make it."

"I'll see you there." It sounded more like a command than an invitation.

THE MISSING KEY

Davenport found his wallet lying on the dresser where he had left it. Nothing was missing. Whether anyone had rifled through it, however, was another matter. But someone had definitely taken his clothes.

He ran through the sitting room where the D'Arcys and Thornhills were playing bridge. To his dismay they ignored him, though he might have been the killer.

Rose was sitting at the kitchen table looking over what appeared to be newspaper clippings. Next to them stood the ever-present sherry glass. "Rose!" he shouted. "Somebody stole my clothes!"

"Now, Louie, you're jumping to conclusions."

"You mean you know who took them?"

"You don't have to shout—I'm not deaf like Alice, remember? Sure I do. They're in the dryer."

"What dryer?"

"The one in the Shed. Where we do all the laundry."

"You washed my clothes?"

"Well, Mr. Special Deputy Sheriff, people were beginning to complain about the smell coming out of your room. It was like you'd been walking around in the dump. And that blueberry stain . . ."

"You mean you could smell them out in the— Never mind. But I locked the door. How did you get in?"

"Why, with the key, of course. Did you think I came through the window?"

Davenport pulled the skeleton key from his pocket and waved it in the air. "Where did you get a key?"

"I've got a duplicate key to all the rooms."

"What? You told me I had the only one!"

"No I didn't. I said you had the only *skeleton* key. I have duplicates of all the other keys in case somebody loses one."

"Well, where do you keep them? Does anybody else know about the duplicates?"

"Well, now, I don't know. Lisa does, of course. And Joey, maybe."

He stared at her in disbelief, quickly assessing certain unpleasant possibilities. But she certainly hadn't fired the rifle shots, and her responses to his questions had been straightforward and consistent. Besides, he reasoned, she herself had been a victim. In any case, he needed help, had to trust someone. "Why didn't you use the duplicate key to get into Mr. Parkening's room when he didn't show up for lunch that day?"

"Because I couldn't find it."

"You mean someone else had it?"

"I didn't say that. I said I couldn't find it."

"Well, is it there now?"

"I don't know. Want me to look?"

Davenport sighed. "As soon as you get a chance. Any other keys missing?"

"I haven't a clue. They're all scattered in a drawer in my room."

"Do you keep it locked?"

"Not until now."

He paced around for a minute. "What are you reading?"

"Some articles about my husband. Lisa said you were asking about him." She glared at him. "Did you think he might be the killer?"

"Of course not. I was just wondering what he was like . . . ."

A distant buzz notified her that the laundry was dry. Without a word she got up and stalked off. In a moment she was back with his clothes. "Here. You'd better put this stuff away." She tossed the basket at his feet. "And by the way, I'd appreciate it if you'd move the bed back to where you found it."

Davenport could think of nothing to say. Before he could murmur his thanks she added, "Then come on back here and I'll get you some supper."

"Supper?"

"You've got a ball game to umpire tonight, remember?"

A scream erupted in the front of the house. Davenport raced through the dining room, gun drawn. D'Arcy was stretched out on the floor of the sitting room.

"What happened?" Davenport demanded.

D'Arcy didn't respond. He appeared to be foaming at the mouth. But he was still smiling. Davenport hoped it wasn't the beginning of some new plague.

"He fainted, Loose. But we all heard them."

"Heard who?"

"The voices of Fred Fairfax and Frank Parkening."

"What are you talking about?"

Maryellen Thornhill pointed toward the bay window. "It's true—they were right out there."

Davenport ran to the screen door and peered outside, but he saw no one. Rushing back to the victim, he bent over the long, prostrate figure and shouted, "Dr. D'Arcy—can you hear me?"

"Yes, yes, I'm all right now. I must have fainted." He sat up.

"Can you tell me what happened?"

"I heard Fred outside the window." He climbed to his feet.

"What did he say?"

"He said I was next!" The diplomat's knees started to buckle.

Davenport caught him. "Help him outside," he grunted.

The others quickly surrounded D'Arcy and led him from the house. They were followed by Davenport, who briefly inspected the ground below the bay window and checked out the Cape Cod. There was no sign of a disturbance.

Suddenly Rose was standing beside him. "What was all the commotion, Louie?"

"They all claimed they heard a ghost."

"How do you account for that, Mr. Special Deputy Sheriff?"

"I don't know. Mass hysteria brought about by stress, I suppose."

D'Arcy was moving toward the Farmhouse on his own, swinging his long arms like a pair of windmills. "C'mon in," said Rose. "Your chowder's ready."

Kill the Umpire

Davenport arrived at the playing field at the same time as the cowboy he'd met in the dump, who gave him a finger. He returned a sideways nod. The horse snorted, though it sounded more like a laugh.

He parked as close as he could get to the diamond, in the driveway of the "Spruce Island Historical Museum," formerly someone's house, and wandered back to the field. A cheer went up from the stands. Self-consciously he turned and bowed, only to find the fans applauding Byron, who, he learned later, had been a major league pitcher in the sixties and seventies. He continued the bow down to his shoes, which he carefully retied.

This must be the most beautiful ball park in the world, thought Davenport. A home run to center field would be in the ocean. The old lighthouse at Nor'east Head was visible over left field, Cormorant Rock beyond right. In between, the water glistened in the late afternoon sun.

The diamond was crowded with boys and girls, and twice as many relatives sat in the stands, where he had watched the fireworks display a few nights earlier. The entire Crane family was present, including several look-alikes he had not yet met, as well as Rog Banner, Art Dazzledorf, Byron Henderson, Doc Houseman, and a few other familiar-looking faces. This time, however, no one jeered him. Nobody waved, either, so as not to prejudice his decisions, apparently.

Though Davenport had seen many Red Sox games on his off-duty hours, and had participated in a few league games himself, he had never umpired one. Nonetheless he knew one thing: the umpire was always right. Promptly at six o'clock he swaggered out from behind the plate and yelled, "Play ball!"

Nor'east Head, as the visiting team, batted first. The Crane boy, who came up with two out, yelled, "Hi, Uncle Louie!" Davenport nodded gravely. Some of the fans chuckled. The kid grounded out to short. Three up and three down.

By the bottom of the fourth the score was 3-0 in favor of Centerville. In the fifth, with the bases loaded, the Nor'east Head batter slammed a curving line drive down the third base line, fair. The ball got past the left fielder and rolled to the fence. The hitter rounded second and headed for third. The outfielder hurled the ball in to the third baseman. The crowd was on its feet as the runner pounded for home. The ball sailed toward the plate, arriving just before the baserunner. Davenport hesitated to make sure the catcher held on to the ball and to wonder briefly whether anyone was being murdered back at Porpoise Bay Cottages. He thumbed the runner out. A few good-natured boos drifted in from the bleachers. The next batter struck out. The game was tied.

It stayed that way until the bottom of the sixth, when the Centerville team scored on a bases-loaded walk. The Nor'east Head pitcher yelled, "What??"

"That was right over the plate, ump," came a cry from the stands. This time the boos were less good-natured. He began to sweat. Fortunately, the inning ended uneventfully with a soft pop-up to second.

Top of the seventh, and final, inning. Bobby Crane was up first. He looked at a called third strike. Slowly his head turned toward Davenport. He didn't say a word, but there was fire in his eyes. He threw his bat toward the dugout. "You're outta the game!" roared the umpire.

"You're blind as a bat!" came the unhappy reply. "I'm sorry I asked you to ump!"

Nor'east Head stranded two runners, and the game ended at 4-3. The stands emptied almost immediately. No one, not even his "nephew" said a word of thanks or good-bye. Even the horse ignored him. Davenport slouched wearily toward the Plymouth. That's life, he thought: hero one day, bum the next.

He saw that the museum was still open, and ducked inside. A blonde girl of ten or twelve greeted him with a sweet smile and demanded two dollars. He paid up and wandered back to an earlier era of fishing boats and nets, a kitchen full of ancient cooking gear and utensils, an apothecary shop with its bottles of colorful liquids and powders. The place smelled faintly tinny and a trifle musty, but into his mind wafted the timeless aromas of baked fish and blueberry muffins. For a moment he wished he had been born a hundred years earlier. Then he realized that, if he had, he would be dead now.

The walls were covered with photographs of life on the island and the sea. Some of the older pictures were of Indians standing beside tents on a beach, or fishing in one of the coves. In later ones Davenport found more familiar faces, the forebears of present-day islanders: unmistakable Blues, Banners, and Hendersons. Island life had changed little in a century or more.

It was just before eight o'clock when the girl flicked the lights a couple of times, though she was only twenty feet away. She smiled broadly at him, exposing well-spaced teeth. Reluctantly, he took his leave.

Noting that the liquor store was still open, he pulled in and bought a bottle of sherry from the clerk, George Banner, the man he had spoken to on the phone a few days earlier. Davenport asked him whether he was related to the Mayor and to Rose and some of the Cranes.

"Might be," he replied. "I lie a *little*."

During the transaction the museum girl came in behind him. "Hi, Daddy," she called out.

"Have you met my daughter, Louis?"

"Just a little while ago."

"Well, here you are. Give my regards to cousin Rose."

"I will."

"And Louis . . . ."

"Yes?"

"It's nice of you to get her the sherry. She doesn't like to be seen coming in here too often."

A Stranger from Away

The cottages were peaceful, with a wisp of smoke curling lazily from the chimney of the Big House, and lights in the windows of the Farmhouse, though it was not yet dark. Davenport checked the sign-out sheet in the sitting room. It was blank. Either no one was out or, as usual, they hadn't signed up.

He placed the bottle of sherry on Rose's little side table and found "The Old Lighthouse," which he dumped onto the ancient card table. I haven't peed since noon, he reflected as he was turning over the pieces. I wonder what that means. The phone rang. He waited to see if someone in the kitchen would get it. No one did. He ran to answer it and recognized the voice of Mayor Banner.

"Hello, Louis! Tough game, eh?"

"I'm sorry about—"

"Can't win 'em all."

"Anything wrong, Rog?"

"Maybe yes, maybe no. That's for you to decide."

"What's the problem?"

"Cousin Worm just called, said there was a stranger came over on the boat today. He isn't staying at any of the B & B's and nobody's seen him since he left the dock. Thought you'd like to know."

"Did the captain get a description?"

"Average height and build. Wearing a red flannel shirt and jeans. Not much to go on, I suppose."

"That's all right. Thanks for the information. If anybody else spots him, have him give me a call, will you?"

"I'll do that."

He had just returned to the puzzle when the phone rang again. He hurried back to the kitchen. "Louis! Good game, didn't you think?"

"*Very* good game, Don."

"That was the first one our boys have lost all year."

"I'm sorry about—"

"Yep. A pity, all right. Anyway, I just called to tell you that one of my cousins down at Fog Cove said he saw a stranger walkin' around on the beach down there. Wouldn't've paid him any mind, but the guy was carryin' a rifle. Wasn't shootin' at anything, just walkin' along the beach and then he went into the woods and disappeared. Thought you might like to know."

"Did he get a description?"

"Said he was about average in size, and wearin' a red flannel shirt and jeans."

"Okay, thanks. And keep me posted if he turns up anywhere else."

"I will."

"By the way, I wonder if you could help me with something."

"If I can."

"You remember we talked the other night about the Project planned for the middle of the island?"

"I remember."

"Tell me: who owns the land around that property?"

"Well, I don't know, and that's the truth. I think it could be some of the Blues, but I'm not sure. I'll tell you how you can find out, though."

"How's that?"

"Stop in at the license bureau some time. Cousin Sherri has a book with all the deeds recorded in it."

"Thanks, Don. I'll do that."

"All right. See you at the Dulse Festival tomorrow."

"Well—"

He was standing in the middle of the dining room staring at the picture of Jack Kelly, who seemed to be wearing the same clothes that Davenport was, when the phone rang again. This time it was Gannet, the Centerville mechanic, who wanted to tell him that his father had seen someone walking up the road toward Nor'east Head carryin' a rifle. A stranger from away. Nobody knew who he was.

"Was he wearing jeans and a red flannel shirt?" Davenport asked him.

"That's amazin'! How did you know that?"

"I'm a detective. By the way, I found my wallet. I'll bring you the—"

"No hurry, Louis."

Certain that the phone was going to ring again, Davenport ambled around the kitchen examining the glass porpoises in the window sills. A little note on one of the refrigerators reminded someone to water the flowers. The pleasant humming gave him a curious sense of well-being. Suddenly he saw a figure in the woods behind the parking lot. The hair rose on the back of his neck. He rubbed his eyes and looked again. No one there. Feeling for the .38, he cautiously proceeded to the sitting room, where the gaping bay window stared back at him.

He sat down at the puzzle and nervously reached for a cigarette. The phone rang. Davenport jumped. He hustled to the kitchen, switched off the light, and answered the damn thing.

"Hello, Louis, it's Henry. At the grocery store."

"Let me guess. You saw someone."

"Nope."

"No? What, then?"

"My wife saw someone out the window just now. A stranger in a red flannel shirt. Headin' up the road toward Porpoise Bay. And Louis?"

"Yes?"

"He was carryin' a rifle."

"Okay. Thanks, Henry. If you see anything else, let me know, will you?"

"Sure will. Don't forget the Dulse Festival tomorrow!"

"Right."

He returned to sitting room, but thoughts of the mysterious stranger crowded everything else out of his mind. Should he go looking for the intruder? Or stake himself out in his car and wait for someone to show up? Should he at least stay up and listen for prowlers? The last seemed the best option. He turned out the light and fumbled to his room. "I should've checked the other cottages," he mumbled. "And now I'm talking to myself. Where the hell is Tate?" He noticed that the flowers on the dresser were drooping, too.

The clean pajamas smelled faintly of detergent, unlike the ones they gave you every Saturday at the orphanage, which never got really clean in the overcrowded machines.... Was that a noise? he wondered. He reassured himself: the stranger could be anyone, and he probably had nothing to do with the murders. Then it occurred to him that he could be the escaped prisoner Tate was looking for. He listened harder, but heard nothing but the distant roar of the surf, and finally fell asleep reliving all the plays of the baseball game that afternoon.

At dawn he awoke to real or imaginary sounds unrelated to those of the sea. Using his revolver to pry open the curtains, he peered sleepily out the window. No one was up and around. A couple of boats were already in the bay. The sea looked rough.

He stuffed a cigarette into his dry mouth and tiptoed out of the room, listened at Rose's door, stood at the bottom of the steps attending to the silence upstairs, crept into the kitchen and checked the back door. Everything seemed to be in order except for the deputy sheriff himself: a vague pain in his chest and another in his abdomen convinced him that he was, at last, in the throes of a terminal illness. Perhaps, he thought, he ought to go see Houseman.

He got back into bed, stared at the ceiling, watched a spider set her sticky trap, listened to the rising wind. At 6:30 he put on some clean clothes and called the sheriff's office. Oscar promised he would leave a note for Tate. Not satisfied with this, Davenport called the sheriff at home. No answer. He wandered out the kitchen door toward the parking lot, noted vast swirls of cirrus clouds in the sky and foamy whitecaps in the cove and beyond. Fishing boats bounced up and down on the waves like toys. A flock of gulls stood in the spruce trees, jeering at him. "What are you doing out there?" Lisa called from the kitchen. He barely managed not to shoot her.

At breakfast the guests of Porpoise Bay Cottages seemed more relaxed than they had been the day before. None of them had been killed or poisoned, none of the cottages had been violated, and no one (except for Davenport himself) had heard noises or seen faces at their windows. Nonetheless, everyone seemed to be content to hang around the Big House reading or playing bridge. Even Baker stayed put, trying to get various slime mold spores to sprout in the dregs of his oatmeal. His wife had formulated a new theory: the killer was merely trying to scare everyone away from the cottages. Davenport reminded her that Fairfax and Parkening were dead.

"Coincidence?" she suggested.

None of the guests wanted to accompany Davenport to the Dulse Festival. Reminding them to remain in close contact with someone else and to keep an eye open for strangers, he rattled off by himself.

THE DULSE FESTIVAL

Booths had sprung up all over the high school parking lot like mushrooms after a summer rain. Despite the big breakfast, Davenport immediately went for a fresh, warm, blueberry muffin, and then another, and a paper cup of coffee to keep him awake. At mid-morning he ran into the retired teachers from Indiana, who looked like two kids at a county fair. "How many times have you been to the Dulse Festival?" he asked them.

"As many years as we've been coming to Spruce Island," the husband answered. "It never changes." The man's dead tooth reminded Davenport that he hadn't seen a dentist in far too long.

"But they still can't seem to remember us from year to year," sighed the wife. "We'll always be from away."

"Coming to the variety show tonight? It always winds up the festival."

Davenport popped a Maalox tablet. "Tonight? Well, I don't know . . . ."

"Try to make it. It's a good show."

The next table was cluttered with huge brown paper bags of dulse, jars of dulse seasonings, and pamphlets extolling the health benefits of a diet supplemented by generous quantities of dulse. Davenport picked up a cookbook titled *Dining with Dulse*. He skimmed through it and found suggestions like:

Dulse Soup	Dulse Treat
Open can of soup (any kind)	Cut up any available fruits
Add powdered dulse	Arrange prettily on bed of dulse
Cook	Serve

Dulse Salad	*Dulse Cake*
Prepare favorite salad	Buy cake mix
Sprinkle with dulse flakes	Prepare according to directions on box
Garnish with rasher of dulse	Blend in chopped dulse
	Bake

"Cap'n Louis!" Hermit shouted around one of the five-gallon bags. Can I interest you in a little dulse?"

"Do you have anything smaller?"

"Well, I have these little samplers for the torrists." He waved a small cellophane bag containing a few strands of the red-brown seaweed.

"For who?"

"For the torrists."

"How much?"

"A dollar."

"How much are the big bags?"

"Five bucks."

Davenport found a dollar, which disappeared at once. "Anything else? Dulse flakes? Dulse powder? Dulse fudge?"

"Fudge?"

"Try a piece. Nicest thing you ever ate!"

Davenport picked up a crumb. It was like nibbling a salt lick. "I think I'll pass on that."

"It's your funeral!" cried the diminutive sea farmer.

Stuffing the little package into his pants pocket, he wandered over to the potato-peeling contest, where islanders of all ages were gathered around Grandma Nan, whose spotted, veiny hands surrounded a large spud. When it was denuded and its coat fell into a nearly-perfect shell at her sturdy feet, she broke into a gummy grin, her eyes disappearing entirely. The crowd cheered, and so did Davenport. Grandma Nan's unbroken peeling was more than twice as long as that of her nearest competitor, a young woman of ninety engulfed in a huge woolen sweater.

After congratulating the winner, who recognized his voice at once, he found a telephone and dialed Porpoise Bay Cottages. Rose informed him that everything was quiet. He told her he wouldn't be back for lunch. She reported that there was still no call from Tate. That business taken care of, he helped himself to a large bowl of fish chowder and several more muffins.

Don Crane found him just as he was mopping his lips, and invited him to participate in some of the fund-raising activities. "You like baseball, don't you, Louis? You can help with the baseball throw. Come right over here."

Davenport followed him to a metal contraption, where he was motioned inside. He found himself seated in a kind of cage dangling over a tank of sea water. "Any sign of that stranger with the rifle?" he asked nervously.

"Nope. He seems to have disappeared. I'll hold your stuff. You prob'ly don't want to get anything wet."

"Uh—" he replied, but found himself handing over the .38 before stripping off his shirt and shoes and socks. "Be careful with that revolver—it's loaded!"

"'Bye for now!" Crane called out, and slammed the door.

Facing him were some of the boys he had called out on strikes the day before. Several of them tried their luck and failed, one or two hitting the target, but with insufficient power. "We'll get you next year, Uncle Louie," shouted Bobby Crane. Davenport grinned smugly.

Then the adults stepped up. It was Crane himself who dunked him the first time, followed by George and Gannet Banner (who reminded him of the $1.50 he owed) and Henry Sanders, and even eighty-two-year-old Art Dazzledorf. The mayor dropped him into the tank twice, to delighted cheers. Davenport learned later that every one of them, almost everyone on the island, in fact, had been a star baseball player in his prime. He was grateful that Byron hadn't shown up.

Crane finally reappeared and let him out of the cage. He slapped Davenport on his wet back, handed him a large towel. "There's a good breeze, Louie," he said. "You'll be dry in no time." He handed him back his gun and belt. "You any good with this thing? There's a skeet shoot at three o'clock. You want to try your luck?"

"Why not?" said Davenport, neglecting to mention that this was the main reason he had come to the festival in the first place: to look for someone who could handle a gun and to check him over for flannel clothing and other signs of familiarity.

"I'll sign you up!"

Davenport wandered along admiring the food, the beautiful quilts and hand-made furniture, the jars of pickles and pears. The sun dried him out quickly and he bought a large cup of rhubarb punch, which led immediately to another antacid tablet.

He sauntered casually toward the skeet shoot and looked over the contestants. Most were wearing red flannel shirts. The $5 entry fee was the last bill he had.

At exactly three o'clock the starter lined up the first contestant. "Pull!" he yelled. A clay disc flew through the air and was instantly blown to smithereens. Davenport studied the man, an obvious Banner. Another disc and another hit. Only one miss in the series.

He studied the next contestant, a Henderson, who had two misses. And the third and the fourth. Almost all of the twenty-one contestants, including the mayor, the druggist, and three women, were excellent marksmen, but none appeared to be the one who had taken a shot at him or the Big Banana.

Then it was Davenport's turn. Someone handed him a shotgun. He stepped nervously to the line, hesitated a moment before yelling, "Pull!" A miss. "Pull!" Another miss. Chuckles from the crowd. The next was a solid hit, and he heard a welcome murmur of approval. More confident now, he blasted most of the remaining discs, for a total of four misses, tying him for last place with the cantankerous geezer, still wearing his sling, he had seen in Houseman's makeshift parking lot just after his arrival on the island.

The three contestants who had hit all the skeets stepped up for a shootoff, but only one managed another perfect round. He asked Crane who the woman was. "Oh, that's Cousin Sherri. I told you about her. Works at the license bureau. She's a Blue," he added, unnecessarily. "C'mon, Louis," he said. "We could use you in the tug o' war."

Davenport begged off. "Sorry, Don. Got to get back to the cottages. Got some work to do."

"That's all right. We'll get you next time. But don't forget about the variety show tonight. We're savin' you a seat."

"I'll try to make it."

"See you at seven-thirty," Crane replied summarily, and hurried off.

Davenport started to leave, but at the fringe of the crowd he paused to watch the three village mechanics, all brothers, take on three of the Cranes. It was a determined effort on both sides, lasting several minutes, with no clear winner, and huge wolf grins at either end.

As he was climbing into the Plymouth the soggy bag of dulse exploded in his pocket, which somehow reminded him to wonder whether Crane might have removed the bullets from his revolver while he was being dunked. But everything was in place. Scratch another suspect, he sighed. Only 898 to go, including the old fart in the sling.

A̲nother T̲hreat

The minute Davenport got to the Big House he put in another unsuccessful call to Tate. "Out campaigning, Lou," yawned Teresa, the weekend receptionist. "Back Monday."

"Any messages?"

"He wants you to say a good word for him on the island."

No one was around, everything was quiet, and Davenport, exhausted, shuffled to his room for a nap, pleased to discover that the sheets had been changed and that someone had placed fresh flowers on his dresser. It must be Saturday, he realized. He climbed happily into his bed, wondering, as always, how far it was from the one he had been born in. The smell of the ocean and the splashing of the waves against the rocks seemed so familiar, almost a part of his being.... He fell asleep thinking about the meadow, the sea, Hermit, the Dulse Festival, the Cranes, baseball, horses, the dump, and Rose, in that order, more or less, and dreamed he was chasing a mysterious stranger in a red flannel shirt, only to discover that the man was also chasing him, in a never-ending circle.

When he woke up it was already late afternoon. He enjoyed a warm, incident-free shower, put on clean under- and outerwear, including a borrowed tie. Refreshed and ready for anything, or so he thought, he strolled into the dining room feeling less like poor relation and anticipating a pleasant, relaxing, semi-formal dinner. D'Arcy, however, had joined Thornhill in boycotting formality, wearing jeans and an open shirt.

Davenport was seated with Alice Barnstable, who harangued him about the Big Banana, demanding to know when it would be ready, asserting that it was the last time she would loan anything to him or anyone else, he was paying for the damages, etc., etc., her eyelids fluttering without surcease. He tried to appease her by offering a ride to the variety show, which she loudly declined. "Seen one, you've seen 'em all," she screeched, forking in a hunk of baked halibut.

None of the guests had left their rooms all afternoon, except, of course, for Baker, who had spent the day in the woods, forgetting even to return for lunch. Davenport asked him where he had gone.

"Over by the bog," he replied. "There are thousands and thousands of sundews and venus flytraps over there! It's beautiful!"

"Finished Chapter Three!" his wife added. "You've just arrived on Spruce Island in the fog. I gave you some personal problems. All fictional detectives have something rattling around in their closets. Want to read it?"

"Later," he promised absentmindedly. He was beginning to think that perhaps she was right: someone was merely out to frighten the guests. Maybe Fairfax's death had been an accident after all, and Parkening had simply died of heart failure. In any case, he reminded himself, he was on vacation. After borrowing ten dollars from Rose he took off for the Spruce Island High School.

There were a few nods, but otherwise no one paid particular attention as he strode into the gymnasium and down the free-throw lane to the folding chair next to the Cranes, who barely acknowledged his arrival. Indeed, the boy whose life he had saved only three days earlier ignored him completely. Grandma Nan quietly gummed a strand of dulse. If she knew he was there she showed no sign of it.

Davenport stretched his legs. He gazed up at the basketball goal hanging above and in front of the curtained stage and remembered his own school days. Though he had not played on the team he had often dreamed of flying through the air and dunking incredible twisting shots, one after the other. This segued, somehow, into a consideration of the finger wave. He had paid close attention and concluded that it was all right to leave the finger up when encountering a string of vehicles, unless the space between them was more than a few carlengths. But you had to be careful—the third or fourth car might be a woman and you had to be ready to pull the finger down at a moment's notice. But a new problem came to mind: do you give a finger to someone coming out a side road?

By seven-thirty all of the folding chairs and the few rows of bleachers were occupied. There was a loud buzz of conversation, though no one was talking to Davenport. He gazed up at the American flag hanging next to that of Spruce Island, a school of herring in a deep blue sea, bordered by a lengthy strand of dulse.

Suddenly the lights went off and the auditorium was plunged into darkness. There was a moan from the crowd, a few giggles. The stage lights came on, to scattered applause. The worn, purplish curtains parted and Mayor Banner appeared, squinting in the glare of a makeshift spotlight. He strode to the lectern and began to speak.

Someone in the audience yelled, "We can't hear you, Rog!"

The Mayor studied the microphone, flipped a switch, tapped the mike. The sound of fingernails striking metal echoed around the gym. "Testing one-two-three-four," he orated, and then backed away when a shrill whistle pierced the air. At once he began, a capella, on the national anthem. Everyone, including Grandma Nan, rose and joined in. Her voice was strong, clear, and, unlike Davenport's, perfectly on pitch.

When that business was taken care of and everyone was seated, the Mayor waited for quiet. "Folks, we have an important visitor with us this evening. You all know him and what he did. Special Deputy Sheriff Louis B. Davenport, would you come up to the stage for a presentation?"

Davenport was surprised and embarrassed. The grins on the faces of those around him, however, suggested that everyone knew this was coming. When he hesitated momentarily, someone started to applaud. It grew as he strode uncertainly toward the stage, looking for a way to climb onto it. Finding none, he vaulted himself up, to a round of cheers. He shook hands with the Mayor, who pinned a sprucewood button labeled "Honorary Spruce Islander" onto his shirt and presented him with a huge bag of choice dulse tied up with a red ribbon.

Davenport stood looking over the audience, dumbfounded. It seemed the whole island was there, including the teenage waitress Marge and her family, as well as Lisa with her current boyfriend, and even Byron. And possibly, he reminded himself, a murderer. The only outsiders he recognized were the old couple from Indiana, who waved cheerfully to him.

The applause finally faded to a clap. "That's all, Louis," said Banner. "You can go." Everyone laughed heartily. Davenport hopped from the stage and returned to his seat, to another round of cheers.

Bobby smiled broadly and shouted, "Congratulations, Uncle Louie!" Grandma Nan gave him a toothless grin. Crane slapped him on the back.

"I thought—"

"We wouldn't have needled you if we didn't like you, Cousin Louis."

Davenport offered him a strand of the dulse.

"Go ahead," Crane insisted. "You take the first piece." Which he did, gorge rising, beads of sweat condensing on his forehead. But he managed to swallow the soggy residue without gagging or spitting it out.

The mayor then introduced a man who needed no introduction, the island cowboy who had spent a year out west and came home a stranger.

He strummed his guitar a few times, tap-tap-tapped his foot, and sang three songs he had written about a cowboy who had spent a year out west and came home a stranger. The crowd applauded wildly after each one. Davenport began to understand that they would applaud a thick album of wedding pictures. Caught up in the enthusiasm, he clapped louder than anyone else.

A folding chair was set up in the middle of the stage. At the mayor's signal all the children in the audience came up the side steps, which Davenport hadn't noticed, and sat down in concentric circles around the chair. Richard Blue wandered out and took his seat.

The crowd began to titter: they knew what was coming. It was the one about Blue's great-grandfather, who had a heart attack just as he was presented with a job to do. "An Indian," Blue concluded, "would rather die than work!" The crowd roared.

"Cousin Richard is a good part Indian himself," Crane reminded Davenport.

Then there was one about a hoopsnake that nobody could catch because, when threatened, it stuck its tail in its mouth and rolled away; and another about a wagon and a team of horses with reins that stretched when they got wet. An old farmer drove the wagon home from the fields one rainy afternoon, but the horses pulled farther and farther ahead, leaving the farmer miles back, where he finally stopped. He wasn't worried, though, because when the sun came out the wagon started to move, bringing the farmer home in time for supper. The children giggled and giggled, as did Davenport.

The last story was about the time he and a few other divers went out to haul up the cargo from a merchant ship that had sunk in the bay with a shipment of bathroom fixtures and Scotch whiskey. When they brought everything up from Davy Jones' locker they opened a bottle and, having nothing else to drink from, poured it into one of the gleaming white commodes, which was passed around. "When it came to me," Blue recalled, shaking his head, "I took one look and I just couldn't do it."

Davenport, the only person in the gym who hadn't heard the story before, finally got it and let out a blurt. Everyone else was waiting for this and laughed with him. The old fisherman, oblivious to the applause, got up and left the stage, and the children scurried back to their seats.

Next came a short, plump woman who lipsynched "Coal Miner's Daughter" and "Stand By Your Man" to the accompaniment of suggestive wiggles and gyrations. The crowd found this hilarious, too. Davenport was puzzled until Crane explained that she was the island undertaker, dead serious every day of the year except this one. He imagined next year's show starring himself telling funny jokes like the one about the boy with peach fuzz on his face, and pretending to be intimidated by a swooping bat....

The next act, to his considerable surprise, was Joey. Someone had combed his hair and he looked much less intimidating than usual. He began with a series of bird songs—a white-throated sparrow, an osprey, a veery and, finally, two gulls squabbling over a piece of decaying flesh at the dump. The audience enthusiastically shouted out the names of each of the birds. Then it was on to a low-flying airplane, a crowd at a baseball game, a stormy sea. He ended up with several perfect imitations of well-known film actors: Bogart, Lorre, Raines, Greenstreet, Henreid, and even Bergman. Davenport applauded loudly when Joey left the stage, marveling that a mentally challenged person could be so talented in so many ways.

The island impressionist was followed by a young man, the grandson (according to Crane) of Art Dazzledorf, who began with: "Talkin' to Cousin Richard backstage a little while ago. Claimed he was puttin' away some money for his burial. I said, 'What for? You think they're gonna let your ugly carcass lay on top of the ground and rot?'"

The laughter was led by a booming guffaw offstage. Davenport glanced at the faces of the Cranes, who had started to chortle even before the young comic began. They were with him a hundred percent. At last he understood why there was no embarrassment, no nervousness among any of the performers on stage. The entire audience was a large extended family, everyone a part of everyone else. And now they had invited him to become one of them. At last he belonged somewhere. His chin began to quiver.

Young Dazzledorf's huge red eyebrows lifted. "Torrist came up to me the other day. Said, 'Do you smoke fish here?'"

"'Yes,' I said, 'when we can't get any tobacco.'"

While the laughter was dying down he made a telescope with his fists and called out, "Where's Byron?"

Everyone turned and pointed to the former major-leaguer, who stood and waved his cap all around. "Ran into Byron the other day—well, almost—he was on the road again.... Anyway, you all know that lobster trap he keeps in his yard." Nods and grunts from the crowd. "Well, he told me he was going to take it back to the dump. I said, 'Why?' He said, 'I've had the damn thing out there for three years now, and haven't caught a single lobster!'"

No one laughed harder than Byron. The young comic went right on: "My brother is such a pain in the butt we call him 'Hemorrhoid.'" [Pause] "Or 'Emorrhoid' for short...."

Davenport shifted uncomfortably in his chair.

". . . show that more than half the people who get married eventually get a divorce. My wife and I have been married nine years." [Pause] "Where did we go wrong?

"One last joke, folks."

Cheers and applause from the crowd, which the performer acknowledged with a cheerful bow. "Hear about the guy who was losing his hair?"

The audience quieted down a little: they hadn't heard this one. Davenport brushed what hair he had left over his bald spot.

"Every day he woke up and found a few more hairs on his pillow. Finally he only had one left. Well, he fed and watered and nurtured that hair for weeks. But one morning he woke up and the hair lay beside him on the pillow. 'Oh, my God!' he cried. 'I'm bald!'" The assistant pharmacist left the stage accompanied by another thunderous ovation.

Byron came on with a guitar and sang several sea chanteys, including the story of the Lady Butterfield. There wasn't a dry eye in the house. He was followed by Hermit, who did a few tricks with strands of dulse: knot tying, origami, magic involving balloons and dulse, handkerchiefs and dulse, etc.

"He's got a few new ones this year," whispered Crane in awe. "I've got to get him to show me how he made that gull appear out of nowhere." Without another word he got up and left the auditorium. Davenport, puzzled, watched him disappear out a side door.

The final act was a barbershop quartet composed of the Mayor, the druggist, and brothers Don and Perry Crane. After a few harmonious numbers Crane returned to his seat. "Nice goin', Dad," said his son. Grandma Nan nodded happily.

Mayor Banner wound up the show by announcing the gardening award, which was won by one of his cousins for her English flower garden. Rose finished second. "That's all for this evening, folks. I leave you with this thought: You need memories so that, the day you die, you can go out with a smile on your face. Take care, now—there's a storm comin'. Good night and we'll see you all next year!"

Davenport wondered where he would be then. Alive, he hoped.

As the crowd rapidly dispersed, Lisa worked her way over to him. "Louie!" she cried out. "Mom just called. Something's happened at the cottages. You'd better get back there quick!"

A Hot Night

The cottages were in another uproar. Thornhill was pacing back and forth in front of the fireplace, cracking his knuckles and thrusting them over the screen from time to time to warm them up, though it was a muggy night and there was no fire. He had found the usual note on his dresser, on the usual paper, with the usual warning, and he anticipated the usual result. Moreover, another decaying gull had been found in the kitchen of the Farmhouse. And, if that wasn't enough, Baker had seen a stranger walking around in the woods.

"Can you describe him, Mr. Baker?"

"Not really. I wasn't paying much attention."

"Was he carrying a gun?"

"I didn't notice."

"Do you know if he was wearing a red shirt?"

"Beats me."

Davenport shook his head. "Anybody else see anything suspicious?" No one had.

"Did you lock your room when you went out, Mr. Thornhill?"

"Of course I did, Loose. You think I'm stupid?"

"Why shouldn't he?" his wife interjected. "You *are* stupid!"

"You shut up, you . . . you . . . slime mold!"

"Who's a slime mold, you miserable—"

"Hold it a minute!" shouted Davenport. "Just sit down, all of you, and try to get hold of yourselves."

After everyone had grudgingly arranged themselves around the sitting room, and Baker had cheerfully noted, for the record, that slime molds are quite wonderful creatures, Davenport turned to Rose. "Do you have a duplicate key to the Thornhills' room?"

"Yes, I do. I checked as soon as Paul found the note. It's in the drawer where it belongs."

"And the drawer was locked?"

"Just like you said."

"Is there any way into the room other than the door?"

"Well, there's the window, but—"

"I took a look at that, Monsieur Da-ven-porrrt. It was locked and no one broke in that way."

"What were you doing in the room, Dr. D'Arcy?"

"I heard Paul yelling and I went over to investigate."

"What I want to know is what you're going to do about this, Loose!"

"Please, Mr. Thornhill, sit down. All we can do is try to see that you're safe and secure so that no one can cause you any harm. Rose?"

"Yes, Louie?"

"Is there another room the D'Armses and Thornhills could have tonight?"

"Well, they could move back to the Cape Cod. Or over to the Blacksmith Shop."

"We're not going back to the Cape Cod, Monsieur. Somebody's already shot a hole in it, remember?"

"Well, that leaves the Blacksmith Shop."

"You found a note in there just before the ladies left!" Cathy Baker pointed out. "That's no more secure than the Farmhouse!"

"There's one other possibility," Rose suggested. "Everyone can stay here until this whole thing blows over."

"You mean the Big House?"

"That's what I said, Louie. The Thornhills can stay in Jack's old study, and the D'Arcys can move into Lisa's room."

"You see what they're doing, Sheriff?" Barnstable piped up. "They're driving us out of our cottages, one by one. Where the hell are we going to go if somebody finds a note in the Big House?"

Davenport sighed. "Well, folks, the ladies found a threatening note and they seem to have found a way out of their dilemma. I suggest you consider a similar solution."

"Monsieur Da-ven-porrrt, if you haven't gotten to the bottom of this situation by tomorrow, I'm going to have to go over your head."

"You mean call the sheriff? If you can track him down, let me know. I'd like to speak to him myself."

"I meant the President. The FBI."

"You go right ahead, Dr. D'Arcy. I need all the help I can get."

"I hate to interrupt these high-level discussions," said Rose, "but it's late, and if we're going to move everyone around, we'd better get started."

Davenport raised a hand. "One more thing," he announced in his most confident manner. "I'd like to have permission from all of you to get into your rooms in the cottages."

"What the hell for, Loose?"

"To see if I can find out how someone else seems to be getting in."

There were some murmurs and grumbling, but no objections.

"Okay, let's all try to get a good night's sleep and maybe things will look better in the morning."

It was still very warm at midnight, when Davenport and the others finally got to bed. He stripped to his shorts and climbed onto the familiar soft mattress. A moment later he threw off the covers. After rolling back and forth for several more minutes he got up, opened the window. The moon was obscured by clouds, and there was only steamy blackness. A hot wind did nothing more than lift the curtains away and expose him to whoever might be sneaking around outside.

After the squeaking of the bedsprings upstairs finally stopped, he imagined he heard noises coming from the general direction of the Farmhouse. It sounded like someone digging a grave. He fervently hoped it wasn't his own.

*D*angerous *G*round

Davenport woke from a fitful sleep to the sound of piercing screams. He leapt from the bed and stuck his head through the curtains. His heart was beating fast, but, he reasoned, at least it was still beating. The noise appeared to be coming from behind the Farmhouse. Kelly's barks echoed around and around the cottages.

After pulling on his pants and shoes he grabbed the .38 and flew out of the Big House, swiveling left and right, gawking for killers behind every spruce and shutter. The sun had not been up long but the air was like a hothouse and he was already sweating profusely.

With intense deliberation he rounded the corner of the ancient cottage and found Maryellen Thornhill peering into a hole in the ground, where the yelps seemed to be coming from. At one end, stuck in a mound of dirt, was a makeshift wooden cross. "How did you get down there?" she yelled into the hole.

"I fell in, you stupid fool!"

"Who's a stupid fool? *I* didn't fall into a hole. *You're* the stupid fool!"

"Ah, shaddup!"

"Stupid fool! Stupid fool!"

Davenport came up behind her, gun still drawn. "What's going on here?"

She whirled around. "Oh my God—you almost scared me to death!"

From the hole: "That you, Loose? Get me out of here, will you?"

Davenport peered into the earth. The victim was sitting at the bottom of the deep, narrow grave. "You hurt, Mr. Thornhill?"

"My ankle is killing me! I want out of here!"

"Take it easy, take it easy. We'll get you out as soon as we can." By this time everyone had arrived from the Big House. One by one they crept toward the disaster.

"Fall into a hole, Paul?" shouted Alice Barnstable.

"What's it look like?"

"Somebody go find Joey and get a ladder," Davenport suggested. Baker jogged off toward the Shed.

"What happened, Mr. Thornhill?" Davenport called into the crater.

"I came over to get my shaver. When I got to the door I heard a noise out back. Sounded like an animal scratching. I came around the Farmhouse to check, and that's when I fell into this damn hole."

"Didn't you see it?"

"Nah—it was covered by grass or something."

"Didn't I warn you to stay with other people, Mr. Thornhill?"

"I told my wife to keep an eye on me, Loose. Can I help it if I'm married to a twit?"

"Who's a twit? I didn't fall into a hole!"

"You didn't keep me from doing it, either!"

"What could I do, you nitwit? You went around the house and then you disappeared."

"Ah, you—"

"All right, all right! You can settle this later."

Joey showed up, in his porpoise underwear, with an aluminum ladder. Baker followed with a flashlight. In another moment the handyman was helping Thornhill out of the trap.

His wife greeted him with, "Stupid fool!"

Davenport's bladder was nearly bursting. "Will someone take Mr. Thornhill to see Doctor Houseman? I'm going to look around." D'Arcy nobly volunteered to chauffeur the unfortunate victim to Centerville.

After finding nothing of importance in the woods except for a place to relieve himself, Davenport returned to the Big House, accompanied by the plaintive call of the lonely winter wren. Something's fishy, he half thought, half mumbled. Then he remembered the rocky ground. *It would have taken a backhoe to dig that grave.* Unless . . .

He hurried to his room to wash up and put on a clean shirt. Before he could do either, he spied the note on top of his dresser. The first thing that crossed his mind was: Why did I answer that goddamn phone call? The familiar palpitations began. This time he was certainly doomed. Clutching the dresser with both hands, he peered with one eye at the threatening note.

THE SHERIFF CALLED. LISA.

A Secret Passageway

Lisa was in the kitchen attending to a vat of oatmeal on one stove, skillets with slabs of bacon and bullseyes of eggs on the other.

"Where's Rose?" Davenport inquired.

"ShewenttoHenry'swe'reoutofbutterdon'tbotherme."

He strode to the little table and picked up the phone. Though the door and windows were opened "to the max," as his granddaughters would put it, the kitchen was as hot as the oven. "H'lo, Olive, it's Davenport. Is the sheriff back yet?"

"Where have you been, Lou? He's been trying to get you all morning."

"It's not even eight o'clock yet! What's up?"

Lochinvar Tate came on the line. "Lou! Sorry, boy, the vacation's over."

"*What* vacation?"

"Hold on to your hat, son. Fairfax and Parkening *both* died of cardiac arrest."

"What? You mean a heart attack?"

"Listen up, Lou. Their hearts just stopped. As if they were scared to death."

"Or maybe they were poisoned."

"Very possibly. You know it takes forever for the lab to find traces of something when they don't know what they're looking for. By then the toxins might have already disappeared. Point is, whatever killed them, it looks bad. I'd suggest you send all the guests at that resort packing before another one falls over. I'm calling the state boys in on this."

"Hold on, Loch. We still don't have anything conclusive. Did you find out who owns the spruce forest?"

"No way to find that out, Lou. The Swiss are tighter than a gnat's ass when it comes to financial matters. We could ask the Feds, but I doubt it would help."

"Any ballistics yet?"

"Uh—here it is. All three bullets came from the same .22-caliber rifle."

"Well, that narrows down the possibilities a little. All we have to do is find out whose rifle they came from. What about your escaped prisoner?"

"Hasn't turned up yet."

"What was he wearing?"

"Prison clothes—what do you think?"

"There's a stranger running around the island in blue jeans and a red flannel shirt."

"Well, he could've stolen them. Maybe you'd better look into it. Gotta run, Lou. Don't let me down, boy. We don't want any screwups this close to the election, do we? Good luck, son."

"Thanks," said Davenport to a dead line. When he looked up, Lisa was returning from the dining room, where she had served the oatmeal. He rushed through the swinging door. D'Arcy and Thornhill had not yet returned form the doctor's office. For everyone else it was already too late. "Folks," he announced in his calmest voice, "I've just learned that Mr. Fairfax and Mr. Parkening might have been poisoned. With what, we don't know. The sheriff advises once again that all of you return to the mainland until we can sort this thing out."

To his surprise the Bakers, Alice Barnstable, and Harriett Quinlan went on with their oatmeal. Even Pat D'Arcy, freed for once from her husband's constraint, silently gobbled down her first breakfast in years. Only Maryellen Thornhill set her bowl on the floor for Kelly and left the room. The cereal disappeared immediately and the dog, tail wagging, looked around for more.

Lisa came in with plates of bacon, eggs, and freshly-baked biscuits. The remaining guests dug in. Davenport, torn between caution and wonderful aromas, reluctantly decided to forgo breakfast. "Lisa, I'm going to check out the other cottages. Don't save me anything. Not hungry."

On her way to the kitchen she called back, "What makes you think I was going to save you anything?"

Maryellen Thornhill was waiting for him in the sitting room. "That's it, Loose," she announced. "We're out of here."

"A wise decision under the circumstances. Does your husband agree with that?"

"The stupid fool can stay here if he wants to. But *I'm* packing." With that she headed toward her room.

Davenport retrieved the flashlight and stepped into the thick haze surrounding Porpoise Bay Cottages. He couldn't see the water, but he could smell and hear it. The wind had picked up considerably and he had a difficult time walking a straight line to the other cabins. Nonetheless, he proceeded at a jaunty, if uneven, pace toward the Blacksmith Shop, certain he had solved the mystery of how the killer got into locked rooms. From the woods came the song of a white-throated sparrow. Davenport smiled and tried to return the greeting, but the wind blew it away.

The screen door creaked open and the wind slammed it against the side of the cabin. He fumbled for his gun and skeleton key. Having been recently painted, the heavy inner door was stuck, but at last he pushed it aside and stumbled in, leaving it ajar. He was greeted by the stuffy odors of paint, ashes, and old furniture.

Special Deputy Sheriff Davenport's eyes panned around the sitting room. Everything was just as he had seen it the night the ladies got their note except that the huge fireplace was cold and the flowers very dead. He gazed dreamily at the watercolor of the cove by the late Lester Topat before continuing his sweep of the room, stopping finally at the rug under the table by the window facing the bay. The only sounds were those of the wind and of gulls and ravens laughing uproariously outside. He removed the dead flowers and shifted the table toward the sofa.

His knees cracked as he squatted down and slowly peeled back the rug. The worn, ancient wood was dark, but lighter where the floor had been covered. He ran his hand over the border between dark and lighter and felt a barely discernible crack. Pulse quickening, he ran a finger all around the rectangular border. On the left he felt a heavy string. Using his pen knife he fished it out of the crack. It was anchored. He pulled. Something gave. He lifted the trapdoor and peered under it. A set of worn dirt steps led down into the mildewy blackness. He clicked on the flashlight and gazed at the makeshift stairway. It didn't go very far. If there had been a tunnel there it had been filled in or collapsed long before.

He repeated the procedure in the Farmhouse, where he found the other end of the tunnel under the train tracks in Frank Parkening's room. Another dead end, another blind alley. The tunnel had been filled in from both ends, and it was impossible to get from cottage to cottage by that route. But whoever dug the hole that Thornhill fell into must have known that a tunnel had once been there, that the dirt would be relatively easy to remove. And Rose surely knew this, too.

The Lights Go Out

He wasted no time in chitchat. "Why did you tell me there's no tunnel between the Farmhouse and the Blacksmith Shop?"

"There isn't."

"C'mon, Rose, I found it."

"I said there isn't any tunnel. I never say there didn't *used* to be one."

Lisa and Marge appeared to pay no attention to this onslaught, but he could tell they were listening.

"So you knew about the tunnel?"

"Of course!"

"What was it for?"

"It was Fred Fairfax's secret passageway between the two cottages."

"You mean for trysts, that sort of thing?"

"A quaint way to put it, Louie, but that's exactly what it was for."

"And you let him dig it?"

She slid a tray of unbaked rolls into the oven. "It was years ago. We needed money to shore up some of the cabins. They're over a hundred and fifty years old, you know."

"And Fairfax gave you the money in exchange for letting him dig a tunnel."

"That's right."

"You let him have access to the ladies?"

"No, it wasn't like that. Fred and his wives used to stay in the Blacksmith Shop. There were others in the Farmhouse."

"Who was there?"

"Things have changed over the years. Some of the people stopped coming. Other times it was the Thornhills or the D'Arcys or the Parkenings."

"Fairfax had affairs with Maryellen Thornhill? And Pat D'Arcy?"

"And Alma Parkening, too, prob'ly. Marge, call the guests into the dining room, will you?" The girl reluctantly complied.

"But why a tunnel? Couldn't he just walk over?"

"Things were different in those days, Louie. Extramarital affairs weren't so open as they are now."

"And you let him get by with this?"

She turned from the stove and whacked her hands to her hips. "Louie, I couldn't care less what my guests do with their sex organs as long as it's between consenting adults. And you shouldn't either. Now get into the dining room. Dinner's almost ready. 'Lunch' to you." He thought he heard a snort from Lisa.

Davenport was annoyed, but he was also starved. He washed the dirt from his hands at the kitchen sink and pushed through the swinging door. The other guests were streaming in from the sitting room. When the roast chicken, rice, and tomatoes with sour cream appeared he gave Kelly a little of everything. When she didn't keel over, he and his dinner companions, the Thornhills, who were silent for once, fell to. The dog ran to another table and sat expectantly, a long drool hanging from her mouth. Outside, the wind hummed and whistled.

Thornhill flung his taped ankle out for inspection. "Doc said it was only a sprain. I just need to stay off it for a few days."

"Stupidest man who ever lived," his wife reminded Davenport.

"Well, it takes one to know one," Thornhill rejoined, spewing rice all over the table. Davenport patiently removed a grain from his chicken breast.

"I thought you two were leaving."

"Can't. The stupid ferry broke down. Won't be fixed until tomorrow."

"We should've left days ago," his wife pointed out. "The idiot wouldn't listen to me."

"Who's an idiot, you old battle—"

"Folks, in my humble opinion you're both idiots. Shut up and eat your goddamn chicken."

"Hear, hear!" whooped Barnstable.

"You shut up, too! All of you could be dead before the ferry is up and running again!"

As if on cue, a bullet crashed through the west window and splintered the frame on the other side. Everyone instinctively jumped up. "Get down!" Davenport barked, and they all plunged to the floor. "Stay here!" The wind was screaming through the broken window.

He ran to the kitchen. Rose, Lisa and Marge were already under a table. He inched up to the screen door and peered out. The sky had grown very dark. With a broom handle he pushed open the door and, when no one fired at it, edged outside. Slowly, his revolver pointing straight ahead, he slunk along the Shed. A raven took off, squawking. He poked his head around the corner of the building. In the woods on the other side of the Farmhouse a red shirt disappeared into the trees. Shit, he thought, as he set off across the freshly-mowed grass. I'm getting too old for this. Maybe they're trying to run me to death.

Kelly appeared out of nowhere and together they chased the culprit up the Red Trail and all the way to the cliff where Fairfax had been tossed over. There they found someone in a red flannel shirt cowering at the edge, pointing a bottle at them. "Don't shoot, Shurff! I won't take another drink, I swear it!" Kelly sniffed at Byron's feet. At that instant Davenport realized he had been decoyed like an amateur, and he turned and panted back down the trail, expecting every step to be his last.

Everyone was standing in front of the Big House, their hair blowing violently in the wind. "Monsieur Da-ven-porrrt!" D'Arcy roared. "The Mayor just called to tell you that a stranger was seen driving down the main road outside Nor'east Head!"

"Did he get a description of the car?" wheezed Davenport.

"Parrr-don, Monsieur?"

"DID HE GET A DESCRIPTION OF THE CAR?"

"HE SAID TO TELL YOU HE WAS DRIVING ART'S CAR," bellowed D'Arcy, "WHOEVER ART IS."

A loud clap of thunder ended the shouting. Davenport and the other guests barely made it inside before sheets of rain fell from the sky. The wind howled and howled. A flash of lightning was followed almost immediately by the crack of a tree splitting. Davenport watched from the bay window. "Damn," he mumbled. "Byron's out there."

"I wouldn't worry about Byron," said Rose, who was standing beside him. "Rain or shine, he's always out there somewhere." At that moment the electricity went off. She fished a box of matches from her kangaroo pocket and began to light the oil lamps. The matchbox, he noted, was identical to the one he had found on the shore wrapped in a piece of Fairfax's bloody shirt.

Davenport made his way to the darkened dining room, where Joey had already replaced the shattered window with a sheet of plywood, and into the kitchen, brightly lit by an Aladdin lamp. The strong smell of kerosene reminded him of a stove everyone huddled around at the orphanage, the one that had finally burned the place to the ground along with the thirteen children who hadn't made it out. Louie had been one of the lucky ones.

A tree branch slammed against the side of the house. He tried the phone. It was dead. The tempest roared.

He returned to the sitting room. Everyone was present except for Baker. "Where's your husband?" he demanded of the amateur sleuth and budding writer. She nodded toward the bay window. In the meadow gamboled Baker, naked as a spruce, jumping and laughing in the wind and rain. Behind him splashed the two-year-old. "Ain't he something?" she asked rhetorically.

All afternoon debris clattered against the house while everyone hunkered down in the sitting room thinking black thoughts and sipping golden sherry, "courtesy of the law," as Rose put it. Davenport, with his host's permission, sat in her late husband's chair, dozing and wondering helplessly where the gunman was. Lisa and Marge managed to come up with sandwiches and coffee, which eased the anxiety and boredom, but it was well after midnight before the gale abated and everyone picked up a lamp or candle and trudged off to bed.

An Assessment of Damages

It was a dark and stormy night. Davenport dreamed that a gull wearing a red flannel shirt was standing outside in the wind and rain, tapping his window with a tree limb....

"Huh? What?" The room was brightly lit. His immediate reaction was: Fire! But it was only the sun.

A tap on the door. "It's Lisa, Louie. Henry's on the phone."

"The grocer?" he shouted from the toilet.

"That's what I said. Somebody broke into the store last night."

"Maybe it was a tree limb," he grunted.

"Not unless it broke into the cash register, too."

"All right. Tell him I'll be down there as soon as I can."

Forgetting to comb his hair over his bald spot, he threw on some clothes, hurried to the kitchen, grabbed a couple of warm scones from a tin sitting on the table, and burst forth from the Big House. It was a cool, crystal-clear day. Not even a wisp of a cloud in the sky, only Harold T. Henderson circling leisurely over the island, searching, Davenport presumed, for damage done by yesterday's storm.

Munching on a scone, he drove slowly into town, avoiding limbs where possible, driving over them when necessary. Someone had already lopped off the top of a fallen spruce tree and dragged it from the road. On the final morsel he felt a dull pain in one of his upper molars, and something sharp on his tongue. Pondering the likelihood of death at the hands of the young dentist/podiatrist who visited the island once a month, he reached in and pulled out an old filling, gray and deformed like a spent bullet.

Henry Sanders, potbellied and jovial, was waiting for him in front of the store, and breathlessly escorted him to the cash register, which had been opened without force and now stood empty, like a clam on the beach. Davenport asked him why the register wasn't locked. "Nobody has ever done anything like this before, Louis. It must be the stranger that's been runnin' around loose, don't you think?"

"Maybe, Henry, maybe. Right now I'd say it was an inside job." He noticed a sign on the wall behind the counter: IF IT MAKES YOU SICK, BRING IT BACK.

"You mean the guy hid in here and stayed when I left for the night?"

"Well, it looks like somebody did, doesn't it? See how the broken window glass fell to the outside?"

"Well, I'll be. I hadn't noticed that before. I'll be more careful from now on when I close up, Louis."

"You do that," nodded Davenport. "Well, I'll be on my way. You see anything funny going on, give me a ring."

"Aren't you going to look for fingerprints or something?"

"I'll come back later for that if need be."

"All right, then. And don't forget your groceries."

"Huh?"

"Lisa gave me her order when I called. Said you would pick them up."

"Oh. Okay. Sure . . . ."

Henry watched patiently as Davenport loaded the back seat of the Plymouth. "Might as well stop at the dump on your way back," he added, tossing a couple of trash bags onto the floor. Davenport rattled off before Sanders could come up with any more chores.

He drove down to the old lighthouse and pier to take a look at the damage for himself. The sea was still choppy, but boats were everywhere, their inhabitants cutting nets away from damaged weirs, dragging vessels stranded on shore back into the water, bailing out others. When he was satisfied that everything was under control he turned around and headed toward Porpoise Bay. The lobster trap on Byron's little lawn lay crushed under a huge tree limb, but the tiny house was intact.

In a few minutes he was careening down the driveway toward the parking lot. Barnstable sprinted out to meet him. "My car's ready, Sheriff—let's go!"

"Hold on a minute, Alice. I've got some stuff in here for Lisa. Then I'm going to have a cup of coffee. Maybe two cups. You can join me if you want."

She skidded to a stop, stared at him for a moment, shrugged, and retorted, "Maybe I will."

Rose was waiting in the kitchen with a pot of coffee and a message: "Rog called. H. T. found Art's car in a ditch on the Dulse Cove Road, but nobody was in it. And Hermit isn't down at the cove, and his dory's gone. Rog thinks he may have drowned in the storm."

"Tell him I'm on my way."

"I don't know why anyone would want to live in this godforsaken place," Barnstable philosophized as they rattled up the driveway. She continued to badmouth the place all the way to the dump and back to Centerville, remarking on the bad weather, the hostility of the people, the filthy gulls, the lack of amenities, and ending with "Why do I keep coming here?"

"You're a masochist, remember?"

"That's true. Always have been. Want to hear my life story, Sheriff? It's fascinating."

"Maybe later." He dropped her off at the garage with: "Tell Gannet to send the bill to the sheriff's office, and to add the $1.50 I owe him," and sped off without waiting to find out the grand total.

The wildflowers in Houseman's yard were bright in the morning sunshine, apparently undamaged by the ravages of the previous night's storm. He pulled into the driveway behind a line of muddy cars. The screen door had been torn off and was lying twisted and broken in the front yard. The waiting room was crowded with people suffering minor cuts and scrapes. They all greeted him warmly, then ignored him as if he were one of their own. Crane's brother Perry was there with a sick kid, who vomited on Davenport's foot. Striving not to inhale whatever organisms might be wafting toward his nostrils, he managed to mumble, to Crane's apology, that it was no problem.

"Find another dead body, Louis?" Houseman inquired pleasantly when he came out to get the next patient.

"Not yet, Doc, but I hear Hermit may have drowned."

"One thing I've learned over the years is that you never pronounce somebody dead until you've seen the corpse. Hermit's disappeared any number of times, but he always shows up. Byron, too. Who's next?" Perry Crane carried his sick daughter into the office. She was replaced by Houseman's big, yellow cat, who lapped the vomit from Davenport's shoe and curled up beside him on the sofa.

It was more than an hour before Houseman got back to him. Just as he had dozed off with the cat in his lap, the doctor's snowy head appeared in the doorway. "C'mon back, Louis."

Wide awake now, he took the chair that was offered and glanced around nervously at the shiny instruments, the packages of syringes and needles.

"Your tics are much improved," the physician observed. "You have a suspect?"

"That's what I came to talk to you about."

"I'm listening."

"What sorts of poisons do you keep in your office?"

"I keep a few drugs that would be poisons if not administered properly. All doctors do. Why do you ask?"

"Because Fairfax and Parkening might have been poisoned."

"That so? What with?"

"The coroner hasn't come up with that information yet."

"I'm curious. Let me know when you find out. Anything else I can do for you?"

"Did you prescribe anything for them?"

"Parkening was taking digitalis. When he spilled his supply all over the floor he came to me for some more."

"That's a heart medicine, isn't it?"

"That's right."

"Could that kill a person if he took too much?"

"Any drug will kill you if you take too much. You ought to know that, Louis."

"And that's all you have to say about Fairfax and Parkening?"

"I only saw them once in a great while."

"What about Thornhill?"

"Bad sprain. I taped him up. Didn't poison him, though."

"He wasn't faking it?"

"Not unless he found some way to stiffen and swell his ankle. Oh, he was some sore, all right."

"Okay, Doc. Thanks." Davenport rose to go, happy, as always, to be leaving a doctor's office.

On the way to the cottages he made a detour to the spot where Art Dazzledorf's car had been abandoned in a ditch on the back road. What he found was a junker with a license plate he recognized, having seen it in the corner of Gannet Banner's lot. He turned the Plymouth around, inadvertently backing into the same ditch and disconnecting the muffler again, and roared slowly back to Porpoise Bay.

On the dresser in his room lay a note. Without giving himself time to think about it, he grabbed it up. GO TO INDIAN CAVE, it commanded.

Delightful aromas greeted Davenport's nostrils as he swung into the kitchen. Lisa was stirring a big pot of soup on one of the stoves. He asked her where Indian Cave was.

"Down near Fog Cove. Ask anybody down there."

"Could somebody hide in there for a while?"

She inhaled a lungful of tars and nicotine and gazed at him with wolf-like eyes. "I guess so. It's kind of hard to get to, though. Why—are you trying to hide from someone?"

"Can you get there by boat? A dory, say?"

"That's about the only way you can. But watch out."

"Why?"

"They say it's haunted."

Indian Cave

Davenport, his stomach filled with garden vegetable soup and chocolate-chip cookies, roared back down the island. Fingers popped up everywhere, perhaps half for him and half for Kelly, sitting tall and alert on the passenger side. He tested his continuous wave theory on a series of cars and pickup trucks, successfully, as far as he could tell, and produced several expert sideways nods to apparent general approval.

A few of the Centerville smokehouses puffed their fragrant haze into a cloudless sky. Houseman's lawn was even rifer with hawkweed and daisies than it was before, fairly bursting with color in the warm afternoon sun. Just outside of town he passed the cemetery filled with former Banners, Hendersons, and Blues.

On a whim, he drove up the narrow path into the final resting place of virtually all the people who had ever lived on Spruce Island, looking idly for a Davenport. As far as he could see, there weren't any. But somewhere along the coast of Maine he knew there would be a few. Some day, if he survived this case, he would find them. Maybe write a book about the experience. *Tripping Over My Roots*, by Louis B. Davenport, came to mind.

Fog Cove sparkled into view. He slowed down and marveled at the brightness of the little village, picture perfect in its valley setting. On the bridge over Rainbow Creek he stopped and asked a pair of ten-year-old girls the way to Indian Cave.

They looked at each other. The one with red hair and a nose saturated with freckles asked, "Why do you want to go *there*? Hi, Kelly!" The dog's tail thumped against the seat.

"Just to check it out."

"It's haunted, you know," said her darker, stockier cousin.

"So I heard."

"Well, all right. You turn left at the church and follow the road to the end. Then you walk down the beach for"—she appealed to her friend for help—"ten minutes?"

The red-haired girl nodded. "I guess. But nobody ever goes *there*."

"Thanks, kids."

"All right. But you be careful, Uncle Louis."

He turned left at the shiny white church with the bright red roof and followed the road to the end. The water, still in some turmoil, splashed hard against the shore. For exactly ten minutes he slogged down the beach to a rocky outcropping stretching across the sand and into the sea. There was no sign of a cave. He walked around and over the rocks to the other side, Kelly sniffing furiously for creatures of any stripe. Then he remembered that the mouth of the cave faced the sea.

He stripped off his shoes and socks and rolled up his pants. Checking to make sure his revolver was where it should be, he plunged into the foamy water. Whooeeee, oh GOD that's cold! he muttered to himself. Kelly was already swimming past him, riding up and down on the swell.

Water up to his knees, Davenport turned the corner around the rock wall and splashed into the mouth of Indian Cave. An intense odor greeted his nostrils, one of smoke and decay and mildew and the sea and a few other things he couldn't identify. But no Hermit, no dory, nothing except for a pile of chicken bones ("Stay out of there, Kelly!") and beer bottles and cigarette stubs, abandoned, no doubt, by some of the island's teenagers. It was then that he saw the walls move.

He rubbed his eyes and looked harder. The entire throat of the cave squirmed with—was crawling with—something . . . little animals . . . thousands of them, every one of them awake now and staring directly at him, or so he thought. The hairs on the back of his neck popped straight up. Leaving Kelly to her own fate, he slapped back into the water and raced around to the shore, expecting, at any moment, to feel the pricks of tiny teeth all over his body.

The bats, however, seemed to be quite indifferent to either him or the dog, who swam leisurely around the bend, having satisfied her olfactory curiosity. He grabbed his shoes and socks, sloshed to the car, and rattled away, mumbling "stupid fool" to himself, at the same time fascinated by the strange, organic feeling of bare feet against pedals.

Halfway up the island he remembered the serenity of Blueberry Hill and was tempted to have a snooze at the sunny crest. Later, he promised himself, and sped on up the road to Centerville, where he paid a visit to the office of the Registrar of Licenses and Deeds.

"Afternoon, Louis," said the woman who had won the skeet shoot at the Dulse Festival on Saturday.

"Hello, Sherri. Nice shooting."

"Thanks. What can I do for you today?"

"I need to know who owns the property adjacent to the spruce forest."

"Well, let me get out my maps." She climbed onto a ladder and pulled a book about the size of a table top from the high shelf. As if it weighed no more than a sparrow she tossed it onto the counter between them, thumbed three or four pages, stopped, traced a boundary with her finger. "Let's see . . . the property to the west—that's about three hundred acres—is registered to Barley Henderson; on the south and east we have Regal Blue; and up here to the northeast it's in the name of Midge—no, *Cliff*—Banner. That's Midge's son. Midge died a while back."

"So you might say all three families would be affected by the Project."

"I think you could say that."

"What about the owners of the spruce forest itself?"

"Well, all I have on that is a Swiss bank in Lausanne. The Swiss are quite private about matters like this."

"So I understand." He gazed at the coal-black hair, the strong arms, the ruddy complexion. Tell me, Sherri, which islanders would stand to lose the most if the Swiss owner decided to sell the property to developers?"

"Is this a trick question?"

"Not at all. Somebody wants to stop the Project dead. I thought you might have some ideas about that."

"Well, if somebody turned the island into a bunch of carnivals and hotels," she retorted, "I imagine that would make almost anybody mad, wouldn't you say?"

"But *some*body must be a little madder than everyone else."

Her coal-black eyes stared at him blankly.

"Who owned the land before the Swiss bought it?"

She put the book back in its place and searched out another. After poring through it for several minutes, she said, "That was Indian land. There was never a deed to it originally. The Swiss filed a claim and that was that."

"Would you say they swindled it from the Blues?"

Coldly: "We were called 'the Bluefoot' then."

Davenport filed this information and carried it back to Porpoise Bay, where uniformly grim-looking people slouched on the chairs and sofa in the sitting room.

"What the hell happened?" he demanded. "Did somebody else get a note?"

"Thanks to you, Loose, we *all* got one!" Thornhill lamented. "WE'RE *ALL* GOING TO DIE!"

A Confession

Dinner was a miserable affair for everyone except Davenport, who hadn't received a threatening note, and the Bakers, who didn't care. Even the intrepid Alice Barnstable seemed nervous, distracted, hardly touching her food. Marge implored everyone to eat, pointing out that Rose and Lisa had worked hard to fix them a nice supper, and had tasted everything to make sure it was all right. They ignored her. Finally everyone wandered into the sitting room for the evening, leaving Davenport and his table companions to linger over dessert and coffee.

"I was hoping to have a chance to talk to you," Cathy told him. Her husband gazed out the window, his lips moving in silent calculations of square roots or molecular arrangements. The two-year-old imitated him, little bubbles of spittle seeping out of her tiny mouth.

"You have another theory?" Davenport inquired through a large mouthful of cheesecake.

"It's not a theory. It's a fact."

"You know who did it?"

"Absolutely."

"Would you care to let me in on your conclusion?"

"Sure. It was Doctor Houseman."

"Pete? What motive?"

"They were both mercy killings. It started with Lester Topat. Remember, he had cancer? He was on his last legs when he got here and the first thing he did was ask the doctor to put him out of his misery. Same with Frank Parkening, only he had incurable heart disease."

"And he asked Houseman to—"

"Or maybe the doctor decided to take matters into his own hands."

Davenport swallowed noisily. "What was Fairfax's misery? And what about Rose? And why all the notes? And—"

"I haven't gotten that far. But I've got chapter four done—you want to read it?"

"What happens in chapter four?"

"You visit the morgue."

"Maybe later."

They retired to the sitting room. "Monsieur Da-ven-porrrt," D'Arcy grinned, "we've all decided to take the first boat in the morning. Furthermore, we're all going to stay here in the sitting room tonight, and we'd like you to spend the night here with us. Would that be possible?"

"It's the first sensible thing any of you has said," Davenport responded. "But first I've got an errand to run. Shouldn't take long."

"Hurry back, Sheriff."

"Yeah, Loose, don't stay away too long."

Flattered by the unexpected attention, he assured them that he would return as soon as possible. "C'mon, Kelly," he sung out.

"We'd rather you leave her here, Monsieur, if you don't mind."

"Well, I guess that's up to her. You want to go with me, old girl?" The dog trotted toward the door.

"Wait!" Maryellen Thornhill hurried to the kitchen and came back with a piece of cake, which the dog readily accepted. Ignoring everyone else, Kelly sat down, tail flapping for further handouts. Davenport, making his way to the Plymouth, mumbled something about the nature of friendship and loyalty.

Near Caitlin's Park he found Byron waddling down the road dragging something behind him. He stopped and offered him a ride. This time Byron accepted. "Sorry if I scared you yesterday on the cliff. I thought you were someone else."

"Nope. It was me."

"What's that, another lobster trap?"

"Yep. Storm broke my other one."

"Where'd you get it?"

"At the dump. You'd be surprised at what you can find in the dump."

Davenport pulled up in front of the tiny house. "Will you be okay?"

Byron jumped out of the car and hauled up his trap. "I'll be okay. Thanks for the ride. I'd offer you a beer, but I'm fresh out."

"Want me to bring you some?"

"That's all right, Shurff. My neighbors keep me well supplied."

"Let me know if you need anything else. We're honorary cousins now, you know."

Byron bared his mottled teeth. "I will."

Davenport backed into the main road and returned Byron's wave with a sideways nod as he pulled away. "Hope you catch something this time!" he shouted.

There were no patients in the waiting room. The evenings were reserved for emergencies, apparently. Nonetheless, Houseman appeared immediately, as if aroused by some secret warning device. He didn't seem surprised to see the Special Deputy Sheriff. "You decide to do something about those tics, Louis?"

"No, this is more of a social call."

"Well, I've got a couple of sick patients to look after. Come on back if you want to talk."

"This is kind of personal."

"Oh, I see. All right. Sit down."

"I'll ask you straight out, Pete. Did you kill any of the guests at Porpoise Bay Cottages?"

Houseman looked him right in the eye. "I didn't kill anybody. Les Topat asked for some help and I gave it to him."

"An assisted suicide?"

"You could call it that."

"Why did you do it?"

"I'm a doctor," replied Houseman, whose eyes had become distinctly moist. "I've never seen anybody in so much pain."

"Why did he come all the way to Spruce Island to die?"

"I asked him the same question. He said none of his doctors back home were willing to stick their necks out for him." He was openly weeping now. The cat came out of nowhere, jumped into the old man's arms, and lapped up the tears.

"But *you* did."

"I told you why."

"Didn't you try any painkillers?"

"Of course I did. Even morphine didn't help much."

"Did you know him very well?"

"Well enough."

"What about Fairfax and Parkening?"

"If they committed suicide, they never asked for my help."

"You didn't give them anything? Or give it to someone else to administer?"

"No, I didn't."

"All right, Pete. Thanks. You'd better get back to your patients."

"Aren't you going to arrest me?"

"What for? The man's been cremated. How could we prove somebody poisoned him?"

Unable to speak, Houseman stuck out his hand. His grip was soft, yet firm. Regaining control, he said, "Thanks, Cousin Louis. If you ever need my help, you know where to find me."

Davenport's left eyebrow shot up. "What kind of help did you have in mind??"

The Missing Dory

Davenport strained to get a good look at the sleeping Walter D'Arcy, but it was too dark and he was turned the other way. And there was another loose end flopping around in his mind as he lay listening to the snorts and whistles of the guests at Porpoise Bay Cottages: why did someone send him to Indian Cave when there was nothing there? Unless, of course, that was what he was supposed to find! As the room clock struck midnight, he suddenly understood why Hermit had disappeared, and he slept peacefully until dawn, when Harriett Quinlan's alarm sounded for her final birdwatch of the summer on Spruce Island. He checked his watch; it had stopped again.

Everyone groaned except for the Bakers, who had chosen to retire to their own room upstairs. Davenport had had no problem with that. He was certain they were in no danger.

The phone rang. It rang again. He trotted to the kitchen. "H'lo?"

"Cousin Louis?"

"Yes. Who's this?"

"Worm Mallory."

"Captain of the Island Haven?"

"Nope. This week I'm the crew. Shep's the cap'n."

"You want to speak to Rose?"

"No, actually I wanted to speak to you."

Davenport waited. He noticed for the first time that it was foggy outside. "Well, go ahead."

"I'm down at the dock in Centerville. Shep just spotted Hermit's dory out in the bay, headed for the mainland. There was someone wearin' a red flannel shirt in 'er, but it wasn't Hermit."

"Who was it?"

"I don't know."

"You notify the Coast Guard?"

"No, I notified *you*. You're the law around here, aren't you?"

"All right, Worm, I'll take care of it."

"One more thing: the ferry is still down. The first trip won't be till around noon."

"Noon. Thanks."

Davenport pressed the receiver button, then dialed the sheriff's office. When he asked Oscar whether Tate had come in yet, the response was, "You'd better speak to Manny."

The deputy sheriff came on immediately. "Lou? Can you get back here right away?"

"Don't think so, Manny. The ferry's down."

"Well, we need help. Sheriff just resigned."

"He *what*? Why?"

"Some dang reporter caught him coming out of a motel room with your Mrs. Fairfax early this morning. It was all over the tube, didn't you see it?"

"Porpoise Bay Cottages doesn't have a TV set."

"Really? How do those people manage to get along over there? Anyway, the bigwigs in the party told him the race for the House was finished, and that he was through as sheriff, too. They're looking for a replacement now. You want the job?"

Rose came through the swinging door, seemingly unsurprised to find Davenport in the kitchen. She waved cheerfully and filled the big coffee pot.

"No thanks, Manny. The case over here has turned out to be more complicated than I thought. It might take quite a while to sort it all out. In fact, as long as you're the acting sheriff, I'm officially requesting you to set up a deputy's office on Spruce Island. I think they need the presence of a law enforcement officer over here on a permanent basis."

"Sure, Lou, if that's what you think."

"By the way, did you find that escaped prisoner yet?"

"We nabbed him a couple days ago. Dressed up like a woman but he didn't fool anybody. Haw haw haw. You should've seen him trying to walk on those high heels!"

"Got work to do, Man. I'll let you know of any developments." He whanged the receiver into the hook. "What's for breakfast, Rose? I'm starved."

"I thought I might make some blueberry pancakes."

"Save me some, will you? I've got something to do this morning."

"You sure it can't wait?"

"I'll be back before long. By the way," he called over his shoulder, "the ferry won't be running until noon."

"Yes," she said. "I know."

Davenport stopped in his room for a quick comb. On the dresser stood the large bag of dulse. He grabbed a strand and stuffed it into his mouth. Either this is a very good batch, he thought, or the stuff's beginning to grow on me.

Despite the 100% humidity, the old Plymouth started right up. As he roared onto the road his lights flashed into the eyes of a pair of deer, one a doe, the other a fawn. They stood their ground. He stopped and waited for them to wander leisurely into the woods.

The main road was nearly deserted. It was as if the whole island were waiting for something to happen. The only sounds were those of his own disconnected muffler and rattling bumper. Eventually he found the church in Fog Cove and turned left toward the beach. Humming softly to himself he took off his shoes and socks, rolled up his pants, and splashed down the shore to Indian Cave. This time the tide was lower, and the water was only up to his ankles. Without bothering to feel for the revolver he came around to the mouth of the cave, where he found, as expected, a dory. Just climbing into it was a short, stocky, dark-haired dulser. He jumped when Davenport spoke.

"Going somewhere, Hermit?"

"Cap'n Louis! Holy Christ, you've got to stop sneakin' up on people like that!"

"Sorry. I just wanted to ask you something."

"I don't have much dulse with me right now, if that's what you—"

"Never mind the dulse. I've got enough to last me quite a while." The bats, awakened by the disturbance, squirmed in annoyance.

"Well, I was just going out to pick. It'll be low tide in an hour or so."

"You move down here for a while, Hermit?"

"Not exactly. It's just that the pickin's better in Fog Cove right now."

"Where you won't find any strangers to steal your boat, is that it?"

"Uh—I don't know anything about no strangers...."

"I think I do, finally. Well, I'll leave you to your picking."

"All right, Cap'n."

Davenport whirled smartly and splashed jauntily back to his car. Halfway there he reached for his nearly empty pack of cigarettes. He rolled it into a ball and threw it as hard as he could toward the sea. My God, he moaned to himself, I think I broke my arm!

A Denouement

Breakfast was over by the time Davenport returned to the kitchen of the Big House. His arm still hurt a little, but he was fairly certain it wasn't a fatal condition. He grabbed a warm pancake and strode into the dining room. The guests, having packed the night before, lingered over coffee. Kelly was asleep in a corner, bulging with food.

"Folks," he mumbled around the pancake, "let's go into the sitting room." Everyone complied without a word. After tossing a spruce log nonchalantly into the smoldering fireplace he took his place in front of it. A hot blaze roared up behind him, and the sweet bouquet of burning spruce filled the room.

He swallowed the last of his breakfast and cleared his throat. The tics, he suspected, were gone for good. "This is the time in the mystery novels when the detective announces who the murderer is."

He saw that he had their full attention.

Sighing loudly, he proceeded. "Unfortunately, I'm not able to do that just yet."

The guests of Porpoise Bay Cottages glanced nervously at one another.

"Let me sum up what we know about this case," he began. Everyone leaned forward. Cathy Baker smiled and got out her note pad. Her husband gazed at the ceiling and the universe beyond. "We've had two possible murders on Spruce Island, and several other close calls. I'm referring to the deaths of Fred Fairfax and Frank Parkening, and the shots taken at me in the shower and another at the Cape Cod when no one was inside, not to mention Ms. Barnstable's car. And, of course, the events precipitating Dr. D'Arcy's fainting spell, Rose Kelly's serious illness, and the painful injury of Paul Thornhill. How's the ankle, by the way?"

"Hurts like hell, Loose."

"That's because you won't take your painkillers, you nincompoop," added his wife.

"How do I know they aren't poisoned, you old bat?" he retorted with a snarl.

Davenport ignored them. "We seem to have an unusual pattern here. Most serial killers use the same modus operandi with all their victims. In this case we seem to be seeing several different methods at work. This might mean either that someone is trying to throw us off the track, or that the murders and the other incidents were committed by more than one individual.

"At present we can't rule out the participation of any one of you, or a hired accomplice, or accomplices, in some of these crimes, and all of you remain suspects, even those who were victims of an attack yourself. My personal opinion, however, is that the perpetrations were carried out by a person or persons unknown, someone who may well be a stranger to Spruce Island." He paused to gauge the impact of these remarks on those huddled before him.

"Don't you even have a clue who might have done these things, Mr. Davenport?" A diamond bracelet glittered in the firelight.

"To be frank, Mrs. D'Arcy, none whatever. Except that he is probably a terrific shot, and also knows something about poisons."

"Doesn't that narrow down the possibilities, Sheriff?"

"Maybe, but not enough. The point is this: you're all leaving the island in a couple of hours. Someone from the sheriff's office will be in contact with you after you return home, where I can practically guarantee you'll be safe. Until then, I would suggest you all take proper precautions. Understood?"

"I must say, Monsieur Da-ven-porrrt," that I'm not very impressed by your investigation, or by the sheriff's department in general. You can be certain I'm going to see that a Congressional probe is initiated into this matter."

"That's up to you, Dr. D'Arcy. However, I would suggest you do this from the relative safety of your home in New Haven. And one more thing. I suspect that this whole business is tied up with the theme park being planned for the center of the island. Until this matter is cleared up, I would suggest that all plans for the APTGAFIA Project be suspended."

"There are a lot of people who are not going to—"

"Dr. D'Arcy, do you value your life? And that of Mrs. D'Arcy?"

"Yes," grinned the diplomat, patting his wife's shoulder. "Yes, I do."

"Then give us a chance to do a thorough investigation before you go any farther, will you? It's possible that we are dealing with some powerful organization we don't know anything about. Give us some time, that's all we're asking."

"What about next summer?"

"Don't depend on it."

"Sickening," murmured Thornhill.

"*You're* sickening," his wife reminded him.

"That's all I have to say. I imagine all of you will want to start gathering up your things."

The guests at Porpoise Bay Cottages drifted slowly from the sitting room. Baker was the last to leave, carrying only a bottle of bright yellow slime mold growing on a medium of oatmeal. He gazed at Davenport and his eyebrows did several rapid pushups.

Now only Rose remained, slouched down in her usual chair. She sighed, "Well, Louie, I'd better go out and take care of the dishes."

"I'll help you."

Kelly was still asleep in the dining room. Davenport pushed open the swinging door and held it for Rose. "Where's Lisa?"

"I gave her the day off." She smiled. "Looks like we're going to have quite a few days off for a while, doesn't it, Louie? Until the August crowd arrives, anyway."

"Sit down, Rose."

"I will, Louie, just as soon as I've put the dishes in the washer."

"Sit down. I'm not quite finished with what I was saying a minute ago."

"But you dismissed all the guests."

"Rose, I think you know who's responsible for the deaths of Fred Fairfax and Frank Parkening."

"I do?"

"You and a few other people."

"What other people?"

"I'm coming to that. First, let me tell you what I think happened here. Correct me if I make a mistake, will you?"

She sank into a chair.

"That was quite a show Joey put on for me, wasn't it?"

Rose's eyes widened, more in appreciation than in surprise. "You mean—"

"Joey is just as smart as you are, isn't he? Maybe even smarter."

"In some ways. How did you know?"

"I was at the variety show, for one thing. Were you there?"

"No, I wasn't. I have a bunch of cottages to run, remember?"

"I realized then that he could have been responsible for all the mysterious voices that certain people heard at various times over the last few days."

"Go on."

"At first I thought somebody put him up to it. Now I think he's just part of the whole conspiracy."

Rose found a bottle of sherry and poured herself a glass. "Conspiracy?"

Davenport poured one for himself. "That's what I said." He lifted the glass. "Cheers!"

"What do you mean?"

"A number of different people fired shots at me and the Cape Cod and the Big Banana, quite possibly with Fred Fairfax's rifle. All of those were intentional misses, and they were fired by an expert. At first I wondered who was the best marksman on the island, but I have since learned that just about everyone here is a crack shot. The women, too. Maybe even you."

"So where does *that* leave you?"

"I believe I know who's behind the whole thing."

"Who?"

"Spruce Island."

"What? What are you talking about?"

"I think that just about every islander knows what has happened here, maybe even the kids. I think the Council of Mayors has had meetings to discuss ways to keep the developers away from Spruce Island. I think they believe that a big thing like a theme park would ruin the island forever, and destroy a large extended family and a unique way of life. Eventually it was decided that when the plans for the park reached a certain stage, drastic action would have to be taken."

"But how do you enlist a whole island in such a thing?"

"First you find a few people who are willing to risk everything for something they believe in. Beyond that, you are encouraged by the certain knowledge that you can count on the support of everyone else if the need arises. If someone is accused of something—anything—every other Spruce Islander would be willing to stand up for him. Give him an alibi and, if necessary, even confess and take the heat. Am I right?"

She gazed at him steadily with a hint of a smile topped by a touch of admiration.

"You faked the poisoning, didn't you, Rose?"

"Not exactly. That was pure coincidence. Pete's been trying to get my gall bladder out for years."

"I figured it was something like that."

"Well? What next?"

"That's up to you. You can't keep them out forever, you know."

"We can sure as hell try!"

The End

A long yellow station wagon led a string of cars down the main road to the Centerville pier. Special Deputy Sheriff Louis B. Davenport, along with Rose, Joey, and Kelly in a bright red pickup truck, brought up the rear. He responded promptly to all waves and nods, until Rose admonished: "Only the driver gets to finger wave, Louie."

The whinnying of Alice Barnstable wafted through the fog from a few carlengths ahead, nearly drowning out the brickbats from the car behind her. "Tell me something, Rose: the Thornhills really love each other, right?"

"Wrong. They can't stand each other. Never could. Even argued at their wedding."

"So why have they stayed together all these years?"

"They're comfortable with each other, Louie. They're comfortable."

The captain and crew were ready for the caravan, and everyone was waved onto the Island Haven immediately. No Spruce Islanders were waiting to board. The word had gone out, apparently, and no one stood in the way of the mass exodus from Porpoise Bay.

The passengers climbed out of their vehicles and wandered aimlessly around the deck. Harriett Quinlan began at once to study the surface of the water through her binoculars. Alice Barnstable continued to rail at the rail. Only Cathy Baker hopped off the ferry and ran back to say good-bye to them, promising to be back in a year or so. "Jim has already signed up with H. T. Henderson for flight lessons next summer, and I should have my novel done by then."

"We'll be here, Cathy," said Davenport. She kissed him on the cheek.

When she was safely back on board, Captain Farmer gave three short blasts on the horn and the boat backed away from the pier and disappeared into the fog, the Bakers, including the two-year-old, waving from the stern. In another minute it was all a memory.

The pickup pulled away from the dock and headed up the main road. "It would be a shame if Alice and Harriett didn't come back next year, Louie. Couldn't you make an exception for them?"

"Don't worry about that. I had a little talk with them last night while everyone else was getting ready to bed down. I told them the whole story. They'll be back on the next boat."

"Good," said Joey, who was driving. "I like Alice and Harriett. They're practically the only people that come here who aren't phonies."

"When did you begin to suspect—?" Rose began.

"Merely a process of elimination, my dear Ms. Watson. I knew that Alice was in on the whole thing from the beginning. She told me she heard Fred Fairfax and Walt D'Arcy from the Lodge the morning of Fairfax's demise, though she's almost as deaf as the Cranes' old dog. Then there was the question of who was putting the dead gulls into the cottages and the threatening notes in the rooms. I thought all along there must be a tunnel or some access. But I couldn't find anything like that. So it had to be something simpler. Like the duplicate keys you have.

"But neither you nor Joey could've fired all the rifle shots, so there had to be others in it with you. The calls I kept getting from everyone on the island about a 'stranger' in their midst was pure hokum, of course. And when Hermit 'disappeared' so his dory would be available for the 'stranger's' benefit, and I found that phony junk car in the ditch on the back road, I knew that a lot of people must be involved.

"As for the warning notes, you and the others mainly wanted to frighten the people who were trying to turn the island into a theme park. But something got out of hand. Fred Fairfax was drunk and probably fell and broke his neck while he was being chased by some someone making animal noises." He glanced toward Joey, who gave him a sideways nod. "Anyway, whoever was with him must have pushed his body over the cliff to make it look like an accident." The driver shrugged.

"What about Frank?"

"I suspect he was literally scared to death. By rattling doorknobs, or tappings on his window. By someone who knew he had a very weak heart."

"And, of course, there was also an attempted murder in progress when I arrived."

"What attempted murder, Special Deputy Sheriff Davenport?" Rose inquired.

"The murder of Spruce Island itself."

"So what are you going to do now, Cousin?" Joey asked him.

"Well, the first thing I'm going to do is finish that damn lighthouse puzzle. Then I'm going to set up a deputy's office on Spruce Island."

She smiled. "Jack used to work that puzzle every summer."

"After all," he continued, "we can't let another murder happen here, can we?"

When they got back to Porpoise Bay Cottages, Kelly jumped from the truck bed and ran into the woods, sniffing for interlopers. The others strode into the mist toward the rocky shore. Davenport couldn't see anything, but he knew that in front of him were myriad flowers and birds, the forest and the sea. Gulls and ravens grumbled and squawked at the top of invisible spruce trees. In the distance a foghorn wailed mournfully, and somewhere above them a small plane droned above the fog. "When did Lisa say gourmet night was, Rose?"

"Wednesday. But we can have it tonight if you like."

He nodded happily. "Anything but chili."

"I don't hear the winter wren any more," Rose observed. "He must have found a mate at last!" She pulled a handful of dulse from the pocket of her red flannel shirt and offered a few strands to him and Joey.

"You know," Spruce Island's Deputy Sheriff Davenport mumbled, after stuffing them into his mouth, "I believe I could get to like it here."

"Louie," she said as they disappeared into the fog, "I think this is the beginning of a beautiful friendship . . . ."

Acknowledgments

I am indebted to the late Gleason Green for the story about the Scotch whiskey, and Dr. Philip Mossman for excellent technical advice. I also thank my usual cadre of relatives, friends, advisors and critics for helping to whip the novel into shape. The good parts, however, are entirely my own creation.

visit the author at www.genebrewer.com

CPSIA information can be obtained
at www.ICGtesting.com
Printed in the USA
BVHW030718100219
539880BV00001B/153/P